P9-BBN-768

Praise for the novels of

STEPHANIE LAURENS

"Laurens's writing shines."
—*Publishers Weekly*

"In an Amanda Quick–style suspense/romance,
Laurens never loses touch with her characters'
deep emotions or the haunting mystery."
—*RT Book Reviews*

"An interesting and absorbing plot…an exciting
and appealing romantic mystery."
—*FreshFiction.com*

"The sensual tension simmers…
and, as always, Laurens delivers the
delicious heat as they fall in love."
—Michelle Buonfiglio, *myLifetime.com*

"Laurens spices up her superbly sensual,
elegantly written love story with a generous
measure of splendidly entertaining."
—*Booklist*

"A fast-paced, action-packed, historical romance.
Stephanie Laurens has another winner
on her hands."
—*The Romance Readers Connection*

"Danger, intrigue and seduction aplenty—
will leave you satisfied yet hungry for more."
—*Romance Reviews Today*

STEPHANIE LAURENS

Impetuous Innocent

HQN™

Recycling programs
for this product may
not exist in your area.

ISBN-13: 978-0-373-77508-8

IMPETUOUS INNOCENT

This edition published by arrangement with Harlequin Books S.A.

For questions and comments about the quality of this book please contact us at Customer_eCare@Harlequin.ca.

® and TM are trademarks of the publisher. Trademarks indicated with ® are registered in the United States Patent and Trademark Office, the Canadian Trade Marks Office and in other countries.

www.HQNBooks.com

Printed in U.S.A.

Impetuous Innocent

CHAPTER ONE

"GEORGIE? GEORGIE! Open this door! Aw—c'mon, Georgie. Jus' a bit of a kiss an' cuddle. D'you hear me, Georgie? Lemme in!"

Georgiana Hartley sat cross-legged in the middle of her bed, fully clothed, a small, slight figure in the huge four-poster. The flickering light of a single candle gleamed on her guinea-gold curls, still dressed in an elegant knot. Her large hazel eyes, fixed on the door of her chamber, held an expression of annoyance; her soft lips were compressed into a disapproving line. Charles was becoming a definite boor.

It was her seventh night in England, her fourth at the Place, seat of her forefathers and home of her cousin Charles. And it was the third night she had had to seek the safety of her bedchamber at a ridiculously early hour, to avoid Charles's drink-driven importunities.

She had done it again.

Pulling a pillow across her lap, and wrinkling her nose at the musty smell that arose when she settled her elbows on it, Georgiana berated herself, for what was certainly not the first time and would undoubtedly not be the last, for her apparently innate impulsiveness. It had been that alone which had driven her to leave the sunny climes of the Italian coast and return to the land of her birth. Still, on her father's death, it had seemed the most sensible course. With a deep sigh she dropped her chin on to her hands, keeping her eyes trained on the door. All was quiet, but she knew Charles was still there, just outside, hoping she might be silly enough to try to slip out.

James Hartley, painter and vivant, had left his only child to the guardianship of his only brother, her uncle Ernest. Uncle Ernest had lived at the Place. Unfortunately, he had died one month before his brother. Georgiana sniffed. Doubtless she should feel something for her uncle, but it was hard to feel grief on the death of someone you had never met—particularly when still coping with a far more shattering loss. And particularly when circumstances had conspired to land her in Charles's lap. For the news of her uncle's death had not reached James Hartley's Italian solicitors in time to stop her instinctive flight from the beauties of Ravello, her home for the last twelve years, now filled with too many painful memories. She had arrived at the Place to find Charles—Uncle Ernest's son, and a stranger to her—in possession.

The solid oak door rattled and jumped in its frame. Georgiana eyed it with increasing concern. The worn lock and the old iron hinges were all that stood between her and her drink-sodden cousin.

"Aw, Georgie, don' be a prude. You'll like't, I promise. Just a bit o' fun." A loud hiccup reached Georgiana's ears. "It's all right. You know I'll marry you. Lemme in and we'll be married tomorrow. You hear me, Georgie? C'mon, Georgie, open this door, I say!"

Georgiana sternly repressed a shiver of pure revulsion. Marry Charles? Feeling panic stir, she deter-

minedly pushed the horrifying thought aside. Now was
no time to go to pieces.

The door bounced, reverberating on its hinges as
Charles made a determined assault on the thick panels.
Georgiana's eyes grew round. As the thumping continued, she scanned the room for some implement, some
weapon. But there was nothing, not even a candelabrum.
With a grimace of resignation, she returned her gaze to
the heavy oak door, philosophically waiting for whatever came next, confident that, one way or another, she
would deal with it.

But the door stood firm. With one last defeated
thump, Charles stopped his hammering.

"Damn you, Georgie! You won't get away! You can't
escape me. You'll see—you'll have to give in, soon or
late." A jeering, drunken laugh crept into the room.
"You'll see."

Unsteady footsteps retreated down the passage as
Charles took himself off to bed, giggling crazily.

Slowly Georgiana raised her brows. She remained
perched on the bed, listening. When five minutes had
passed with no sound from beyond her door, she hurled
aside the pillow and slipped from the bed. A determined
frown settled across her heart-shaped face. She fell to
pacing the room. Can't escape?

For five minutes she walked the unpolished boards.
The wind whistled and moaned, little blasts worming
their way through the ill-fitting shutters to send the curtains skittering. Absent-mindedly Georgiana dragged
the patched quilt from the bed and flung it about her
shoulders. She reviewed her options. There weren't
many. She knew no one in England, had no one to turn
to. But one thing was certain—she could not stay here.

If she did, Charles would force her to marry him—by hook or by crook. She couldn't hide behind locked doors forever.

With the dogged and purposeful air which had carried her across an unstable Continent unharmed, she threw off the quilt and crossed to the wardrobe. Setting the door wide, she struggled to pull her trunk free. Once she got it to the floor, she tugged the cumbersome corded box to the side of the bed. She opened the heavy lid and propped it against the bed.

A scratching at the door startled her.

Slowly Georgiana straightened and eyed the scarred oak panels with misgiving.

The noise came again.

"Miss Georgie? It's me, Cruickshank."

Georgiana let out the breath she had been holding and went to the door. It was a fight to turn the heavy key. After much tugging, the bolt fell back and she eased the heavy door open. "Cruckers! Thank goodness you've come. I was racking my brains to think of how to get hold of you."

Maria Cruickshank, a thin, weedy woman, tall and lanky, with iron-grey hair tightly confined, sniffed loudly. Originally maid to Georgiana's mother, she was the closest thing to a family retainer Georgiana had.

"As if I'd not come running with all that racket. He may be your cousin, but that Charles is no good. I told you so. *Now* do you believe me?"

Together they pushed the door shut. Cruickshank wrestled the lock home and turned to face the child-cum-lovely young woman she adored. She placed her hands on her hips and frowned grimly. "Now, Miss Georgie, I hope you're convinced. We've got to leave this house. It's no place for the likes of you, what with Master Charles as he is. It's not what your father intended, dear me, no!"

Georgiana smiled and turned back to the bed.

Cruickshank's eyes widened. She drew full breath, girding her loins for battle. Then she saw the trunk. Her breath came out with a soft whistle. "Ah."

Georgiana's smile grew. "Precisely. We're leaving. Come and help."

Cruickshank needed no further urging. Ten minutes later, all of Georgiana's possessions were back in her trunk. While Cruickshank tightened the straps, Georgiana sat on the lid, biting the tip of one rosy finger and plotting her escape.

"Now, Cruckers, there's no point in setting out before dawn, so we may as well get some sleep. I'll stay here, and you go back downstairs and warn Ben. Charles must be dead to the world by now. I'm sure I'll be safe enough."

Georgiana waited for the inevitable protest. Instead, Cruickshank merely snorted and clambered to her feet.

"True enough. A whole decanter of brandy he poured down his gullet. I doubt he'll be up betimes."

Georgiana's hazel eyes widened in awe. "Truly? Heavens!" She wriggled her toes, then jumped to the ground. "Well, that's all the better. The longer he sleeps, the farther we'll get before he finds out."

Cruickshank sniffed disparagingly. "D'you think he'll follow?"

A worried frown drew down Georgiana's fine brows. "I really don't know. He says he's my guardian, but I don't see how that can be." She sank on to the bed, one hand brushing gold curls from her forehead in a gesture of bewilderment. "It's all so confusing."

Her tone brought Cruickshank to her side, one large hand coming up to pat Georgiana's shoulder comfortingly. "Never you worry, Miss Georgie. Ben and me, we'll see you safe."

Fleetingly, Georgiana smiled, her hand rising to grip that of her maid. "Yes, of course. I don't know what I'd have done without my two watchdogs."

Bright hazel eyes met faded blue, and Cruickshank's stern features softened. "Now, lovey, do you have any notion where you should go?"

It was the question Georgiana had spent the last three days pondering. To no avail. But her tone was determined and decisive when she said, "I've thought and thought, but I can't think of anyone. As far as I can see, the best thing I can do is throw myself on the mercy of one of the ladies of the neighbourhood. There must be someone about who remembers Uncle Ernest or Papa and will at least advise me."

Cruickshank grimaced, but did not argue the point. "I'll be back before first light. I'll bring Ben for the trunk. You get some rest now. Enough excitement for one night, you've had."

Obediently Georgiana allowed Cruickshank to help her into her nightgown, then clambered into the big bed. Cruickshank resettled the quilt and tucked the sheets under the lumpy mattress. Again the maid sniffed disparagingly.

"Even if 'twas your grandpa's house, miss, all I can say is the accommodation leaves much to be desired." With a haughty glance at the aged bedclothes, Cruickshank clumped to the door. "Just to be on the safe side, I'll lock you in."

With the problem of Charles already behind her, and her immediate actions decided, Georgiana's mind slowed. With a sigh, she snuggled deeper into the mattress and curled up tight against the cold. Her lids were already drooping as she watched the door close behind the faithful Cruickshank. The lock fell heavily into place. Georgiana yawned widely and blew out her candle.

"SHHH!" Cruickshank held a finger to her lips and with her other hand indicated a door giving off the dimly lit passage.

Georgiana nodded her understanding and slipped silently past the room where Charles's slatternly housekeeper and her equally slovenly spouse snored in drunken unison. The Pringates were new to the Place, and Georgiana could not conceive how Charles had come to hire them. They seemed to know little to nothing of managing a household. None of the old servants had remained after her uncle's death. Presumably it was hard to get good help in the country. And, even to her untutored eyes, the Place was in sorry condition, hardly an attractive proposition to experienced staff.

Mentally shrugging, she hurried on. The dank corridor ended in a huge stone-flagged kitchen. Cruickshank was struggling with the heavy back door. As she eased it open, the tell-tale sound of a horse whickering drifted in with the wet mist. Galvanised, Georgiana hurried out into the yard, Cruickshank close behind.

Her own travelling carriage, battered and worn after the long journey from Italy, but thankfully still serviceable, stood in the muddy yard, her two powerful carriage horses hitched in their harness. She spared the time to bestow a fond pat on each great grey head before allowing Ben to help her into the coach.

As the door shut, sealing her within, with Cruickshank on the seat opposite, Georgiana settled herself on the padded leather with a weary sigh. She had hoped to enjoy a rest after the jolting roads of the Continent. True, the English roads were in much better condition, but she had looked forward to keeping her feet on firm ground and her bottom on softer seats for some time. Fate, however, had clearly decided otherwise.

The carriage rocked as Ben climbed to his perch. Without his customary whistle, he set the team moving. The coach rumbled quietly out of the yard and turned into the lane.

As the miles fell slowly behind them, Georgiana wondered anew at the oddity of the Place. The old house stood in its own extensive grounds, overgrown and choked with weeds, amid fields and meadows, all lying fallow as far as she had seen. She lifted the window flap and peered through the early morning gloom. There was no sign of livestock anywhere. Fences were broken and gates hung crazily on ruptured hinges. An air of decay hung like a pall across the estate. Heaven knew, it wasn't all that large as estates went. But the Place had hit hard times, and neglect had taken its toll. She was sure her father had not known the state of his family's property. If he had, he would never have suggested she seek refuge there. Or, alternatively, he would have made some provision to restore the Place to its former glory.

As the carriage drew to the crest of a hill which

marked the limit of the estate, Georgiana, leaning past
the leather flap, caught a last glimpse of the grey roofs
of the Place. Then the horses started on the downward
slope and trees blocked her view. In truth, from what
she had seen in her three days there, she doubted the
Place was worth saving.

Her only regret in leaving was that she had failed to
unearth the set of paintings her father had told her he
had left there. Close to twenty finished canvases, he had
said. The only one she was really interested in was a
portrait of her mother which he had painted shortly after
their marriage. He had always maintained it was the
best of the handful of portraits he had done of his wife.
Georgiana had looked forward to seeing again the face
of her gentle mother, otherwise no more than a misty
memory. But Charles had denied all knowledge of the
paintings, and her surreptitious searches had failed to
find any trace of them. Now, as she didn't fancy staying
within Charles's reach, the paintings would remain lost
to her. Philosophically, she sighed. She knew she'd made
the right choice. But she had so wanted that portrait of
her mother.

The lane which led to the Place was long and wind-
ing. It followed a strange line, around the boundaries of
the holdings of a neighbouring estate, eventually joining a road which ultimately led to Steeple Claydon.
The morning mists were lifting by the time the coach
trundled into the small village of Alton Rise, no more
than a cluster of cottages nestling at the first cross-
roads. Ben pulled the horses up before the tiny inn. He
jumped down from his perch and came to the carriage
window.

Georgiana pushed aside the window flap and

leant out. "Can you ask where the nearest magistrate lives? If that sounds too far, ask for the nearest big landowner."

Ben nodded and disappeared into the inn. Ten minutes later he was back. "They said best to go on up to Candlewick Hall. It's owned by a London swell, name of Lord Alton. His family's been hereabouts for generations, so it seems a safe bet. The innkeeper's missus thought you'd be safe enough asking for help there."

"Heavens, Ben!" Georgiana looked at her faithful henchman in horror. "You didn't tell them about…?"

Ben shrugged his old shoulders. "'Tweren't no news to them. By all accounts, that cousin of yourn's not much liked."

Georgiana considered this view. It was not hard to believe. Charles, in three days, had proved his colours beyond question. "How far is it to Candlewick Hall?"

"No more'n a couple of miles," said Ben, hauling himself up.

As the coach lumbered forward, Georgiana sat back and rehearsed her explanation. Doubtless she would have to be frank with Lady Alton. She was not sure what she expected her ladyship to do for her. Still, at the very least, surely Lady Alton would be able to recommend a hotel in London where she could safely stay?

The coach had picked up speed on the better-surfaced road. Georgiana's wandering attention was reclaimed by the slowing of the vehicle as Ben turned the horses sharply to the left. Drawing closer to the window, she rolled up the flap and fastened it above the frame so she could gaze unimpeded at the landscape. And a very different landscape it was. In just a few miles, all evidence of rot had vanished. The fields they now passed were well tended; sheep and cattle dotted the pastures. All was neat and pleasant perfection. As if to give its blessing, the sun struck through the clouds, bathing the scene in warmth and brightness.

Georgiana was even more impressed when they reached the park of Candlewick Hall. Two stone eagles, perched atop tall gateposts, stood guard. Between them, massive wrought-iron gates hung wide. A neat gravelled drive led onwards, curving away between two lines of beech trees. The horses appreciated the even surface and trotted easily onward. Georgiana looked about her and was pleased to approve. This was how she had imagined an English gentleman's country residence would look, with trimmed shrubberies and manicured lawns falling away on one side to an ornamental lake, a white summer-house perched on an island in the middle. The vista had about it an air of peace and tranquillity. As the coach swept around a bend, she caught a glimpse of colour through the green of the trees—presumably the gardens, which meant the house was near. She scooted to the other side of the coach and looked out.

Her eyes grew round and her lips formed an "Oh" of delight.

Candlewick Hall rose before her, its cream stone walls touched here and there with bright creeper. Three storeys of square-paned windows looked down on the gravel court before the front steps. In the morning light, the house was cloaked in a still serenity, a peaceful solidity, which tugged oddly at her. Candlewick Hall embodied everything she had come back to England to find.

The pace of the coach was checked, and they rocked to a stop before the white steps leading up to two massive front doors. Ben swung down and came to assist her to alight. He escorted her up the steps and plied the heavy knocker.

Georgiana faced the heavy wooden doors. It had seemed much easier to claim help from an unknown lady when she had been sitting in her bed last night. But the memory of Charles's ravings stiffened her resolve. As the sound of footsteps drew nearer, she took a deep breath and fixed a confident smile on her lips.

"Yes?"

A stately butler looked majestically down upon her.

"Good morning. My name is Georgiana Hartley. I wonder if I might have a word with Lady Alton?"

Georgiana was pleased with her tone. She sounded confident and in control, despite the fact she was inwardly quaking. If the butler was this starchy, what was his mistress like? She kept her chin up and waited.

The butler did not move. Georgiana felt her confidence draining, dissipating like the morning mist under the intensity of his scrutiny. She wondered if the man was hard of hearing, and was gathering her courage to repeat her request in more strident tones when he smiled, quite kindly, and bowed. "If you will step into the drawing-room, Miss Hartley, I will inform Lord Alton immediately."

Buoyed by her success, Georgiana was across the threshold before she analysed his words. She came to an abrupt halt. "Oh! But it was Lady Alton I wished to see."

"Yes, of course, miss. If you would take a seat?"

Unable to resist the deferential and strangely compelling courtesy of the impeccable butler, Georgiana found herself ushered into a beautifully appointed room and made comfortable in a wing-chair. Having ascertained that she was not in need of any refreshment thus early in the day, the dignified personage withdrew.

Feeling slightly dazed, Georgiana looked about her. The interior of Candlewick Hall did justice to its exterior. Exquisite taste and a judicious eye had chosen and arranged all the furnishings, creating and enhancing a mood of peace and serenity to match that of the gardens. Her hazel gaze wandered over the room, coming to rest on the large painting in pride of place above the mantelpiece. As a painter's daughter, she could not do otherwise than admire Fragonard. She was intrigued, nevertheless, to find a picture incorporating numerous naked female forms so publicly displayed. A more private room would, she thought, have been more appropriate. But then, she reminded herself, she knew nothing of the latest whims of English social taste. And there was no doubt the Fragonard was an exquisite work of art.

The subtle colours of the room slowly eased her tension, seeping into her sight and mind. Georgiana smiled to herself and settled back in the chair. Candlewick Hall seemed designed to calm the senses. With a grateful sigh, she relaxed.

The effects of three late nights dragged at her eyelids. She would close them. Just for a moment.

"THERE'S A YOUNG LADY to see you, m'lord."

Dominic Ridgeley, fifth Viscount Alton, lifted his blue eyes to his butler's face. Around him, on the polished mahogany table, the remains of a substantial breakfast bore mute testimony to his recent occupation.

But the dishes had been pushed aside to make way for a pile of letters, one of which his lordship clasped in one long-fingered hand.

"I beg your pardon?"

"A young lady has called, m'lord." Not a quiver of emotion showed on the butler's lined face.

Lord Alton's black brows rose. His features became perceptibly harder, his blue gaze perceptibly chillier. "Have you taken leave of your senses, Duckett?"

Such a question, in such a tone, would have reduced most servants to incoherent gibbering. But Duckett was a butler of the highest standing. And he had known the present Lord Alton from the cradle. He answered the question with an infinitesimal smile. "Naturally not, m'lord."

His answer appeared to appease his master. Lord Alton regarded his henchman with a puzzled and slightly wary frown. "Oh?"

At the prompt, Duckett explained. "It seems the young lady requires assistance with some difficulty, m'lord. She asked to see Lady Alton. She appears to be in some distress. I thought it wise not to turn her away. Her name is Miss Hartley."

"Hartley?" The black brows drew down. "But there aren't any Miss Hartleys at the Place, are there?"

In response to his master's quizzical look, Duckett graciously informed him, "I have heard that Mr James Hartley's daughter has been visiting the Place for the past few days. From the Continent, I believe."

"Staying with frightful Charles? Poor girl."

"Exactly so, m'lord."

Lord Alton fixed Duckett with a suspicious look.

"You said she was distressed. She's not weeping and having the vapours, is she?"

"Oh, no, m'lord. Miss Hartley is perfectly composed."

Lord Alton frowned again. "Then how do you know she's distressed?"

Duckett coloured slightly. "It was her hands, m'lord. She was clutching her reticule so tightly, her knuckles were quite white."

Suitably impressed by his butler's astuteness, Lord Alton leant back in his chair, absent-mindedly laying the letter he had been reading on the pile before him. Then he glanced up. "You think I should see her?"

Duckett met his master's eye and did not misunderstand his question. No one who was acquainted with Lord Alton could fail to comprehend the delicacy of the matter. For a young lady to meet a gentleman alone, particularly in the gentleman's house, with no other lady anywhere about, was hardly the sort of behaviour someone as conservative as Duckett would normally encourage. And when the gentleman in question was Lord Dominic Alton, the situation took on an even more questionable hue. But Duckett's perception was acute. Miss Hartley was in trouble and out of her depth. His master could be relied upon to provide the answer to her troubles. And, regardless of his reputation, she stood in no danger from him. She was too young and too green, not his type at all. So, Duckett cleared his throat and said, "Despite the—er—conventions, yes, m'lord, I think you should see her."

With a sigh, Lord Alton rose, stretching to his full six feet. Relaxing, he shook out his cuffs and settled his dark blue coat over his broad shoulders. Then he looked up and wagged an admonitory finger at Duckett. "If this lands me in scandal, old friend, it'll be all your fault."

Duckett grinned and opened the door for his master. "As you wish, m'lord. She's in the drawing-room."

With one last warning glance, Lord Alton passed through the door and crossed the hall.

GEORGIANA'S DREAM was distinctly disturbing. In it, she had transformed into one of the nymphs depicted in the Fragonard canvas. Together with her unknown sisters, she cavorted freely through a sylvan glade, blushing at the cool drift of the breeze across her naked skin. Abruptly, she halted. Someone was watching her. She glanced around, blushing even more rosily. But there was no one in sight. The sensation of being watched grew. She opened her eyes.

And gazed bemusedly into eyes of cerulean blue.

Her gaze widened, and she saw the man behind the eyes. She stopped breathing, no longer sure which was reality and which the dream. For the man watching her, a gleam of undisguised appreciation in the depths of those beautiful blue eyes, was undoubtedly a god. And even more disturbing than her erotic dream. His shoulders were broad, filling her sight, his body long and lean and muscular. His face was strongly featured, yet held the clean lines painters adored. Thick dark hair cloaked his head in elegant waves, softening the effect of his determinedly squared chin. Finely drawn lips held the hint of a disturbing smile. And his eyes, glorious blue, set under strongly arched brows and framed by lashes too long and thick for a man, seemed to hold all the promise of a summer's afternoon.

"Oh!" It was the most coherent response she could muster.

The vision smiled. Georgiana's heart lurched.

"You were sleeping so peacefully I was loath to disturb you."

The deep tones of his voice enclosed Georgiana in a warmth reminiscent of fine velvet. With an effort, she straightened, forcing her body to behave and her mind to function. "I… I'm so sorry. I must have drifted off. I was waiting for Lady Alton."

The gentleman retreated slightly to lean one elegant arm along the mantelpiece, one booted foot resting on the hearth. The blue eyes, disconcertingly, remained trained on her face.

"I'm desolated to disappoint you." The smile that went with the words said otherwise. "Allow me to introduce myself. Lord Dominic Alton, entirely at your service."

He swept her an elegant bow, blue eyes gleaming.

"But alas, I've yet to marry. There is, therefore, no Lady Alton."

"Oh, *how* unfortunate!"

The anguished assessment surprised Dominic. He was not used to such a response from personable young women. His lips twitched and his eyes came alight with unholy amusement. "Quite!"

His tone brought the hazel gaze to his face. But she showed no consciousness of her phrasing. Seeing real consternation in the warm hazel eyes, Dominic rejected the appealing idea of explaining it to her. Clearly, Duckett's assessment of her state was accurate. She might be sitting calmly, rather than indulging in hysterics, as females were so lamentably prone to do, but he had no doubt she was seriously adrift and knew not which way to turn. The expression in her wide hazel eyes said so. In response, he smiled beguilingly. "But I gather you have some problem. Perhaps I could be of help?"

His polite query flustered Georgiana. How could she explain…? To a man…?

"Er—I don't think…" She rose, clutching her reticule tightly. As she did so, her gaze went beyond Lord Alton to the Fragonard. Georgiana froze. What sort of man, with no wife, hung a scandalous masterpiece in his drawing-room? The answer threatened to scuttle what wits she still possessed.

Unknown to Georgiana, her thoughts passed clearly across her face, perfectly readable to the accomplished gentleman watching her. All Dominic's experience told him to accept her withdrawal as the blessed release it doubtless was. But some whimsical and unexpected impulse pushed him to learn what strange story, what quirk of fate, was responsible for depositing such a very delightful morsel on his doorstep. Besides, he didn't entirely like her assumption that he was powerless to help her. He drew himself to his full height and fixed her with a stern eye. "My dear Miss Hartley, I do hope you're not about to say you '—doubt that I can be of assistance—' before you've even told me the problem."

Georgiana blinked. She had, of course, been about to say just that. With the ground cut from under her feet, she struggled to find some acceptable way out.

Lord Alton was smiling again. Strange, she had never before encountered a smile that warmed her as his did.

"Please sit down, Miss Hartley. Can I get you some refreshment? No? Well, then, why don't you just tell me what your problem is? I promise you, I don't shock easily."

Georgiana glanced up, but the blue eyes were innocent. Sinking once more into the wing-chair, she considered her choices. If she insisted on leaving Lord Alton without asking for his advice, where would she go? And, more importantly, how far behind her was Charles? That thought, more than any other, drove her to speak. "I really wanted to ask for some advice…on what I should do, finding myself in the situation I… I now find myself in." She paused, wondering how detailed her explanation need be.

"Which is?" came the soft prompt.

The need to confide in someone was strong. Mentally shrugging, Georgiana threw caution to the winds. "I recently returned to England from the Continent. I've lived for the last twelve years in Italy with my father, James Hartley. He died a few months ago, leaving me to the guardianship of my uncle, Ernest Hartley."

She looked up. Lord Alton's expression was sympathetic. He nodded encouragingly. Drawing a deep breath, she continued. "I returned to England immediately. I…didn't wish to remain in Italy. On my arrival at Hartley Place, I learnt that my uncle had died a month or so before my father. My cousin Charles owns the Place now." Georgiana hesitated.

"I'm slightly acquainted with Charles Hartley, if that's any help. I might add that I would not consider him a fit person for a young lady such as yourself to share a roof with."

His cool, impersonal tone brought a blush to Georgiana's cheek.

Seeing it, Dominic knew he had struck close to the truth.

Keeping her eyes fixed on the empty fireplace, Georgiana struggled on. "I'm afraid...that is to say, Charles seems to have developed a fixation. In short," she continued, desperation lending her words, "he has been trying to force me to marry him. I left the house this morning, very early."

She glanced up and, to her surprise, found no difficulty in meeting his lordship's blue gaze. "I've no one in England I can turn to, my lord. I was hoping to ask your wife for advice as to what I should do."

Dominic's gaze rested on the heart-shaped face and large honey-gold eyes turned so trustingly towards him. For some perverse reason, he knew he was going to help her. Ignoring the inner voice which whispered he was mad even to contemplate such a thing, he asked, "Have you any particular course of action in mind?"

"Well, I did think of going to London. I thought perhaps I could become a companion to some lady."

Dominic forcibly repressed a shudder. Such a glorious creature would have no luck in finding that sort of employment. She was flexing her fingers, her attention momentarily distracted. His eyes slid gently over her figure. The grey dress she wore fitted well, outlining a pair of enticingly sweet breasts, young and firm and high. Her skin was perfect—peaches and cream. As she was seated, he had no way of judging her legs, although, by the evidence of her slender feet, he suspected they would prove to be long and slim. Her waist was hidden by the fall of her dress, but the swell of her hips was unmistakable. If Georgiana Hartley became stranded in London, he could guess where she'd end. Which, all things considered, would be a great shame. Her candid gaze returned to his face.

"I have my own maid and coachman. I thought that might help."

Help? A companion with her own maid and coachman? Dominic managed to keep his face impassive. There was no point in telling her how ludicrous her ideas were, for she wasn't going to hire out as a companion. Not if he had anything to say in the matter. The wretched life most paid companions led, neither servant nor family, stranded in limbo between stairs, was not for Miss Hartley.

"I will have to think of what's best to be done. Instant solutions are likely to come unstuck. I've always found it much more useful to consider carefully before committing any irrevocable act."

Listen to yourself! screamed his inner voice.

Dominic smiled sweetly. "I suggest you spend an hour or so with my housekeeper, while I consider the alternatives." The smile broadened. "Believe me, there are alternatives."

Georgiana blinked. She wasn't sure what to make of that. She hoped she hadn't jumped from the frying-pan into the fire. But he was turning her over to the care of his housekeeper, which hardly fitted with the image revolving in her mind. There was another problem. "Charles might follow me."

"I can assure you this is one place Charles will never look. And I doubt he'd pursue you to London. You're perfectly safe here." Dominic turned and tugged the bell-pull. Then he swung back to face Georgiana and smiled reassuringly. "Charles and I don't exactly get on, you see."

A pause ensued. While Miss Hartley studied her hands, Dominic studied Miss Hartley. She was a sweetly turned piece, but too gentle and demure for his taste. A damsel in distress—Duckett had been right there. Clearly, it behoved him to help her. The cost would be negligible; it would hardly take up much of his time and might even afford him some amusement. Aside from anything else, it would presumably annoy Charles Hartley, and that was a good enough reason in itself. He determinedly quashed his inner voice, that advocate of self-protection at all costs, and returned to his agreeable contemplation of Miss Hartley.

The door opened, and Georgiana came slowly to her feet.

"My lord?"

Dominic turned. "Duckett, please ask Mrs Landy to attend us."

"Yes, m'lord." Duckett bowed himself from the room, a smile of quiet satisfaction on his face.

AFTER A PLEASANT and reassuring hour spent with Mrs Landy, Georgiana was conducted back to the drawing-room. The motherly housekeeper had been shocked to learn of Georgiana's plight and even more moved when she discovered she had missed her breakfast. Now, fortified with muffins and jam and steaming coffee, and having been assured her two servants had been similarly supplied, Georgiana faced the prospect of her interview with Lord Alton with renewed confidence. No gentleman who possessed a housekeeper like Mrs Landy could be a villain.

She smiled sweetly at the butler, who seemed much less intimidating now, and passed through the door he held open for her. Lord Alton was standing by the fireplace. He looked up as she entered, and smiled. Georgiana was struck anew by his handsomeness and the subtle aura of a deeper attractiveness that owed nothing to his elegant attire, but derived more from the quality of his smile and the lights that danced in those wonderful eyes.

He inclined his head politely in response to her curtsy and, still smiling, waved her to the wing-chair. Georgiana seated herself and settled her skirts, thankful she had this morning donned one of her more modish gowns, a grey kerseymere with a fine white linen fichu, edged with expensive Italian lace. Comfortable, she raised expectant eyes to his lordship's dark-browed face.

For a full minute, he seemed to be looking at her and thinking of something else. Then, abruptly, he cleared his throat.

"How old are you, Miss Hartley?"

Georgiana answered readily, assuming him to be considering what employment might best suit her years. "Eighteen, my lord."

Eighteen. Good. He was thirty-two. She was too young, thank God. It must just be his gentlemanly instincts that were driving him to help her. At thirty-two, one was surely beyond the stage of lusting after schoolroom chits. Dominic smiled his practised smile.

"In light of your years, I think you'll find it will take some time to discover a suitable position. Such opportunities don't grow on trees, you know." He kept his manner determinedly avuncular. "I've been thinking of what lady of my acquaintance would be most useful in helping you. My sister, Lady Winsmere, is often telling me she pines for distraction." That, at least, was the truth. If he knew Bella, she would leap at the opportunity for untold distraction that he intended to offer her in the charming person of Miss Georgiana Hartley.

Georgiana watched Lord Alton's face intently. Thus far, his measured statements made perfect sense, but his patronising tone niggled. She was hardly a child.

"I have written a letter to her," Dominic continued, pausing to draw a folded parchment from his coat, "in which I've explained your predicament." His lips involuntarily twitched as he imagined what Bella would make of his disclosures. "I suggest you take it and deliver it in person to Lady Winsmere in Green Street." He smiled into Miss Hartley's warmed honey eyes. "Bella, despite her occasional flights of fancy, is quite remarkably sane and will know precisely how you should go on. I've asked her to supervise you in your search for employment, for you will be sadly out of touch with the way things are done. You may place complete confidence in her judgement."

Relief swept over Georgiana. She rose and took the letter. Holding it carefully, she studied the strong black script boldly inscribed across the parchment. Her fingers moved across the thick, finely textured paper. She felt oddly reassured, as if a confidence placed had proved to be well founded. After her problems with Charles, the world seemed to be righting itself. "My lord, I don't know how to thank you. You've been more help than I expected, certainly more than I deserve." Her soft voice sounded so small in that elegant room. She raised her eyes to his, smiling in sincere gratitude.

Unaccountably irritated, Dominic waved one fine hand dismissively. "It was nothing, I assure you. It's entirely my pleasure to be able to help you. Now one more point." He hurried on, strangely unwilling to bear more of Miss Hartley's gratitude. "It seems to me that if Charles is out there scouting about he'll be looking for your carriage, with your coachman atop. I've therefore given orders for you to be conveyed to London in one of my carriages, together with your maid. One of my coachmen will drive you and will return with the carriage. After a few days, when Charles has given up, your coachman will follow you with your coach. I trust such an arrangement is satisfactory?"

Georgiana felt slightly stunned. He seemed to have thought of everything. Efficiently, smoothly, in just one short hour he had cleared the obstacles from her path and made all seem easy. "My lord, you overwhelm me. But surely—you might need your carriage?"

"I assure you my carriage will be…better used conveying you to London than it otherwise would be," Dominic responded suavely, only just managing to avoid a more subtly flattering selection of words. God! Dealing with an innocent was trying his wits. A long time had passed since he had engaged in social discourse with a virtuous young lady of only eighteen summers. It was too abominably easy to slip into the more sophisticated and seductive modes of conversation he used almost exclusively to females these days. Which, he ruefully reminded himself, was a definite reflection on the types of ladies whose company he currently kept.

With another dazzling smile, Georgiana Hartley inclined her head in acceptance. At his intimation, she fell into step beside him, gliding towards the door on tiny, grey-slippered feet.

Still bemused, and with the feeling that events were

suddenly moving rather faster than she could cope with, Georgiana could nevertheless find no fault with his arrangements.

Duckett met them in the hall with the information that the coach stood ready.

Dominic could not resist offering her his arm. With gentlemanly courtesy he conducted her to the coach, pausing while she exchanged farewells with Ben, surprising everyone, Ben included, by breaking off her words to give him a quick hug. Then Dominic handed her into the luxuriously appointed coach, wherein her maid was already installed, and stood back. Duckett shut the door firmly. The coachman, Jiggs, gave the horses the office. The coach pulled smoothly away.

Dominic Ridgeley stood on the steps of his manor house, his hands sunk in his pockets, and watched his coach roll out of sight. Then, when he could no longer see the swaying carriage roof, he turned to go inside, pausing to kick at a piece of gravel inadvertently, inexcusably resident on the steps. With a sigh and a pensive smile, as if some pleasant interlude had come to its inevitable conclusion, he went inside and shut the door.

CHAPTER TWO

NIGHT had descended by the time Lord Alton's travelling carriage drew to a halt on the cobbles before the elegant town house of Lord and Lady Winsmere. Georgiana glanced up at the tiers of lamplit windows reaching high above the street. Beside her, Cruickshank sat silent, her lips set in a severe line. The groom swung down and trotted up the steps to jangle the doorbell before returning to help them to the pavement.

A portly butler appeared. One glance at the groom's livery was apparently enough to effect instant entrance for Georgiana and Cruickshank.

Georgiana allowed the butler to remove her pelisse. Then she turned and, in a voice tinged with nervousness, said, "I wish to speak with Lady Winsmere, if you please. I have a letter of introduction from Lord Alton."

Despite the butler's gracious bow and solemn face, Georgiana was instantly aware of his avid interest.

"I will convey your letter to Lady Winsmere, miss. If you would care to wait in the drawing-room?"

Shown into a reception-room of pleasing proportions, Georgiana stopped and blinked. The door shut behind her. Cruickshank had dutifully remained in the hall. Georgiana scanned the room, then, finding nothing of greater moment to consider, gave her attention to a careful appraisal of the white and gilt décor. The room was well stocked with furniture, and every available flat surface sprouted at least one ornament. The rule seemed to be that if it wasn't white it had to be gilded. Not even the ornate cornices had escaped. The effect was overpowering. With a sigh and a shrug for English fashions, Georgiana chose a stiff-backed, spindle-legged chair, heavily gilded and upholstered in white damask, and gingerly sat down.

Her gaze roamed the walls once more, but there was no Fragonard to provide distraction.

She folded her hands in her lap and tried to subdue the uncomfortable feeling of encroaching upon those whom she had no right to call on. But Lord Alton had seemed unperturbed by her request for help. Maybe, despite her misgivings, there was nothing so very peculiar about her predicament. At least, not to an English mind. Determined to be optimstic, she endeavoured to compose herself to meet Lady Winsmere's questions. Doubtless, she would have a good few. What was she making of her brother's letter?

Only then did Georgiana realise she had no idea in what light Lord Alton had presented her to his sister. The thick parchment had been fixed with a heavy lump of red wax, on which the seal of the Viscounts Alton had been imprinted. Georgiana frowned. A wave of tiredness rose up to envelop her. Not for the first time since leaving the comfort of Candlewick Hall, she wondered at the wisdom of her actions. She was too impulsive. Often she had landed herself in the suds by rushing headlong on her fate—witness her flight from Ravello. But it was too late to draw back now. She grimaced. The more she thought of it, the more clearly she perceived

her inability to influence the course of events Lord
Alton had charted for her. These, presumably, would
determine her immediate future. Somehow she had
placed herself in Lord Alton's hands.

Georgiana stifled a despondent sigh. She hoped she
looked more confident than she felt.

ON THE FLOOR ABOVE, Bella, Lady Winsmere, was in
the middle of her toilette, preparatory to attending the
theatre. A knock on the door of her boudoir was followed by a whispered conference between her dresser,
Hills, and her butler, Johnson.

Distracted from the delicate task of improving on
nature, Bella frowned. "What is it, Hills?"

Her black-garbed dresser produced a folded parchment, inscribed to herself in her brother's unmistakable scrawl. Intrigued, Bella immediately laid down her
haresfoot. Bits of red wax scattered in all directions as
she broke open the seal.

Five short minutes later, she was crossing her front
hall in a froth of lacy peignoir, rendered barely respectable by a silk wrapper. Johnson, having anticipated her
impetuous descent, stood ready to open the drawing-
room door for her.

As the door shut, bringing her guest to her feet,
Bella's bright blue eyes, very like her brother's, surveyed
her unexpected visitor.

Unconsciously clutching her reticule, once again in
a tell-tale grip, Georgiana beheld an enchanting vision,
fashionably slender and no taller than she herself was.
But there the resemblance ended. Lady Winsmere was
dark-haired, her fine skin was alabaster-white. Her
blue eyes Georgiana had seen before. And the elegance

of her lacy gown made Georgiana feel awkward and abominably young.

For her part, Bella saw a girl on the threshold of womanhood. Her innocence shone beacon-clear. She was all honey and cream, from the top of her curls, tinged with the sun's kiss, to her delicately tinted complexion. Her golden eyes contained a quality of unusual candour. And she had no more inches than Bella herself. Bella's face brightened. A little sigh escaped her. With a generous and genuine smile, she floated forward, both hands outstretched to capture Georgiana's cold fingers in a warm clasp.

"My dear! So you are Georgiana Hartley! Dominic has written me all about you. You poor dear! What a dreadful thing to happen, and you newly returned to England. You must let me help you."

At Georgiana's murmured, "My lady," Bella broke her stride. But when Georgiana attempted to curtsy, Bella held on tightly to her hands, preventing it.

"No, no, my dear. You're among friends here. You must call me Bella, and I hope you won't think me terribly forward if I call you Georgiana." She tilted her small head to one side, blue eyes twinkling.

Georgiana found her engaging manners difficult to resist. "Why, of course not, my... Bella. But truly, I feel as if I'm imposing dreadfully upon you."

"Oh, pooh!" Bella pulled a face. "I'm always bored; there's so little to do in London these days. I'm positively thrilled Dominic thought to send you to me! Why—" she paused, struck by a wayward thought "—just think. If you'd grown up at the Place, we would have been neighbours." Bella waved Georgiana to the chaise and sank to the white damask beside her. "So, you see, there's no need for you to feel at all bothered about staying with me."

Georgiana's head reeled. "Oh! But I wouldn't dream of imposing—"

"Not at all! It's the very thing. You have nowhere to go and we have plenty of room." Bella gazed intently at Georgiana. "Truly, it's no trouble at all."

"But—"

Bella shook her head. "No buts. Just consider it as doing me a favour. We'll have such fun. I'll take you about and introduce you to all the right people."

Despite a sudden tug of impetuosity, urging acceptance of the exciting offer, Georgiana, grappling with the flow of Bella's burgeoning plans, felt constrained to protest. "But my la… Bella. I don't think Lord Alton can have properly explained. I need to find a post as a companion."

Recalling the specific instructions contained in her brother's letter, Bella assured Georgiana that he had, indeed, explained fully. "But my dear, in order to find the right post for you, particularly considering your age, you must first become established in society."

Bella watched the frown gathering in Georgiana's fine eyes. Before her guest could raise any further objection, she raised one slim, restraining hand. "Now before you start arguing—and I do so hate people who must forever be sniping and finding fault—I must tell you that you will be doing me the biggest favour imaginable in allowing me to help you. You can have no idea how boring it is to pass the Season with no real purpose. The Little Season is coming up in a few weeks. I implore you to relieve my frustrations and stay with me and allow me to present you. Surely that's not too much to ask?" Bella's big blue eyes pleaded eloquently.

Bemused by the sudden twist the situation seemed to have taken, with Lady Winsmere now begging the favour of her company, and feeling too drained by the day's events to fight a fate so apparently desirable, Georgiana found herself weakly acquiescing. "If it's really not too much trouble… Just until I can find a position."

"Splendid!" Bella grinned in delight. "Now the first thing we must do is get you settled in a bedchamber. A hot bath is just what you need. Always so soothing after travelling."

With a magic wave of one small bejewelled hand, Bella took charge. In short order, Georgiana, her luggage, Cruickshank, dinner on a tray and a large tub together with steaming hot water to fill it had been conveyed to the best guest chamber on the floor above.

An hour later, after she had closed the door of Georgiana's room behind her, having seen her young guest settled in bed, Bella Winsmere's face took on a pensive frown. Slowly she descended the stairs, so deep in thought that she was halfway across the hall towards the front door before she recalled her intended destination. Swinging about, she turned her steps towards the library at the back of the house.

At the sound of the door opening, Lord Winsmere looked up from the pile of documents he was working on. His lean face lit with a smile of great warmth. He laid aside his pen to reach out a welcoming arm to his wife.

With a quick smile, Bella went to him, returning his embrace and dropping a quick kiss on his greying hair.

"I thought you were bound for Drury Lane tonight?" Lord Winsmere was more than twenty years older than his beautiful wife. His staid, sometimes regal demeanour contrasted sharply with her effervescent charm. Many had wondered why, from among her myraid suitors, Bella Ridgeley had chosen to bestow her dainty hand on a man almost old enough to be her father. But over the years society had been forced to accept the fact that the beautiful Bella was sincerely and most earnestly in love with her eminently respectable lord.

"I was, but we have an unexpected guest."

"Oh?"

His lordship pushed his papers aside, consigning them to the morrow. If his Bella had sought him out, then she had some problem to discuss. He rose and, Bella's hand still in his, led her to the two armchairs stationed before the fireplace.

Bella sat, chewing the tip of one rosy finger, a habit when thinking profoundly.

Smiling, Lord Winsmere seated himself opposite her and waited for her to begin.

"It's really most intriguing."

Inured to his spouse's methods of explanation, Lord Winsmere made no response.

Eventually Bella gathered her wandering mind and embarked on her story. "Dominic's sent a girl to stay."

At that, Lord Winsmere's brows rose sharply. But the knowledge that, despite his apparent lack of moral concern, Dominic Ridgeley had never permitted the slightest breath of scandal to touch his sister's fair name held him silent.

"She's a would-have-been-neighbour. Her name's Georgiana Hartley. Her father was a painter, one James Hartley. He died in Italy some months ago and Georgiana was left to her uncle's care. Most unfortunately, her uncle, who lived at the Place—you know, it's that funny estate that was made by selling off a piece of Candlewick—well, he died too. Just before her father, only she didn't know that, being in Italy. The long and the short of it is, Georgiana travelled all the way from Italy, only to find her uncle dead and her cousin Charles in charge. It only needs to add that Charles is an out-and-out bounder and you have the picture." Bella spread her hands and glanced at her husband.

"How did Dominic come to be involved?"

"It seems Georgiana was forced to flee the Place at dawn this morning. She doesn't know anyone—no one at all. She asked at the Three Bells, thinking to find a sympathetic lady in residence at a neighbouring estate. Of course, the Tadlows sent her to Candlewick. You know how all our people are about Dominic."

Lord Winsmere nodded sagely, a thin smile hovering about his lips at the thought of the godlike status his far from godly brother-in-law enjoyed on his own lands.

"Well, she went to the Hall and met Duckett. And then Dominic came and persuaded her to tell him all." Bella suddenly broke off. "Oh—are you imagining she must be some encroaching mushroom?" Her ladyship leant forward slightly and fixed her big eyes on her husband. "Truly, Arthur, it is not so. She's the most engaging little thing. So innocent and green and so… so trusting."

Lord Winsmere's fine brows rose slightly.

Abruptly Bella dropped to her knees, draping her

silk-clad arms over her husband's knees. She smiled, impish and seductive all at once. "Please, Arthur. Please say she may stay. You know how bored I am. She's perfectly presentable, I give you my word. I could take her about and present her to the *ton*… Oh—I'd have such fun! The balls and parties are so tame, if one's not part of the game. Please, my love. Say she may stay."

Lord Winsmere smiled down into his wife's upturned face while his mind canvassed the possibilities presented by her unknown guest. Their son and only child was ensconced in the country, happily growing out of short coats. Jonathon's constitution was not sickly but did not cope well with the stale air of the capital. But his own work necessitated his presence in London. Bella, torn between the two men in her life, had chosen to remain by his side. As he doubted he could live without her, he would willingly make any sacrifice to alleviate the boredom he knew she found in the predictable rounds of tonnish entertainment. But an unknown girl? And, if he knew his Bella, she meant to fire the chit off with all flags flying. Not that the expense worried him. But was the girl truly as innocent as Bella, herself not much more experienced for all her matronliness, believed?

He reached out a finger to trace the graceful curve of his wife's brow. Impulsively, she caught his hand and kissed it, then continued to hold it in a warm clasp, her eyes on his face.

"You needn't worry about the cost. Dominic said to charge everything to him."

"Did he, indeed? How very magnanimous, to be sure." Lord Winsmere's mobile lips twitched. Dominic Ridgeley had inherited a fortune of sizeable proportions and could easily afford to underwrite the launching of an unknown damsel into the *ton*. The question that exercised Lord Winsmere's mind was *why* his hedonistic brother-in-law should wish to do such a peculiar thing.

"I think perhaps I should meet this paragon before I allow you to take her under your wing."

Bella's eyes grew round. "Are you thinking she is one of Dominic's paramours? I must admit, I did, too, at first. Well, whoever would imagine him having any contact with an innocent young girl? But I assure you she's just what Dominic says—young and innocent and…and hopelessly lost. I dare say she'll have no idea how to go on, having lived in Italy all this time."

Lord Winsmere's face remained impassive. The possibility that his brother-in-law had sent Bella a lady needing help to cover some lapse of acceptable conduct had certainly occurred, only to be immediately dismissed. Few knew better than himself that, despite Viscount Alton's reputation as a well heeled, insidiously charming and potentially dangerous rake, underneath, Dominic Ridgeley adhered most assiduously to a code of conduct that, if it were more widely recognised, would see him hailed as a pillar of society. But it was the veneer society saw—a façade erected to hide the boredom of a man who had never had to exert himself to win any prize. Born with the proverbial silver spoon tightly clamped between his jaws, and with the compounding assets of a handsome face and an athletic frame, there was little Dominic Ridgeley needed in life. And what he did want came easily. Society adored him. His well born mistresses fell at his feet. With ready charm, Dominic moved through it all, and with the years his boredom grew.

"What, exactly, did Dominic say?"

Bella smiled and shifted to sit at his feet, her hand still holding his, her shining blue eyes turned lovingly on him. "Well…"

Fifteen minutes later, Lord Winsmere felt he was in possession of all the salient facts. The only puzzle remaining was his brother-in-law's motives. A whimsical start? Dominic was hardly in his dotage. Nevertheless, young and girlish and innocent was assuredly not his style. The spectrc of Elaine, Lady Changley drifted into Lord Winsmere's mind. Involuntarily, his face assumed an expression of distaste. Lady Changley was definitely not young and girlish, and not by the remotest stretch of the most pliable imagination could she be described as innocent.

Bella saw the disapprobation in her husband's face. Her own face fell. "You don't like the idea?"

Recalled, Lord Winsmere smiled and confessed, "I was thinking of something else." At his wife's fond smile, he continued, "If the girl is all you and Dominic seem to think, I have no objections to your taking her under your wing. Aside from anything else, she'll have to be terribly innocent to swallow this yarn of yours about the way to securing a position being to make a splash in society."

Bella met his sceptical look with a bright grin. "Oh, I'll manage it—you'll see."

Five minutes later Lord Winsmere returned to his desk to tidy his papers away for the night. The memory of Bella's bright eyes remained with him. She was more animated than she had been in months. Perhaps Dominic's damsel in distress was an angel in disguise. He smiled fondly. All in all, he was looking forward to meeting his wife's protégée.

THE SHARP CALL of the orange sellers woke Georgiana. Bemused, she stared about her, then remembered where she was and how she came to be there. Despite the evidence of her eyes, reality retained the aura of a dream. She was lying propped in her pillows, still wondering, when Cruickshank came bustling through the door with her early-morning chocolate.

Georgiana waited silently for her maid's comment. No one could size up an establishment faster or more accurately than Cruickshank.

No sniffs were forthcoming. Not even a snort.

As she accepted the tray across her knees, Georgiana was taken aback to hear the dour maid humming.

Catching sight of her mistress's startled look, Cruickshank smiled. "A right proper place they keep here, Miss Georgie. No need to teach them anything. Mrs Biggins, the housekeeper, is a tight old bird, but fair, mark my words. Runs the place just as she should. And Johnson—he's the butler—and her ladyship's dresser, Hills, are everything they ought to be. A relief, it is, after the Place."

"So you're comfortable here?"

At the wardrobe, Cruickshank nodded emphatically. She drew out a violet morning gown trimmed with fine lace and laid it ready across a chair, then went to search for the accessories.

Georgiana sipped her chocolate. As the sweet warmth slid down her throat and heat seeped through her body, she sighed. So wonderful—to have real chocolate again. She closed her eyes and was immediately back on the terrace at Ravello, her father opposite, across the breakfast-table. Abruptly she opened her eyes, blinking rapidly. Enough of that! She had shed all the tears she possessed long ago. Her father had wanted her to get on with her life. He had warned her not to grieve for him. He had had a good life, so he had said, and wanted his daughter to have the same. That was why she was to return to England and the bosom of her family. Some bosom Charles had turned out to be. At the thought, Georgiana wriggled her toes. The idea of Charles scouring the countryside for her, only to return, dusty and beaten, to the damp and musty Place, brought a glow of satisfaction to her honey-gold eyes. Serve him right.

"How long are we staying here?"

Cruickshank came to draw back the covers. Georgiana slid from the bed, busying herself with washing and dressing while she considered how best to answer. She had not discussed her plan to get a position with either of her servants, sure they would veto the idea as soon as they heard it. Come what may, she was determined to keep them with her. They were all that remained of her parents' happy household.

So, standing patiently as Cruickshank laced her gown, she answered airily, "I'll have to discuss the matter with Lady Wins... Bella. She seems to wish us to stay for a while."

Cruickshank snorted. "So I gathered. Still, she seems a real lady; none of your hoity-toity airs about that one."

Georgiana grinned, remembering Bella's fussing the night before. It had been a long time since anyone other than Cruickshank had fussed over her.

After Cruickshank had settled her curls in a knot

on the top of her head, Georgiana tentatively made her way downstairs. Johnson found her in the front hall and, gracious as ever, directed her to the breakfast parlour overlooking the rear gardens.

"There you are, my dear!"

Georgiana had the feeling Bella had been waiting for her to appear. Her hostess surged across the Turkey carpet in a cloud of fine-figured muslin. Georgiana returned her smile.

"Are you sure you've recovered from your ordeal?"

Georgiana flushed slightly and nodded. A man, somewhat older than Bella, had risen from the table to watch them, an affectionate smile on his thin lips. She felt forced to disclaim, "It was hardly an ordeal, ma'am."

"*Ma'am?* I thought I told you to call me Bella." Bella smiled mischievously. "And of course it was an ordeal. Fleeing from horrible Charles was always an ordeal."

Georgiana stopped and stared. "You know Charles?"

Bella's big blue eyes opened wide. "But of course. Didn't I mention it last night?"

When Georgiana shook her head, Bella tucked her arm in hers and drew her guest to the table.

"But we were neighbours; you know that. Of course, Charles came over to play sometimes. But he never got on with Dominic and the other boys, mainly because he was younger and always tried to show off. He used to tease me unmercifully. At least, he did if Dominic wasn't around. So, you see, I know just what it feels like to run away from your cousin Charles. And I can't think he's improved with age."

Standing by the chair beside her new friend,

Georgiana shook her head. "I expect you're right." She looked expectantly at the man. He smiled and bowed slightly.

"Permit me to introduce myself, my dear. I'm afraid, if we wait for Bella to remember my existence, we might not be introduced until dinner."

"Oh, fustian!" said Bella, catching his hand and giving it a little shake. "My dear Georgiana, allow me to present my husband, Arthur."

Georgiana dropped a demure curtsy, hiding her surprise. She had not thought about Bella's husband at all, but would never have imagined the youthful Bella married to a man so much older. As she straightened, her eyes met his, grey and kindly, and she had the feeling of being read like a book. But then he smiled, such a sweet smile, and suddenly it no longer seemed so odd that Bella should be his wife.

"Miss Hartley. Might I say how pleased we are to welcome you to our home?"

Georgiana murmured her thanks.

Over breakfast, Lord Winsmere made little comment, but contented himself with listening as Bella and she discussed feminine interests.

"I see you are out of blacks," said Bella. "So fortunate."

Georgiana hesitated, then explained, "Actually, it's only four months since my father died, but he made me promise that I wouldn't go into mourning for him. But—" she shrugged slightly "—I thought greys and lilacs were a reasonable compromise."

Bella's candid gaze assessed her dispassionately. "I must say, if your father was a painter, I can understand why he was so insistent you stay out of black. With your skin, it would certainly not suit."

Georgiana grinned. "I'm not certain that wasn't at the back of his mind when he made his request."

As she turned her attention to her piece of toast, she was conscious of his lordship's grey eyes resting on her with approval.

In fact, Lord Winsmere was pleased to approve of his wife's prospective protégée. Georgiana Hartley, he decided, was a neat little thing. His eye had seen too many beauties to class her as one, but her features were pure and, with the gloss of a little animation, presently lacking, she could lay claim to the appellation of attractive with ease. She was petite, but her figure was full and delicately curved, not unlike Bella's curvaceous form. And, more important than any other quality, the girl from Italy was not missish. Which was just as well, if she was to deal with his forthright Bella. All in all, Bella's assessment had been accurate. Miss Georgiana Hartley was eminently acceptable.

When the ladies left him to his coffee and the morning's news-sheet, he spent some time in a blank study of the parlour door. Undoubtedly, Dominic had done right in sending Georgiana to Winsmere House. There was little hope such an attractive miss could find decent employment without subjecting herself to dangers he, for one, did not wish to contemplate. Dominic's plan to introduce her into society was a wise one. Thus far, the young lady seemed of a most amenable disposition. And, although not highly born, her lineage was not beneath consideration. He had checked for himself in the Register of Landowners. The Hartleys had been an unremarkable family for generations, but they were nevertheless of good stock. She would make some young squire an unexceptionable wife.

However, more importantly from his point of view, her presence would ease Bella's boredom. His darling had talked non-stop since rising this morning, a sure sign of happiness.

With a smile at his own susceptibilities, Lord Winsmere rose and, taking up his unread news-sheet, retired to the library. For once, Dominic seemed to have bestirred himself for purely philanthropic reasons. His scheme was in the girl's best interests and would keep Bella amused. There was no reason to interfere. Bella could entangle herself in the chit's life to her heart's content. Neither would take any ill. As his shrewd brain began to sort through the potential ramifications of his brother-in-law's plan, Lord Winsmere's brows rose. His lips curved slightly. In the end, who knew what might come of it?

"NOW, GEORGIE, promise me you won't put me to the blush," said Bella, firmly drawing on her gloves as the carriage drew to a standstill. "I couldn't endure it in front of Fancon. The woman's a terror. Lord only knows what damage she could do to your chances if she heard you asking about the price of a gown."

Georgiana blushed. The slight frown on her friend's face told her Bella was not yet convinced she had won their last battle. Georgiana simply couldn't see the necessity for new gowns for herself. Surely it was not a requirement for a companion to be fashionably dressed? But Bella had been adamant.

"Just wait until you *are* a companion before you start dressing like a dowd."

At Georgiana's instinctive and forlorn glance at her demure grey gown, Bella had been instantly contrite. "Oh, I don't mean that! Your gowns are perfectly acceptable, you know they are. It's just that for going out into society you need more...well, more society clothes. This is London, after all."

Finally, worn down by Bella's arguments, strengthened by the defection of Cruickshank, who had deciphered enough of their conversation to give her a hard stare, Georgiana had consented to accompany Bella to the salon of the modiste known as Fancon. It was her third day in London, and she was beginning to feel at home in the large mansion on Green Street. Lord Winsmere was all that was kind. And Bella, of course, was Bella. Georgiana was overwhelmed by their kindness. But not so overwhelmed that she would consent to Bella's buying her new gowns.

"If I must have new gowns to go about and become known, then of course I'll pay for them." Her calm statement had caused Bella to look at her in concern.

"But, my dear Georgie, gowns, you know...well, they're not all that... I mean to say..." The garrulous Bella had flustered to a halt.

The drift of her thoughts had reached Georgiana. "Oh! Did you think I have no money?"

Bella's eyes widened. "Well, I thought you might not be exactly flush, what with your trip and expecting your uncle to be there to help at the end of it."

Georgiana smiled affectionately. They had thought her a pauper but had still wanted to help. She knew enough of the world to appreciate such sentiments. "Not a bit of it. My father left me reasonably well to do—or at least, that's how my Italian solicitors described it. I don't know what exactly that means, but I have funds deposited here on which I may draw."

To her relief, Lord Winsmere had insisted on accompanying her to the bank her father had patronised. She had little doubt it was his lordship's standing that had resulted in such prompt and polite service. There had been no difficulty in establishing her *bona fides* through papers she had carried from Italy.

While waiting for the carriage to stop rocking, Georgiana glanced at Bella's profile. They had taken to each other as if each were the sister the other had never had. "Only two gowns, mind."

Bella turned, her eyes narrowing. "Two *day* gowns *and* an evening gown." She stared uncompromisingly at Georgiana.

With a wry grimace, Georgiana acquiesced. "All right. *And* an evening gown. But nothing too elaborate," she added, as the groom opened the door.

Together they entered the discreet establishment of Fancon. A woman dressed in severe black glided forward to greet them. Her black hair was pulled back and, it appeared to Georgiana, forcibly restrained in a tight bun. Black eyes, like gimlets, sharp and shuttered, assessed her. This, she soon learned, was the great Fancon herself. Imbued with suitable awe, Georgiana noted a certain restraint in the woman's manner and was careful to give no cause for offence.

Half an hour passed in the most pleasant of occupations. Fancon had numerous gowns to choose from. Georgiana tried on a great many. There were fabrics, too, which could be fashioned to any style she wished. Georgiana found Bella's interest infectious. And she could not resist the temptation to indulge in Fancon's elegant creations. However, true to her word, she chose only two day dresses, one in softest lilac, the other a deep mauve. Both suited her well, their high waists outlining her youthful figure. She feared that Fancon would be irritated by her meagre order, particularly after the woman had been so insistent she try on such a great number of gowns. Yet nothing but the most complete equanimity showed on the modiste's stern face.

Much discussion went into the creation of an evening gown. The styles which favoured her were easy enough to decide. Yet there was nothing suitable made up.

"Your colouring, Miss Hartley, is less pale than the norm. It is no matter. We will decide on the fabric, and I will have my seamstresses work up the gown by tomorrow." With a calm wave of her hand, Fancon summoned her underlings. They brought bolts of fine cloth, in mauves and lilacs. While Georgiana stood, wreathed in fabric, Bella and Fancon studied her critically. Georgiana, too, watched proceedings in the mirror.

"It must show you off to your greatest advantage," declared Bella.

Georgiana seriously doubted that companions were chosen for the picture they made in the ballroom.

Fancon turned and murmured a command. A minute later, a fresh selection of materials arrived. Sea-green gauze, spangled and shimmering, was draped around Georgiana. The assistant stood back, and Georgiana raised her eyes to the mirror. She gasped. Was the slim, slender mermaid she saw there really herself? The green brought out the lights in her hair and eyes, and emphasised the creaminess of her skin. She stood and stared. Then, slowly, she shook her head sadly.

"Not yet. I'm still in mourning, remember?"

Another murmur from Fancon saw a deep topaz silk replace the sea-green gauze. Again, Georgiana stared. This time she looked almost as worldly as Bella. The silk added an air of allure, of mystery. She looked… enticing. But again she refused.

Apparently resigned to using the purplish hues, Fancon next produced a pale amethyst silk. Georgiana regarded it critically. The colour suited her well enough, making her appear soft and feminine. But the amethyst simply did not do for her what the previous two shades had. In this, she simply looked passably pretty. She turned and looked longingly at the topaz and the sea-green, lying discarded beside her. Still, she couldn't allow herself to be distracted from her purpose. Doubt-less ladies who needed companions would approve of the amethyst silk.

"Yes. I'll take this fabric. And the pattern we agreed on."

Georgiana turned in time to catch the look that passed between Bella and Fancon. It was a look that bespoke an understanding, but she got no further clue to assist in its interpretation.

While they waited for the two day dresses to be packed, Georgiana reflected that Madame Fancon had not seemed anywhere near as dragon-like as Bella had led her to believe.

Settled in the barouche, with Fancon's boxes on the opposite seat, Bella leant forward and spoke to her coachman. "Once around the park for luck. Then back to Green Street."

The carriage moved off. Georgiana sat quietly, wondering a little at the revelations of the sumptuous sea-green and topaz silks. Could she really appear like that? Her? Little Georgiana?

Bella also sat quietly, smugly satisfied with the outcome of her scheming. She had been to see Fancon the day before, while Arthur had taken Georgiana to see her banker. The modiste knew her well; she was, after all, one of her best customers. Fancon had been most helpful, particularly after she had let fall the information that a certain peer was most desirous that Georgiana should be well presented, and hence money was no option. Dominic could hardly take exception to that. Bella grinned. She had little doubt Fancon would guess who the gentleman was. Who other than her brother would be likely to leave a young girl in her care?

"Bella, there's been some mistake. We have six boxes instead of two."

Georgiana's words reclaimed Bella's attention. She turned and found Georgiana frowning at the offending extra boxes. "No, no," said Bella. "It's all right. I bought some gowns, too. I couldn't resist after seeing you in them, and we're much of a size." All of which, Bella told her conscience, was perfectly true.

Georgiana raised her brows but said no more.

Bella returned to her absent-minded contemplation of the pavements. Undoubtedly she'd have to argue hard and fast to get Georgiana to accept the gowns she had bought. But none of them were in colours she, so much darker of hair and fairer of skin, could wear. The sea-green gauze and topaz silk would look hideous on her. They were to be delivered tomorrow, along with the amethyst silk. Surely Georgie would see what a waste it would be simply to throw them away?

As the barouche turned into the park, Bella sat up

straighter. She looked across at Georgiana, sitting qui-etly beside her. Demure she might look, but Georgiana Hartley had a mind of her own. Stubborn to a fault, she was sure to balk at accepting what she would prob-ably class as charity. Still, Bella was perfectly certain Dominic would have wanted her to spend his money as she had. She was sure he would approve, when he saw Georgiana in the topaz silk. And, after all, Georgiana should be grateful enough to want to please her brother. She made a mental note to remember Dominic, if she had need of further ammunition to force Georgiana to accept the gowns.

"IT'S MY 'at home' this afternoon." Bella came bustling into the downstairs parlour.

Georgiana looked up from the magazine she was idly leafing through. She felt supremely confident this morning, arrayed in one of her new gowns, a soft bluey lilac cambric. Bella's elegance seemed less daunting now. She caught Bella's eye as it rested pensively upon her. Georgiana raised one fine brow in invitation.

"About the story we should tell about you. To account for your being here."

"What about the truth?" asked Georgiana, not quite sure what her friend meant.

"Well, yes. The truth, of course. But…do you think the whole truth's wise?"

When Georgiana looked her confusion, Bella contin-ued, "You see, if you tell about how you met Dominic, people might get the wrong idea. To support your story, you'd have to explain about Charles. And, my dear, if you're looking for a position, the last person you would want to claim kinship with is Charles."

Bella had put a great deal of thought into how best to broach this most delicate of subjects. Now she watched Georgiana carefully to see how the younger girl took her suggestion. Georgiana was frowning, her thoughts clouding her big eyes.

"You mean…?"

"What I mean," said Bella, candid to a fault, "is that Charles is hardly a gold-plated reference. But there's really no need to mention him at all. All we have to do is decide how you came to stay with me. I think the most sensible thing to say is that we had met, years ago, at Candlewick, before you went to Italy. We became such friends that we've been corresponding ever since. Naturally, when you returned to England and found your uncle dead, you came back to London to stay with me. That should be believable enough, don't you think?" When Georgiana made no reply, Bella pressed her final argument. "And you wouldn't want to put Dominic in a difficult position, would you?"

Put Lord Alton in a difficult position? For a minute, Georgiana could make no sense of her friend's allusion. Then the Fragonard materialised in her mind's eye… and the image of his lordship as she had last seen him, a vision that had not yet faded from her memory.

"Oh."

Of course. Georgiana gave herself a mental shake. She wasn't so innocent that she couldn't follow Bella's drift. While her visit with Lord Alton had been utterly without consequence, society, if it heard of it, might view it otherwise. She raised her gaze to Bella's face. "I'll do whatever you think best. I wouldn't want to cause your brother any trouble."

Bella grinned, entirely satisfied.

"Oh, and one last thing. It will be better, at this stage, if we make no mention of your wish for a position. Such things are better negotiated after you're known."

Georgiana nodded her acceptance, Lord Alton's assurance that his sister knew what was best echoing in her mind.

That afternoon three matrons came to tea, bringing with them a gaggle of unmarried daughters. Georgiana did not succeed in fixing which young ladies belonged to which mama. In the end, it made little difference. To a woman, they accepted Bella's charmingly phrased explanation of her presence. Quick eyes surveyed the latest entrant in the marriage game. The ladies found no reason not to be gracious. Miss Hartley was no beauty.

Miss Hartley had difficulty subduing her mirth. They were really so blatant in their pursuit of well heeled and preferably titled son-in-laws.

To her surprise, Georgiana found conversing with the younger ladies almost beyond her. Used to dealing with the gracious conversation of the Italian aristocracy, among whom she had spent much of her life, used to the subtle ebb and flow of polished discourse, she found it hard to relate to the titters and smirks and girlish giggles of the four very proper English maids. However, she did not make the mistake of attempting to join the matrons. Stoically, she bore her ordeal as best she could.

Bella, watching her, was pleased by her confidence and innate poise. Innocent and trusting Georgiana might be, but she was no mindless ninny, scared to open her mouth in company. Her manners were assured, unusually so for a girl of her age.

When the guests had departed, Bella grimaced

at Georgiana. "Witless, aren't they?" She smiled at
Georgiana's emphatic nod. "They're not all like that,
of course. Still, there are a lot of unbelievably silly girls
about." Bella paused, considering her words. "Just as
well, I suppose. There are an awful lot of silly men,
too."

They shared a grin of complete understanding.

Five minutes later, just as they had settled comfortably to their embroidery, Johnson entered. "Lady Winterspoon, m'lady."

Bella rose. Georgiana was disconcerted to see perturbation in her friend's blue eyes. Then Lady Winterspoon
was in the room.

"Bella! Haven't seen you in ages! Where've you been
hiding yourself?"

Lady Winterspoon's trenchant accents reverberated
through the room. Bella suffered a hug and a hearty
kiss and, looking slightly shaken, settled her ageing
guest in an armchair. Lady Winterspoon was, Georgiana
guessed, quite old enough to be Bella's mother. Who
was she?

"Amelia, I'd like you to meet Georgiana Hartley.
She's an old friend of mine from the country. Georgiana,
this is my sister-in-law."

Georgiana met the clear grey gaze and found herself
smiling warmly in response. Lord Winsmere's sister, of
course.

"Hartley, hmm? Well, I probably knew your father,
if he's the one I'm thinking of. Painter fellow. Jimmy?
James? Married Lorien Putledge."

Georgiana nodded, eager to hear more of her parents.
She had never before met anyone who had known them
in their younger days.

Reading her interest in her eyes, Lady Winterspoon waved one hand in a negative gesture. "No, my dear. I can't tell you much about them; I didn't know them that well. I take it they've passed on?"

Disappointed, Georgiana nodded. Bella promptly stepped in with their agreed explanation for her presence in Green Street. Lady Winterspoon's shrewd eyes remained on Georgiana throughout Bella's speech. Whether she accepted the story, neither young woman felt qualified to say.

"Hmph!" was all the response she made.

After a moment of silence, during which both Bella and Georgiana racked their brains to think of something to say, Lady Winterspoon commented, "Dare say you'll make quite a hit. Not just in the common way. In the circumstances, not a bad thing to be."

Georgiana decided that was meant as a compliment. She smiled.

Lady Winterspoon's lips twitched. She turned purposefully to Bella. "But that's not why I came. Bella, you've got to have a word with that brother of yours. Elaine Changley's becoming entirely too much, with her airs and graces and subtle suggestions she'll be the next Viscountess Alton." Lady Winterspoon snorted.

Bella frowned and bit her lip. She cast a slightly scandalised look Georgiana's way. But Georgiana was too engrossed in Lady Winterspoon's disclosures to notice.

"If I thought there was any chance of it coming to pass, I'd insist Arthur break the connection. Elaine Changley! Why, she's…" Amelia Winterspoon became aware of Georgiana's clear hazel gaze. She broke off.

"Well, you know what I mean," she amended, glaring at Bella.

Relieved at the opportune halt to her sister-in-law's tirade, Bella gracefully seated herself on the sofa. "Amelia, you know I have no influence whatever with Dominic."

"Pshaw! You'd have influence enough if you chose to use it!"

Bella coloured slightly. "I assure you I share your concern about Lady Changley, but mentioning her to Dominic is entirely beyond me."

"Well, Elaine Changley is beyond the pale! Just bear that in mind. You'll look no-how if you wake up one morning to find her your sister-in-law."

Lady Winterspoon heaved herself up. "Must go. Just wanted to let you know things need a bit of push from you." She fixed her grey gaze firmly on Bella.

Despite her annoyance, Bella could not help grinning back. She rose.

Lady Winterspoon paused to nod to Georgiana. "I'll see you at Almack's, my dear." She turned to Bella. "I'll get Emily to send you vouchers."

"Thank you," said Bella, taken aback. She had forgotten Amelia had the ear of several of the patronesses of Almack's. She went out with Lady Winterspoon.

Minutes later, returning to the back parlour, Bella found Georgiana staring into space. She shut the door with a click, jolting her guest to attention. "Well!" she said, with determined brightness. "Vouchers for Almack's without even having to charm one of the patronesses. We'll go just as soon as Lady Cowper sends them."

"Yes, of course," said Georgiana. But it was plain to Bella that her friend was absorbed in distant thoughts... thoughts she made no move to share.

CHAPTER THREE

BELLA HEARD the door of her boudoir open and shut, but, absorbed in brushing the haresfoot delicately over her cheekbones, she did not turn around. In her mirror, she saw Hills obediently drop a curtsy and leave. Finally, satisfied with her appearance, she swung about. "Arthur— Oh! Dominic!"

She was out of her chair and across the room on the word.

Half laughing, half frowning, Dominic held her off. "No! Compose yourself, you hoyden. What will staid Arthur think? And I can't have you ruining my cravat as you did the last time."

So Bella had to make do with clasping his hands. "Oh, thank you, dearest Dominic, for sending Georgie to me! We're having such a wonderful time!" She drew him down to plant a sisterly kiss on one lean cheek.

Dominic suffered the embrace, using the moment to cast a knowledgeable eye over his sister. "So you and Miss Hartley have hit it off?"

"Famously!" Bella sat with a swirl of her satin skirts. "But whoever would have thought you'd…?" She broke off, biting her lip.

Dominic's black brows rose. There was a disconcerting glint in his eye, but his voice was gentle when he softly prompted, "I'd…?"

Bella flushed and turned back to her dressing-table, skirts rustling, and busied herself with a pot of rouge. She refused to meet his eye. "That you'd behave so uncommonly sensible, if you must know. From everything I've heard, it must be the first time in weeks!"

"Weeks?" The arrogant black brows rose again. Dominic considered the point for all of ten seconds. "Feels more like years."

Bella, surprised by his weary tone, chanced a glance at him in the mirror. He raised his head at that moment, and she was caught in his chilly blue gaze. "That aside, dear sister mine, you would be well advised not to listen to gossip—about myself, or anyone else, for that matter."

Eyes wide, Bella knew better than to remonstrate. Dominic was ten years her senior and had been the strictest of guardians in the years preceding her marriage. She half expected some more pointed rebuke, but he turned aside, a far-away look settling over his handsome face. To her, that pensive look was far more frightening than Amelia's bluster. Surely he wasn't serious about Elaine Changley?

She waited, but he made no further remark. Finally she asked, "Will you stay for dinner?"

He looked up.

Bella fidgeted with her hairbrush. "Georgie and I are going on to Almack's later, so you needn't fear you'll have to kick your heels in my drawing-room."

Her tone brought a smile to her brother's face, dispelling the withdrawn look which had so concerned her. Still, she was sure he would refuse.

Instead, after a moment's hesitation, she heard him murmur, "Why not?"

As it seemed a purely rhetorical question, Bella made no attempt to answer it.

Dominic shrugged, then turned his sweetest smile full on her. "Since you ask, dear sister, I'll stay. It might be interesting to meet my...*your* protégée."

As Bella reached for the bell-pull to summon Hills, Dominic surveyed a nearby chair through his quizzing-glass. Reassured, he carefully disposed his long limbs in the delicate piece.

"So how came you to get vouchers for the Marriage Mart so soon?"

"Well! It was the most fortunate thing!" Bella seized on the question to lead the conversation on to lighter ground, hoping her intrusion into her brother's private life would be the quicker forgotten. Dominic had never allowed her any speculation on the possible candidates for the position of Viscountess Alton. And she had long ago learned that any mention of his mistresses, past, present or potential, was sure to invite one of his more painful set-downs. Still, after Amelia's warning, and her own unfortunate gaffe, she had felt justified in at least trying to broach the subject.

While Hills informed Johnson of the necessity of setting an extra place and returned to twist her hair into an elegant knot, Bella described the recent history of Georgiana Hartley. As she prattled, she watched her brother's face in the mirror. He sat quietly studying his nails, paying scant attention to her words. His lack of interest worried her. She had hardly expected him to be seriously concerned with Georgiana. After all, he had barely met her and she was certainly not the sort of woman to hold his attention. But his introspection was unusual and disquieting, suggesting as it did the existence of some weightier matter dragging on his mind. Like matrimony. But surely, *surely,* he wouldn't choose Elaine Changley?

It was with relief that Bella finally rose from her dressing-table. What with the distraction of Dominic's arrival, the hour was well advanced. He accompanied her down the wide staircase and entered the drawing-room by her side.

Georgiana was talking to Arthur. Warned by his face that someone unexpected had entered, she turned and was trapped, once again without warning, in the blue of Lord Alton's eyes.

The same eyes that haunted her dreams.

For Georgiana, it was a definite case of *déjà vu.* Her breathing stopped; her heart contracted. Her gaze was oddly restricted, the rest of the room fading away, leaving one strong face to impress itself on her mind. Her stare widened to take in his immaculate evening clothes, and the way his dark hair sat in elegant waves about his head. A cornflower-blue sapphire winked in his cravat, its colour no more intense than his eyes.

Then, thankfully, Arthur moved forward to greet his guest.

The worst was past. Georgiana's natural poise reasserted itself and she could function again. Then Lord Alton turned to take her hand. His clasp was cool and gentle. He smiled and bowed elegantly.

"Miss Hartley. So we meet again. I do hope Bella hasn't been tiring you out with her gadding."

To Georgiana's intense chagrin, her tongue promptly tied itself in knots and her voice deserted her. She managed to force out a weak, "Of course not, my lord," around the constriction in her throat. What on earth was the matter with her?

Luckily, Johnson entered to announce dinner. Inwardly, Georgiana heaved a sigh of relief. But relief died a sudden death when she discovered Lord Alton was dining at his sister's board. Naturally, he sat opposite her. Throughout the meal, which could have been the meanest fare for all she noticed, Georgiana struggled to avoid looking directly at the gentleman opposite, with mixed success. Arthur unwittingly came to her rescue, turning the conversation into political waters. He engaged his brother-in-law in a detailed discussion of the Corn Laws, leaving the ladies to their own interests.

As Bella seemed abstracted, Georgiana confined her gaze, if not her attention, to her plate. As course followed course, and the gentlemen's discourse continued unabated, she was conscious of a growing irritation. Admittedly her awkwardness in the drawing-room had hardly been encouraging, but Lord Alton could at least make the effort to address some remark to her. Perhaps, in England, it was not done to talk across the table, even at family meals.

When the sweets appeared before her, Bella shook herself and glanced about. Only then did she notice that her husband and brother had embarked on a most tedious discussion, leaving poor Georgie to herself. It was on the tip of her tongue to call attention to their lapse of manners, when she recalled that neither gentleman would feel the least inhibited about alluding to her own brown study of the past hour, nor in asking the subject of said study. As she had no intention of once again drawing her brother's fire, she turned instead to Georgiana.

"You see what it is to dine *en famille* in Winsmere House? Pearls before swine, my dear. Here we sit, only too willing to be enthralled, and all they can think of is their political problems." Her eyes twinkled at her husband, sitting opposite her at the head of the table.

Unperturbed by her attack, he smiled back. "In truth, I'm surprised to see you still here. I had thought you were off to Almack's tonight."

Bella's eyes swung to the clock, peacefully ticking away on the sideboard. "Heavens! I'd no idea. Georgie, we'll have to bustle. Come. We'll leave our two fine gentlemen to their port."

Both men stood as she rose.

Georgiana perforce rose too. She could not resist throwing one last glance at the tall figure opposite her. To her confusion, she found he was watching her. But his face bore nothing more than a remotely polite expression. He returned her nod with genial but distant civility.

As the ladies departed the room, Arthur turned to his brother-in-law. "If you have the time, I'd value your opinions on how best to go about this business."

Dominic started slightly, as if his mind had wandered from the matter they had been discussing for the past hour. "Yes. Of course." His usual, sleepily bored smile appeared. "I'd be only too delighted, naturally."

Arthur, not deceived, laughed. "Which means you'd much rather be elsewhere, discussing more enthralling subjects, but you will, of course, humour your host. You, Dominic, are a complete hand. Why you must belittle your efforts in this I know not."

By unspoken agreement, they moved to the door. Dominic waved one languid hand, and a priceless sapphire caught the light. "Perhaps because my—er—efforts, as you term them, are so undemanding as to be positively valueless."

Arthur was surprised into a snort. "Valueless? Who else, pray tell, has succeeded in even introducing the subject in Prinny's presence?"

They entered the library and made for the two large armchairs by the hearth.

"Introducing the subject's hardly the same as gaining His Highness's support." Dominic sank into one chair, stretching his long legs before him and emitting a weary sigh.

Arthur glanced sharply at him. "You know that's not necessary. Just as long as His Highness is aware of how things stand. That'll be more than enough." He handed Dominic a cut-crystal glass filled with his oldest port, then settled comfortably in the chair opposite.

Silence fell, broken only by the ticking of the long case clock in the corner and a sudden crackle as a log settled in the grate. Arthur, who had had plenty of opportunity to observe his brother-in-law over dinner, and to note the arrested expression in those startlingly blue eyes whenever they rested on Georgiana Hartley, continued to watch the younger man, waiting patiently for whatever came next, confident that something, indeed, would be forthcoming.

Finally, Dominic's gaze sought his face. "This Miss Hartley I've foisted on you… I assume you approve?"

Arthur nodded. "Georgiana is exactly the sort of company Bella needs. You have my heartfelt thanks for sending her to us."

The black brows rose. "Seemed the least I could do." Dominic's face showed evidence of distraction, as it frequently had that night. Arthur's lips twitched. He sternly repressed the impulse to smile.

Eventually Dominic shook off his abstraction sufficiently to comment, "Bella was saying she's becoming rather stubbornly taken with this idea of hiring out as a companion. She seemed to think that she, Miss Hartley, might take things into her own hands. That, I need hardly say, will simply not do."

Arthur nodded gravely. "I entirely agree. Also, I have to concur with Bella on her reading of Georgiana's character." He paused to steeple his fingers, and stared into the fire over the top of the structure. "Georgiana is clearly unused to relying on the bounty of others. It irks her, I think, to be living, as it were, on our charity. She has some money of her own, but not, I suspect, the requisite fortune. She has spoken to me about the best way to go about hiring herself out. I returned an evasive and, I hope, restraining answer. Luckily, the fact that she has been out of England for so long makes it relatively easy to make excuses which on the face of it are reasonable, without going into over-many details. However—" he smiled at Dominic "—beneath that demure exterior lies a great deal of strength and not a little courage. From what I gather, she made her way to England virtually unaided—not an inconsiderable feat. I seriously doubt she'll accept our vague answers for much longer."

A black frown of quite dramatic proportions dominated the Viscount's face.

Arthur suppressed a grin. Finally he asked, "Do you have any ideas?"

Still frowning, Dominic slowly shook his head. Then he glanced at Arthur. "Do you?"

"As a matter of fact, I do." Arthur straightened his

shoulders and prepared to explain. His grey gaze rested thoughtfully on Dominic's face. "Bella, of course, needs distraction. Essentially, that means a companion. But can you imagine how she would feel if I insisted she hire one?"

Dominic's frown lightened.

"Bella has been most assiduous in helping Georgiana and, from what I've seen, Georgiana is truly grateful. I plan to suggest to Georgiana, in confidence, that she become Bella's companion in truth. However, in order to spare Bella's quite natural feelings, the arrangement will be a secret between the two of us. To all outward appearances, which of course must include the servants, she will continue as a guest in this house." Arthur's brows rose interrogatively. "Do you think that'll pass?"

Dominic grinned. "I'm sure it will. How useful to be able to turn your talents to something other than politics." His grin broadened into a smile. "And no wonder you're so invaluable in your present capacity."

Arthur smiled and inclined his head. "As you say." For a moment he regarded the younger man intently. Then, almost imperceptibly, he shrugged. "I'll speak to Georgiana in the morning. It would be wise, I suspect, to ensure she has no opportunity to take the bit between her teeth."

"THANK YOU, MY LORD." Georgiana curtsied and watched young Lord Mortlake mince away across the floor. Still, at least he had danced well.

She flicked open her fan and plied it ruthlessly. The large, sparsely furnished rooms which were Almack's were crammed with bodies dressed in silks and satins of every conceivable hue. The day had been unseasonably warm, and the evening, initially balmy, had turned sultry. The air in the rooms hung oppressively. Ostrich feathers wilted. As a particularly limp pair, dyed puce, bobbed by, attached to the head-dress of an extremely conscious beauty, Georgiana hid her smirk behind her fan.

Her eyes scanned the company. Other than Bella, standing by her side, engaged in a low-voiced conversation with an elderly matron, Georgiana knew only those few people Bella had thus far introduced her to. And, she reflected, none of them needed a companion.

As her eyes feasted on the spectrum of colours mingling before her, she spared a smile for her sartorial elegance. By comparison with many about her, she was underdressed. The pattern of Fancon's amethyst silk robe was simple and plain, with long, clean lines uncluttered by frills and furbelows. Her single strand of pearls, inherited from her mother, shone warmly about her neck. Originally uncertain, she now felt smugly satisfied with her appearance.

Thoughts of dresses brought her earlier discovery to mind, together with the subsequent argument with Bella. How on earth could she accept the sea-green gauze and topaz silk dresses from Bella, to whom she was already so deeply indebted? Yet it was undeniable that Bella could not wear them. Both dresses were presently hanging in the wardrobe in her chamber. She had been quite unable to persuade Bella to repack and return them. What was she to do about them?

The idea that, if she had been wearing the topaz silk gown that evening, Lord Alton would have paid more attention to her flitted through her mind. Ruthlessly, she stamped on the errant thought. She was here to find employment, not ogle lords. And what possible interest could Lord Alton have in her—an unremarkable country lass, not even at home in England?

Depressed, by that thought and the lowering fact she had not yet made any headway in finding a position, Georgiana determinedly looked over the sea of heads, pausing on the occasional powdered wig that belonged to a previous generation. Maybe, beneath one, she would find someone to hire her?

"Here, girl! Georgiana, ain't it? Come and help me to that chair."

Georgiana whirled to find Lady Winterspoon beside her. The old lady was leaning on a cane.

Seeing her glance, Amelia Winterspoon chuckled. "I only use it at night. Helps me get the best seats."

Georgiana smiled and obediently took her ladyship's arm. Once settled in a gilt chair by the wall, Lady Winterspoon waved Georgiana to its partner beside her.

"I can only take so much of this place. Too much mindless talk addles the brain."

Georgiana felt the sharp grey eyes assessing her. She wondered whether she would pass muster.

A wry smile twisted Amelia Winterspoon's thin lips. "Just as I thought. *Not* in the common style."

The old lady paused. Georgiana had the impression she was reliving long-ago evenings spent under the candlelight of ballroom chandeliers. Then, abruptly, the grey gaze sharpened and swung to her face.

"If you're old enough to heed advice, here's one piece you should take to heart. You ain't a beauty, but you're no antidote either. You're different—and not just because you're fair when the current craze is for dark. The most successful women who've ever trod these boards were those who were brave enough to be themselves."

"Themselves?"

"Themselves," came the forceful answer. "Don't put on airs, nor pretend to be what you ain't. Thankfully, you seem in no danger of doing that. Don't try to ape the English misses. Don't try to lose your foreignness—use it instead. All you need to make a go of it is to smile and enjoy yourself. The rest'll come easy."

"But—" Georgiana wondered whether she should explain her situation to Arthur's sister. Maybe she could help her find a position?

"No buts, girl! Just do it! There's no point in wasting your life away being a wallflower. Get out and enjoy yourself." Lady Winterspoon used her cane to gesture at the dance-floor. "Now go on—off you go!"

Despite the conviction that she should feel piqued at such forthright meddling, Georgiana found herself grinning, then laughing as Lady Winterspoon nodded encouragingly. Rising, Georgiana swept a curtsy to her ladyship, now comfortably ensconced, and, a smile lingering on her lips, returned to the throng. She made her way to where she had left Bella.

But Bella was no longer in sight.

Perturbed, Georgiana stood still and wondered what to do. She could go back and sit with Lady Winterspoon, only she would probably drive her off again. English social strictures were not Georgiana's strong suit. Still, she rather suspected she should not wander about the rooms alone. Suddenly she realised she was frowning.

Lady Winterspoon's strong voice still echoed in her mind. "Enjoy yourself!"

Georgiana lifted her head. She had been introduced to Italian society at the age of sixteen. Surely, at the ripe old age of eighteen, she could manage such a simple social occasion as this? Consciously drawing about herself the cloak of social calm her father's female patrons had impressed on her was the hallmark of a lady, she stepped out more confidently to search for Bella—not hurriedly, in a frenzy, but in a calm and dignified way, smiling as she went.

As she moved slowly down the room, truly looking about her for the first time that evening, she heard snatches of conversation wafting from the groups she passed.

"Did you see that Emma Michinford? Making such sheep's eyes at…"

"Well, we all know what *he's* after!"

"She's really rather pathetic, don't you agree?"

"Not that it'll come to anything, mark my words. The likes of him…"

Waspish, biting, cutting gibes… The comments blurred into a melody typical, Georgiana suspected, of the place. Her smile grew.

"Oh!" Her elbow jogged that of another stroller. "I'm so sorry. Pray excuse me."

"Gladly, my dear, if you'll tell me what could possibly be so amusing in Almack's."

The languid tones of the gentleman bowing before her were, Georgiana judged, devoid of menace. He was very neatly and correctly attired, soberly so. His blue coat was well cut, his satin breeches without a crease. Brown hair, stylishly but not rakishly cut, framed a pleasant face. There was nothing one could put a finger on to account for the air of elegance which clung to him.

As he continued to look at her with mild curiosity, Georgiana, Lady Winterspoon's dictum still fresh in her mind, answered him truthfully. "It was merely the conversation, caught in snippets as I walked about. It's—" she put her head on one side as she considered her words "—rather single-minded, if you know what I mean."

A quirky grin twisted the gentleman's lips. "I do indeed know what you mean, Miss…?"

Having embarked on her course, Georgiana dispensed with caution, "Hartley. Georgiana Hartley. I'm staying with Lady Winsmere. I seem to have lost her in the crush."

"Ah, the lovely Bella. I think I saw her over by the door, in earnest conversation with Lady Duckworth. Permit me to escort you to her."

With only a single blink, Georgiana laid her gloved hand on the proffered sleeve. If she was going to be escorted by any gentleman tonight, she was quite content that it should be this one. He hadn't told her his name, but he seemed thoroughly at home.

"From your comment, you seem almost to laugh at the purpose of this great institution. Yet surely you propose to avail yourself of its services?"

This was the sort of conversation Georgiana had cut her social eye-teeth on. "I most certainly intend to avail myself of its services, but not, I think, as you might assume."

Her companion digested this riposte, before countering, "If that means you are not here to snare a title, or a fortune, what possible other use for this place can you have found?"

"Why, that to which I was putting it when you met me."

A pause developed, followed by a great sigh. "Very well. I confess myself stumped. What is it you've discovered within these faded grey walls?"

Georgiana smiled, eyes dancing. "Why, enjoyment, of course. I was enjoying myself." To her surprise, she realised this was true. She turned to glance into her companion's grey eyes. In them, she saw thunderstruck amazement.

"Enjoyment? In Almack's?"

Georgiana laughed. "Of course. I'm enjoying myself now. Aren't you?"

Her gentleman stopped stock-still, a ludicrous mixture of horror and humour in his face. "Dreadful! I'll never live this down." Then his face cleared and he smiled, quite genuinely, at Georgiana. "Come, Miss Hartley. Let me restore you to Lady Winsmere. You're clearly too potent a force to be let loose for long."

Perfectly content, Georgiana strolled by his side through the crowd, who, she now noticed, seemed to part before them. Even before she caught sight of Bella's surprised face, she had started to question the identity of her escort. But she was determined not to worry. And, thankfully, whoever he was, her escort seemed to find nothing amiss.

Bella curtsied and chatted animatedly, but Georgiana still heard no name. With a final, *sotto voce,* "Enjoying oneself in Almack's. Whatever next?" the very correct gentleman withdrew.

Georgiana turned to Bella, but, before she could utter

her question, Bella was exclaiming, albeit in delighted whispers, "Georgie! However did you do it?"

"Do what? Who is he?" Instinctively, Georgiana whispered too.

"Who? But…don't you know?" Bella stared in disbelief, first at her, then at the elegant retreating back.

"No. No one introduced us. I bumped into him and apologised."

Bella fanned herself frantically. "Heavens! He might have cut you!"

"Cut…? But who on earth is he?"

"Brummel! George Brummel. He's one of society's most powerful arbiters of taste." Bella turned to survey Georgiana appraisingly. "Well! Obviously he's taken to you. What a relief! I didn't know what to think when I saw you with him. He can be quite diabolical, you know."

Georgiana, conscious now of the envious eyes upon her, smiled confidently. "You needn't have worried. We were just enjoying ourselves."

Bella looked incredulous.

Georgiana laughed.

"GOODNIGHT, Johnson."

"Goodnight, my lord."

The door of Winsmere House shut softly behind Dominic. The night continued mild, but the low rumble of distant thunder heralded the end of the unseasonal warmth. Still, Alton House in Grosvenor Square was only five minutes away. Dominic set off, swinging his slim ebony cane, his long strides unhurried as he headed for North Audley Street.

The evening had left him with a sense of dissatisfaction which he was hard put to explain. He had broken his journey to Brighton to check on Miss Hartley, although, to be precise, it was more to relieve his mind over whether Arthur and Bella had been put out over her descent on them. Thankfully, all had turned out for the best. Arthur's scheme would undoubtedly pave the way for Georgiana Hartley to spend the upcoming Little Season with Bella, after which it would be wonderful if she had not received at least one acceptable proposal. The girl was not a brilliant match, but a perfectly suitable connection for any of the lesser nobility who made up the bulk of the *ton*. He had checked on her antecedents and knew them to be above reproach. Yes, Georgiana Hartley would very likely soon be betrothed. Which was far more appropriate than being a companion.

As he swung south into North Audley Street, Dominic grinned. How typical of Arthur to concoct such a perfect solution to the girl's troubles. And Bella's. Everything seemed set to fall smoothly into place. Which, all things considered, should leave him feeling smugly satisfied. Instead, he was feeling uncommonly irritated. The grin faded. A frown settled over his features.

A watchman passed by unobtrusively, unwilling to draw the attention of such a well set up and clearly out-of-sorts gentleman to his activities. Dominic heard him but gave no sign.

Why should he be feeling so disillusioned, so disheartened? He'd been living this life for the past twelve years. Why had it suddenly palled? The circumstances that had driven him to seek the peace of Candlewick drifted into his mind. All the glamour and glitter and laughter associated with the doings of the Carlton House set. And the underlying vice, the predictability, the sheer falsity of most of it—these were what had sent him scurrying for sanctuary. But even Candlewick had failed to lift his mood. While its serenity had been comforting, the huge house had seemed lonely, empty. He had never noticed it before; now its silence was oppressive.

The corner of Grosvenor Square loomed ahead. Dominic swung left and crossed the road to the railed garden. The gates were locked at sunset, but that had never stopped him strolling the well tended lawns by night. He vaulted the wrought-iron railings with accustomed ease, then turned his steps across the lawns in the direction of his town house on the south side of the Square. Tucking his cane under his arm, he thrust his hands into his coat pockets and sank his chin into the soft folds of his cravat. Doubtless, if he were still in the care of his old nurse, she would tell him to take one of Dr James's Powders. The blue devils, that was what he had.

A vision of honey-gold eyes crystallised in his brain. Why on earth Georgiana Hartley's eyes, together with the rest of her, should so plague him he could not understand. He was not a callow youth, to be so besotted with a female's finer points. He had hardly exchanged two words with the chit, yet, throughout the evening, had been aware of her every movement, every inflexion, every expression.

Leaves from the beech trees had piled in drifts and softly scrunched underfoot. Dominic paused to regard his feet, lightly covered with golden leaves. Then he shook his head, trying to rid it of the memory of curls sheening guinea-gold under candlelight. God! What was this? The onset of senility?

Determined to force his mind to sanity, he removed his hands from his pockets and straightened his shoulders. Ten long strides brought him to the fence, and he vaulted over to the pavement beyond. A few days, not to mention nights, of Elaine Changley's company would cure him of this idiotic fancy. As his feet crossed the cobbles, he commanded his memory to supply a vision of Lady Changley as he had last seen her, reclining amid the much rumpled sheets of the bed he had just vacated. Of course, Elaine's ambitions were on a par with her charms. But as he was as well acquainted with the former as he was with the latter he felt justified in ignoring them. A smile played at the corners of his fine lips as he trod the steps to his front door.

In the instant he raised his cane to beat a tattoo on the solid oak door, an unnerving vision in which Georgiana Hartley was substituted for Elaine Changley flooded his brain. So breathtaking was the sight that Dominic froze. The gold top of his cane, yet to touch the door, remained suspended before him.

The door opened and Dominic found himself facing his butler, Timms.

"My lord?"

Feeling decidedly foolish, Dominic lowered his cane. He sauntered past Timms, one of Duckett's protégés, as if it were perfectly normal for him to stand rooted to his own doorstep. He paused in the hallway to draw off his gloves, then handed the offending cane to Timms.

"I'll be leaving for Brighton early tomorrow, Timms. Tell Maitland to be ready about nine."

"Very good, m'lord."

Frowning, Dominic slowly ascended the gently curving staircase, pausing, as was his habit, to check his fob watch against the long case clock on the landing. Restoring his watch to his pocket, he reflected that, if nothing else could cure him of his disturbing affliction, the decadent amusements to be found within the Prince Regent's pavilion at Brighton would.

BY THE TIME the Winsmere House ladies were handed into their coach for the drive home from King Street, Georgiana had had proved to her, over and over again, the truth of Lady Winterspoon's dictum. If she enjoyed herself, then her partners seemed to enjoy her company. If she laughed, then they laughed, too. And, while such overt behaviour did not sit well with one brought up to the self-effacing manners expected of young Italian girls, it was a great deal better, to Georgiana's way of thinking, than simpering and giggling. Her upbringing clearly had not conditioned her for English social life. Nevertheless, the unrufflable calm she had been instructed was a lady's greatest asset certainly helped, allowing her to cloak her instinctive responses to some of those she had met—like Lord Ormskirk and his leering glances, and Mr Morecombe, with his penchant for touching her bare arms.

"The Sotherbys are holding a ball next week. Lady Margaret said she'd send cards." Bella's voice came out of the gloom of the seat opposite. "After tonight, I've no doubts we'll be kept busy. So fortunate, your meeting with Brummel."

The unmistakable sound of a smothered yawn came to Georgiana's ears. She smiled into the darkness. Despite her tiredness, Bella seemed even more excited by her success than she was. She had originally found her hostess's claim of boredom difficult to believe. Now she could find it in her to understand that, without any special interest, the balls and parties could indeed turn flat. Still, to her, everything was too new for there to be any danger of her own interest flagging before Bella's did. Hopefully Bella would not feel too let down when she found a position and moved away. Into obscurity. Georgiana frowned.

If she had been asked, five days previously, whether she had any ambition to enter the *ton,* she would unhesitatingly have disclaimed all such desire. However, having now had a small sample of the diverse entertainments to be found amid the social whirl, she rather thought she might enjoy being able to savour these, in moderation, by way of a change from the quieter lifestyle she considered her milieu. A saying of her father's drifted past her mind's ear. "Experience, girl! There's nothing quite like it and no substitute known.'

As the clop of the horses' hoofs echoed back from the tiered façades of the houses they passed, Georgiana puzzled over her change of heart. Still, nothing could alter the fact that she would need to earn her way, at least to some extent. That being so, perhaps she should take this opportunity of experiencing the *ton,* of enjoying herself amid the glittering throng? According to Bella, she needed to be known to find a position. So, until she secured one, she could, and perhaps should, follow her father's and Lady Winterspoon's advice.

Bella yawned. "Oh, dear. I'd forgotten what it was like." Another yawn was stifled behind one slim white-gloved hand. Then, "I wonder if Dominic has managed to convince Charles to sell the Place yet?"

The question jolted Georgiana out of her reverie. "Lord Alton wishes to buy the Place?"

"Why, yes. Didn't I mention it?"

Her friend's voice was sleepy, but Georgiana's curiosity was aroused. "No. Why does he want it? From what I saw, it's terribly run down."

"Oh, it is. Run down, I mean. Even when Charles's father was alive… And now…"

Georgiana waited, but Bella's mind had clearly drifted. "But why does he want it?" she prompted.

"The Place? Oh, I keep forgetting you don't know all that much about it." Bella's skirts rustled as she sat up. "Well, you see, the Place didn't exist a hundred years ago. It used to be part of Candlewick. But one of my ancestors was something of a loose screw. He gambled heavily. One of his creditors was one of your ancestors. He agreed to take part of the Candlewick lands in payment. So that was how the Place came about. My spendthrift ancestor didn't live long, much to the family's relief. Ever since then, the family has tried to buy back the Place and make Candlewick complete again. But your family have always refused. I don't know how long it's been going on, but, generally, both families have always dealt amicably despite all. That is…" Bella paused dramatically; Georgiana sat enthralled "—until my father's death. Although he had always talked of rejoining the Place to Candlewick, my father hadn't, as far as Dominic could discover, done much about it. So when he inherited, Dominic wrote to your uncle to discuss the matter. But your uncle never replied. He was, by that time, something of a recluse. Dominic could never get to see him. After a while, Dominic gave up. When he heard of your uncle's death, he wrote to Charles. Charles didn't reply either. Mind you," Bella added on a reflective note, "as Charles dislikes Dominic as much as Dominic dislikes him, I can't say I was surprised at that. Still, from what you've said, the Place is falling down about Charles's ears. I really can't see why he won't sell. Dominic's prepared to pay above the odds, and Charles must know that."

"Perhaps it's mere stubbornness?"

"Maybe," Bella conceded, tiring of her brother's problems. She lapsed into silence, the better to consider the doors the evening had opened for her protégée.

Georgiana puzzled over Charles's behaviour. In the few days she'd had to observe him, her cousin had given the impression of being addicted to the good things in life, or rather, that he had a liking for the finer things but had little of the wherewithal required to pay for them. Which made his refusal to sell the Place, in which he demonstrably took no interest, stranger still.

From consideration of Charles, it was a short step to thoughts of the man so inextricably linked in her mind with her escape from her cousin. The demands of her début at Almack's had precluded her thinking of her earlier meeting with Lord Alton, beyond the wish that she had made a better impression. Undoubtedly she had appeared as a gawky, tongue-tied, awkward child. Where on earth had two years of experience gone? Certainly, nothing in her previous existence had prepared her for the odd effect he had on her. She had never reacted to a man in such a way before. It was both puzzling and unnerving. When it came to Bella's brother, her carefully nurtured Italian calm deserted her. Hopefully, by the time they next met, the peculiar effect would have worn off. She did not wish to be forever appearing as a graceless schoolgirl to the gentleman before whom, more than all others, she wished to shine. Still, no doubt she was refining too much on their meeting. Lord Alton would have seen her merely as a child he had assisted in her time of trouble. She could be nothing more than that to him. The thought that she would like to be a great deal more than that to Lord Alton she ruthlessly decapitated at birth. He was a noted Corinthian and, from what she had heard at the dinner-table, one of the Carlton House set. She had nothing to recommend her to his notice—not beauty, nor fortune, nor birth. To him, she would be no more than a passing acquaintance, one he had perhaps already forgotten.

Besides, it seemed he was on the verge of contracting an alliance, although Lady Winterspoon certainly seemed to think the lady in question was rather less than suitable. But she had heard more than enough in Italy to distrust the conclusions of society. Who knew? Maybe Lord Alton was genuinely fond of Lady Changley. She tried to imagine what the lady Lord Alton was in love with would look like, but soon gave up. She knew so little of him that it was impossible to guess his preferences.

As she ruminated on the twist of fate that had caused them to meet, Georgiana reflected that it was perhaps as well she would get few chances to be in Viscount Alton's company. He was the stuff schoolgirl dreams were made of. Unfortunately, she was no longer a schoolgirl. And she did not have the capital to indulge in dreams.

CHAPTER FOUR

"MY LORD, I'm most truly sensible of the honour you do me, but, indeed, I cannot consent to becoming your wife."

Georgiana watched as Viscount Molesworth, an earnest young man more at home on his ancestral acres than in a London ballroom, rose awkwardly from his knees.

Dusting off his satin breeches, he sighed. "Thought you might say that."

Georgiana swallowed a giggle and managed to look politely interested.

Seeing this, the Viscount obligingly continued, "Told m'mother so. But you know what women are. Wouldn't listen. Said you'd be bound to accept me. Said you were just the thing I needed. Must say, I agree with her there." He glanced once more at Georgiana. "Sure you won't change your mind?"

Shaking her head, Georgiana rose and put her hand on the Viscount's sleeve. "Truly, my lord, I don't think we would suit."

"Ah, well. That's it, then." Lord Molesworth, heir to an earldom of generous proportions, lifted his head as music drifted from the ballroom down the hall. "Best get back to the dancing, then, what?"

Unable to command her voice, Georgiana nodded.

Strolling back into the ballroom on his lordship's arm, she could not keep a happily satisfied smile from her face. She had known the Viscount was bordering on a declaration, had been teetering on the brink for the past week. And, as with her two previous proposals, Georgiana had dreaded having to hurt his feelings. But it had all passed off easily, even more easily than the others. Her first proposal had been from young Lord Danby, who had been truly smitten but so very young that she had felt she were dealing with a younger brother, not a potential lover. Her second offer had come from Mr Havelock, a quiet man of thirty-five summers. She was sincerely fond of him, but in a friendly way, and doubted she could ever think of him other than as a friend. He had accepted her refusal philosophically, and they continued friends, but he had impressed on her that, should she have need of support or even something more, he was forever at her disposal.

Relieved at having weathered yet another proposal with no bones broken, Georgiana gave silent thanks that she had attracted only true gentlemen. Some of the more dangerous Corinthians had certainly looked her over—almost, she had felt, as if she were a succulent morsel they were planning to gobble up. But when they learned she was staying with the Winsmeres they usually smiled and passed on.

However, there were a few who had remained long enough to enjoy a light flirtation, a moment of dalliance. Such a one was Lord Edgcombe, who now approached to claim her for the waltz.

Georgiana smiled and curtsied. "My lord."

His lordship, resplendent in a dark green coat which leant a deeper tinge to his golden locks, bowed easily over her hand. "My lovely." His cool grey eyes flicked to the Viscount, still hovering by her elbow.

Georgiana realised he must have seen them re-enter the room, and wondered how much he guessed. She was now too experienced to take umbrage at his outrageous but calculated greeting. Instead, she spoke confidently, succeeding in distracting his lordship from his contemplation of the hapless Viscount. "I take it that means you approve of my gown?"

Lord Edgcombe's grey gaze swung slowly to her face. His lips twitched. Then, to pay her back for her temerity, he raised his quizzing-glass and embarked on a minute inspection of her person. "Mmm," he murmured. "The style, of course, is superb. Fancon, I trust?"

Georgiana, far from blushing and dissolving into a twittering heap, the prescribed reaction to his behaviour, could not restrain her smile. She understood his lordship's tactics only too well.

Far from being put out by her refusal to succumb, Lord Edgcombe responded with a smile of genuine enjoyment and offered his arm. "Come, sweet torment, the dance-floor awaits and the musicians will soon grow weary."

As she twirled down the room in Lord Edgcombe's arms, Georgiana wondered again at the success, for her part unexpected but none the less flattering, which had resulted in her receiving the attentions of one such as his lordship. He was well born, with a comfortable estate, and could be pleasant enough when it suited him. However, as it only suited him to behave so with a select circle of acquaintances, he was generally thought to be beyond the reach of the matchmaking mamas. Georgiana did not entirely understand his interest in her, but instinctively knew she was in no immediate danger of receiving a proposal from Lord Edgcombe. At least, she amended, as she looked into his smiling grey eyes and correctly divined the thoughts behind them, not a proposal of marriage.

"Relieve my curiosity, my dear. What could possibly be so interesting that you needs must be alone with the noble Viscount?"

Georgiana opened her eyes wide. "Why, we were merely strolling, my lord."

The grey gaze remained on her face for a full minute. Then his lips curved once more. "I see." After a moment he added, his voice low, "I don't suppose you feel like taking a stroll with me."

Georgiana's eyes danced. Keeping her face straight, she shook her head primly. "Oh, no, my lord. I don't think that would be at all wise."

They executed a complicated turn at the end of the room, pausing to allow two younger and more enthusiastic couples to pass by. When they were once more proceeding up the long room, his lordship's attention refocused. "Now why is that, I wonder? Surely you don't mean to say that you fear my company would be less... scintillating than the Viscount's?"

Georgiana laughed lightly, her eyes still holding his. "Oh, no—far from it. My fear is more that your company might prove rather *too* scintillating, my lord."

Lord Edgcombe was no more immune to the flattery of a beautiful young woman than the next man, even if he fully understood her machinations. So he smiled again, sharing in her laughter. "My dear, you're a minx. But a delightful minx, so I'll let you escape the set-down you undoubtedly deserve."

Schooling her features to reflect a suitable gratitude, and reducing her voice to a breathless whisper, Georgiana replied, "Oh, thank you, my lord."

"Gammon!" said Lord Edgcombe.

Returning three dances later to Bella's side, Georgiana was given no time to draw breath. Her mentor immediately demanded to be told what Viscount Molesworth had had to say.

Georgiana regarded Bella warily. "He proposed."

"And?" Bella's face was alight.

Georgiana knew it was her friend's dearest wish that she contract a suitable alliance, and Viscount Molesworth was certainly that. But she had no real ambition to marry where she did not love, not even for her best friend. So she drew a deep breath and confessed. "I refused him."

"Oh." Bella's face fell. "But why?"

Seeing the real consternation in Bella's big eyes— eyes that constantly reminded her of another—Georgiana was tempted to make a clean breast of it. But the approach of the gentleman to whom she was promised for the next dance reminded her of their surroundings. "I'll explain later. Not now. Please, Bella?"

Now Bella saw Mr Millikens and smiled and nodded, adding in an undertone for Georgiana's ears only, "Yes, of course. Later. But Georgie, we really must talk of this."

Georgiana nodded her agreement and moved forward to take Mr Millikens's arm.

The rest of the evening passed in a blur before Georgiana's eyes. She spent much of her time examining and assessing the changes the past two weeks had wrought in her life. Arthur's quietly worded request that she remain in Green Street, theoretically a guest, but in truth as a companion for Bella, had been a turning point. His explanation of Bella's need for purpose in an otherwise frivolous existence had struck a chord of sympathy. After that, she had no longer pursued the idea of finding employment with an older lady. Bella, of course, was kept in ignorance of the arrangement, for it was generally only much older women who had companions.

That first night at Almack's had set the seal on her success. From that evening, a steady flow of invitations had poured into Green Street, and she and Bella had been immersed in a tide of balls and parties, routs and breakfasts. Her popularity, both with the gentlemen and the ladies of society, had made Bella crow. For her part, Georgiana wryly thanked her less than perfect looks. Because she was no beauty, she was not a challenge to the reigning *incomparables*. Thus she was accepted without any great fuss, nor was she the butt of any jealousies. Her natural vivacity, which, thanks to Lady Winterspoon and Beau Brummel, she had discovered, carried her through. In her heart, she strongly suspected it was this, together with her unconventionally un-missish behaviour, which made her so attractive to the gentlemen. Certainly, they flocked about her. And, if she were to be truthful, she could not deny a happy little glow of self-satisfaction whenever she thought of her court. She might not be a hit, or a beauty, but she had her own little niche, her own place in the scheme of things. As Lady Winterspoon had suggested, there were many roads to success.

They were among the last to leave the ball. As she had anticipated, Bella returned to the subject of

Viscount Molesworth as soon as the carriage door was shut upon them.

"Why, Georgie? I thought you liked him."

Georgiana leant back against the fine leather upholstery and resigned herself to the inevitable. "Viscount Molesworth is all that is amiable. But truly, Bella, do you think that's enough?"

"Enough? But, my dear, many girls marry with far less than—er—liking for their husbands."

Georgiana stifled a sigh. She would have to try to make Bella understand. "Bella, did you marry like that?"

Bella shifted in her seat, her satin skirts shushing. "Well, no. But…well, you know it's not the done thing, to marry for love. And," she hurried on, "you've no idea the trouble I had, in marrying Arthur. No one could understand it. Oh, it's accepted now. But if Dominic had opposed the match everyone would have agreed with him. Love is simply not a…a determining factor in marriage in the *ton*."

Hearing the sincere note in Bella's voice, Georgiana debated whether to tell her the truth. But, even as the idea formed, she shied away from it. Instead she tried another tack. "But you see, dearest Bella, I didn't come to London to marry. I've given no thought to marrying into the *ton*. I'm not at all sure it would suit me."

To this, Bella returned a decidedly unladylike snort. "Not marry? Pray tell, what else are you going to do with your life? Oh—don't tell me you'll be a companion to some old lady. You'll never convince me you would rather be that than married to some nice, considerate gentleman who'll shower you with everything you desire."

Under cover of the dark, Georgiana grinned. Well, she was a companion, although Bella didn't know it and the lady wasn't old. But would she really prefer to be married, regardless of the man, to have to tend to the comfort and consequence of some faceless gentleman? Georgiana sighed. "You make it all sound so straightforward."

"It is straightforward. It's simply a matter of making up your mind to it and then, when a suitable gentleman comes along, saying yes instead of no."

Georgiana gave a weary giggle. "Well, if the right gentleman comes along, I'll promise to consider it."

Bella wisely refrained from further pushing, hopeful that she had at least made her errant protégée think more deeply on her future position within the *ton*. For Bella was quite determined her Georgie should marry well. She was attractive, which was more to the purpose than beautiful. And the gentlemen liked her—as evidenced by three proposals within two weeks. She had held great hopes of Mr Havelock, but Georgie had refused him without a blink. All she could do now was to hope Georgie's elusive right gentleman came along before her protégée got the reputation of being difficult to please.

A GENTLE BREEZE cooled Georgiana's warm cheeks as she accompanied Lord Ellsmere back to his phaeton. She deployed her sunshade to deflect the glances of any curious passers-by as they left the secluded walk and crossed the lawns to the carriageway. Her hand resting gently on his sleeve, she cast a tentative glance up into his lordship's handsome face. He was watching her and, catching her gaze, smiled ruefully.

"Forgive me, my dear, if my actions seem somewhat importunate. You'll have to make allowances for my—er—strong feelings in this matter."

For the first time since that night at Almack's, now more than three weeks ago, Georgiana felt flustered. Only this morning she had been congratulating herself on having managed to keep her earnest suitors from making any further declarations. How could she have guessed what his lordship had planned in the guise of a perfectly decorous drive in the park?

"Oh, yes, of course," she muttered incoherently. She noticed his lordship's slightly smug expression, and her temper, usually dormant, stirred. As she allowed him to help her up to the high seat of the phaeton, she made a heroic effort to pull herself together.

She could hardly claim that no gentleman had tried to kiss her before. But, in Italy, the flowery speeches and extravagant gestures that usually preceded such an attempt gave any lady all the warning she could need, should she wish to avoid the outcome. But Lord Ellsmere had given no indication of his intent. One minute they had been strolling comfortably along a secluded walk, screened by the lush growths of a long summer from the more populated carriageway and lawns, and the next she had been trapped in his arms, quite unable to free herself—not that she had struggled, stunned as she had been. Lord Ellsmere had, unfortunately, taken her lack of reaction for acquiescence and acted accordingly. Then she had struggled.

To give him his due, Lord Ellsmere had immediately released her, only to capture her hand. He had then proceeded to declare his undying love for her, to Georgiana's utter confusion. Her mind had been miles distant before he had acted, and she had struggled to manage even the most feeble disclaimer.

And now, of course, he merely felt he had acted precipitately and swept her off her feet. He had made it clear he did not accept her refusal of his suit. He would, he had said, live in the hope she would, with time, see its advantages.

As he climbed to the seat beside her, Georgiana turned impulsively towards him. "My lord…"

Lord Ellsmere's eyes followed his diminutive tiger as the boy left the horses' heads to swing up behind them. Then he turned and smiled at Georgiana. "I'll see you at the ball tonight, my dear. We'll continue our discussion then, when you've had more time to consider."

His words were kindly, and Georgiana inwardly groaned. This was precisely the sort of situation she had been trying to avoid. But with the tiger behind, she could do nothing other than acquiesce to his lordship's plan.

In truth, as she felt the cooling breeze ripple past, she welcomed the time to marshal her arguments better. Lord Ellsmere was not Mr Havelock, nor Viscount Molesworth. He had every right to expect her serious consideration of his suit. He was eminently eligible— title, fortune, property and connections. Oh, heavens! What would Bella say this time?

Any thoughts Georgiana might have entertained of keeping her latest offer from her friend died a swift death when, re-entering Winsmere House, she made her way to the back parlour. Bella was there, reclining on the sofa, flicking through the pages of the latest *Ladies' Journal*. She looked up as Georgiana entered. And frowned.

"I thought you were driving with Lord Ellsmere."

Georgiana turned aside to lay her bonnet on a chair. "I was."

Bella's frown deepened. "Didn't he come in?"

"No." Georgiana would have liked to add an excuse which would explain this lapse of good manners on his lordship's part, but could think of nothing to the point. Under Bella's close scrutiny, she coloured.

"Georgie! *Never* say it! He's *offered?*" Bella sat up abruptly, the magazine sliding unheeded from her lap.

Bright cheeks made it unnecessary for Georgiana to answer.

"Oh, my dear! *Ellsmere!* Whoever would have thought it? Why, he's..." Georgiana's lack of response suddenly struck Bella. She stopped in mid-exclamation, disbelief chasing elation from her face. "Oh, no!" she moaned, falling back against the cushions. "You've *refused* him!"

Georgiana smiled weakly, almost apologetically. But she wasn't to be let off lightly. Not this time.

Half an hour later, Bella threw her hands up in the air in defeat. "But I *still* don't understand! Danby was one thing; even Mr Havelock I could sympathise with. But Molesworth...and now, of all men, Ellsmere. Georgie, you'll never live it down. No one will believe you're turning Ellsmere down for the ridiculous reason that you aren't in love with him. They'll start saying there's something wrong with you, I know they will." Bella's voice quavered on the edge of tears.

Georgiana wasn't entirely composed herself. But she endeavoured to keep her tone even as she replied, "But

I don't mean to make them propose. I do everything I can think of to avoid it."

Bella frowned, aware this was so. She had watched her protégée like a hen with one chick, and had puzzled over Georgiana's apparent uninterest in her suitors as suitors, rather than acquaintances. To her mind, the offers were coming in thick and fast precisely because, in comparison with most of the other débutantes, the gentlemen found Georgie so comfortable to be with. Then the oddity in Georgiana's declaration struck her. Her head came up. "*Why* don't you wish them to become attached? You can't possibly have decided you can't love any of them. You can't expect me to believe you truly consider the single state preferable to being married."

There was no possibility of avoiding Bella's stern gaze. Georgiana had, in fact, spent the last weeks fantasising on marriage, albeit marriage to one particular gentleman. She felt her cheeks warm as she blushed guiltily.

And Bella, being Bella, and every bit as impulsive as Georgiana herself, immediately leapt to the correct conclusion. "Oh, Georgie!" she wailed. "You haven't formed a…a *tendre* for some unsuitable gentleman, have you?"

Driven to the truth, Georgiana nodded dully.

"But who?" Bella was nonplussed. She had conscientiously vetted those to whom she introduced Georgiana. There had been no one unsuitable. None of the truly dangerous blades had approached her, and, in the circles they frequented, there was precious little chance for any outsider to gain access to her charge. So who was this mysterious man?

"He's not actually unsuitable, exactly," put in

Georgiana, anticipating Bella's train of thought. At her friend's interrogative glance, she looked down at her hands, clasped tightly together in her lap, and continued, "It's more a case of…of unrequited love. I fell in love with him, but he doesn't love me."

"Well, then," said Bella, perking up at this, "we'll just have to see to it that he changes his mind."

"No!" squeaked Georgiana. She drew a deep breath and went on more calmly, "You don't understand. He doesn't know I love him."

Bella looked thunderstruck. Then, after a moment, she ventured, "Well, why not tell him? Oh, not in words. But there are ways to these things, you know."

But Georgiana was adamantly shaking her head. "He's in love with someone else. In fact," she added, hoping to shut off the terrifying prospect Bella seemed set on exploring, "he's about to offer for another."

"Oh." Bella digested this unwelcome news, a frown settling over her delicate face. For the life of her, she still could not fathom who Georgie's mystery man could be. In the end, she looked again at Georgiana where she sat on a chair, twisting the ribbons of her bonnet in her fingers, an uncharacteristically desolate look in her eyes.

Bella's kind heart was touched. She had been thrilled at Arthur's scheme to hire Georgiana as her companion and truly grateful for the way Georgie had tactfully gone along with the charade. Inwardly, she vowed she would do everything possible to learn who it was who had stolen Georgie's heart and, if possible, change his mind. Unlike Georgiana, she did not imagine a man about to contract an alliance was necessarily in love with his prospective bride. Hence, she did not consider

Georgie's case lost. But, if it was, she must look to protect her friend's best interests. She now knew enough of Georgiana to know she would never consider alternatives until, perhaps, it was too late. So, in a gentle way, Bella asked, "I don't mean to pry, my dear. But do you not feel you could tell me who the gentleman is?"

Georgiana hung her head. Her feelings of guilt were increasing by the minute. How could she repay Bella's kindness in this way? How could she tell Bella she was in love with her brother? Slowly she shook her head. Then, feeling some explanation was due, she said, "You know him, you see. And, as I said, he doesn't know I love him. I...think it would be unfair to tell you—unfair to you and unfair to him."

Bella nodded understandingly. "I won't push you, then. But perhaps, in the circumstances, it would be best if I spoke to Lord Ellsmere this evening." Georgiana's startled look had Bella hurrying on. "Oh, I won't tell him what you've told me. But there are ways and means. I'll just hint him away. It would be best, I think, for all concerned if I had a word with him."

Georgiana thought over this offer. Perhaps, in this case, she would be wise to accept Bella's superior knowledge of how things were done. She raised her eyes to her friend's blue gaze, wishing, for the umpteenth time, that Bella and her brother had taken after different parents in that respect. "If you don't mind speaking to him..."

"Not at all." Bella rose and impulsively hugged Georgiana. "Now! I'm going to ring for tea, and we'll talk about something quite different."

Georgiana summoned a smile and tried to tell herself that the peculiar emptiness within was only hunger.

TWO HOURS LATER Georgiana escaped to the sanctuary of her chamber. She did not ring for Cruickshank, wishing only to lie down and rest her aching head.

Quite when it was that she had finally realised she was in love with Lord Alton she could not be sure. Certainly, her social success and the proposals of Lord Danby and Mr Havelock had precipitated her thoughts on marriage. Only then had her feelings crystallised and gained substance. But, given that Lord Alton was so much older than she, and was shortly to marry Lady Changley, aside from having no inkling of her attachment and certainly no reciprocal emotions, she had originally decided her infatuation, for surely that was all it could be, was bound to pass. In such circumstances, and knowing Lord Alton was unlikely to spend much time in his sister's house, or dancing attendance on them, she had not seen her position as Bella's companion to be in any way compromised.

That had been before the shock of this afternoon had opened her eyes. Lord Ellsmere was all any young lady could desire. He was handsome, considerate, worldly and charming. And rich and titled... The list went on. But he was very definitely not the man she desired. When his lordship had taken her in his arms, she had been deep in a daydream in which she was walking with Bella's brother. The disappointment she had felt on realising that it was not Lord Alton kissing her had been acute.

She could no longer delude herself. What she felt for Viscount Alton was what her mother had felt for her father. She had seen them together often enough, laughing happily in a world of their own, to have an innate sense of the emotion. Love. That was what it was, plain and simple.

How had it happened?

Ridiculous it might be. Impossible it might be. But it was real.

With a great sigh, Georgiana burrowed her head into the soft pillow. How she was going to cope when next they met, as it seemed certain they would, she did not know. But cope she would. She had no intention of letting Bella guess the truth, nor of running away and leaving Bella alone. Arthur had offered her a way out of her troubles, and she had accepted in good faith. She would not let him down. Somehow she would manage.

Worn out, she closed her eyes. She needed to rest her troubled mind. And her troubled heart.

THE DUCHESS OF LEWES was holding her Grand Ball three nights later.

"One has to be a Duchess to call your ball 'Grand,'" Bella acidly remarked. "Still, one has to be seen there. It's one of the compulsory gatherings, you might say."

She had arrived in Georgiana's chamber just as that damsel emerged from her bath. Drifting to the bed, Bella fingered the lilac silk gown laid out there. Then, as if making up her mind, she turned to Georgiana. "Georgie, I know your feelings on this, but I really think you should consider wearing the sea-green gauze. You know I can never wear it. Please, wear it to please me."

Georgiana looked up, arrested in the act of towelling herself dry. Golden curls, dampened with steam, wreathed her head. For one moment she hesitated, considering Bella's plea.

"Wouldn't it cause comment, being so soon after my father's death?"

"But your father said you weren't to go into mourning, remember? And although it's common knowledge that your father has recently died, I haven't told anyone how recently. Have you?"

Georgiana shook her head. She considered the sea-green gauze. Stubbornly, she had bought three more evening gowns from Fancon, all in lilac shades, rather than wear the two gowns Bella had surreptitiously bought. But really, what right had she to refuse? It was a simple request and, after all Bella's help, it was a small price to pay. In reality, it was only her pride that forbade her to wear the delicate creations hanging ownerless in her wardrobe. So she smiled, fleetingly. "If it would please you."

Bella grinned happily. "Immensely." Her objective gained, she did not dally but whisked off to place herself in the hands of Hills.

Some three hours later, when they had finally gained the ballroom of Lewes House, Georgiana stood beside Bella and wondered why she had not overturned her stubborn pride weeks ago. The approbation in Arthur's eyes when she had entered the drawing-room that evening had assured her that her decision to wear the gown had been the right one. And the unusually intent attention of her court, and of numerous other gentlemen she had not previously encountered, bore testimony to their approval of her change in style.

As she accepted Lord Mowbray's arm for the first waltz, she smiled happily, laughingly returning his lordship's pretty compliments. To her surprise, she had discovered she could preserve the façade of a young lady enjoying her first London Season, free of care and the tangles of love, despite her empty heart. She had never been encouraged to think her own troubles of particular note. Hence, she continued to observe the lives and foibles of those about her with interest. She treated all her court in the same friendly style she had always affected. True, there were few among the débutantes she could yet call friend, but Bella was there to supply that need, for which she would always be thankful.

Georgiana had no idea what exactly Bella had said to Lord Ellsmere. Whatever it was, he had gracefully withdrawn his suit, simultaneously assuring Georgiana of his lifelong devotion. For a whole evening, she had speculated on what Bella could have said. In the end, she decided she didn't need to know.

Despite Bella's fears, her refractory behaviour in the matter of her suitors had not given rise to any adverse effects. She was still "that most suitable Miss Hartley" to the hostesses, and the cards and invitations continued to flood in. She could hardly claim she did not enjoy the balls and parties. Yet, somewhere, some part of her was detached from it all, aloof and unfulfilled, empty and void, waiting. But, as she sternly lectured herself in the long watches of the night, what she was waiting for had no chance of arriving. Lady Winterspoon's dictum had come to her rescue. There was nothing she could do but enjoy herself, thereby pleasing Bella and, as her father would have told her, extending her own experience. So, with typical abandon, she did.

By the end of the third dance, a cotillion, the rooms were starting to fill. Georgiana was escorted back to Bella's side by her partner, Mr Havelock, and he remained beside them, chatting amiably of social happenings. When he finally made his bow and left them, Georgiana turned an impishly animated face to Bella. But what she had intended to say regarding Mr Havelock remained unsaid. In fact the words melted from her mind. Her lips parted slightly in surprise as her gaze locked with Viscount Alton's.

Dominic had made his way to Bella's side through the crush, intending to learn what had become of the golden girl he had left in her care. Only when she turned to face him did he recognise in the exquisite woodland nymph, standing slim and straight in silver-green gauze beside his sister, the same young girl whose heart-shaped face and warmed-honey eyes inhabited his dreams. The realisation left him momentarily bereft of words.

It was Bella who came, unwittingly, to their rescue. She uttered a small squeal of delight and, remembering to restrain her impulsive habit of throwing her arms about his neck, grabbed both of Dominic's hands instead. He looked down at her, and the spell was broken. Smoothly, suavely, he raised her hands, first one, then the other, to his lips. "Dear Bella. Clearly in fine fettle."

"But I thought you were fixed in Brighton." Bella received her hands back, but had eyes only for her brother. She saw his gaze had moved past her to Georgiana. When he made no reply but continued to stare at Georgiana, she felt constrained to add, "But you remember Georgiana?"

"Assuredly." Dominic couldn't help himself. His voice had automatically dropped to a deeper register. He smiled into those huge honey-coloured orbs in a manner perfected by years of practice and, taking her small hand, raised it fleetingly to his lips.

Barely able to breathe, Georgiana blushed vividly and sank into the regulation curtsy.

Her blush recalled Dominic to his senses. When she straightened, his face had assumed its usual, faintly bored mien. He turned slightly to address Bella. "As you see, I've decided to exchange the extravagant but questionably tasteful entertainments of His Highness for the more mundane but distinctly more enjoyable pursuits of the *ton*."

"Shhh!" said Bella, scandalised. "Someone might hear you!"

Dominic smiled sleepily. "My dear, it's only what half of the Carlton House set are saying. Hardly fodder for treason."

Bella still looked dubious.

But Dominic's attention had wandered. "Perhaps, Miss Hartley, I can steal a waltz. Judging by the hordes of gentlemen hovering, you have few to spare."

By this time, Georgiana had regained her composure and was determined not to lose it again. "The fruits of your sister's hard work, my lord," she responded readily. She placed her hand on his lordship's sleeve, suppressing by force the shiver that ran through her at that simple contact. How on earth was she to survive a waltz?

Thankfully, Lord Alton seemed unaware of her difficulties. One strong arm encircled her waist, and she was swept effortlessly into the dance. As her feet automatically followed his lead, she relaxed sufficiently to glance up into the dark-browed face above hers.

He intercepted her glance and smiled. "So you've been filling in time with all manner of social gadding?"

Georgiana shrugged lightly. "The pleasures of the *ton*

have yet to pall, though I make no doubt they eventually will."

The dark brows rose. "What a very novel point of view." Dominic's lips twitched. "Surely my sister has taught you that all débutantes must, of necessity, profess addiction to all *tonnish* pursuits?"

A small and intriguing smile lifted Georgiana's lips. "Indeed, Bella has tried to convince me of the irreparable harm my lack of long-term enthusiasm might do to my chances. Still, I prefer to hold my own views." Georgiana paused while they twirled elegantly around the end of the room, before continuing, "I find it difficult to imagine being satisfied with a routine composed entirely of balls and parties and such affairs. Surely, somewhere, there must be some greater purpose in life?"

She glanced up to find an arrested expression on the Viscount's face. Suddenly worried she had inadvertently said more than she intended, Georgiana made haste to recover. "Of course, there may be a hidden purpose in such affairs—"

"No. Don't recant." His voice was low and betrayed no hint of mirth. His eyes held hers, unexpectedly serious, strangely intent. "Your views do you credit. Far be it from me to disparage them."

Georgiana was left wondering whether there was, underlying his seriousness, some fine vein of sarcasm she had failed to detect. But she got no chance to pursue the matter; the music ceased and Lord Alton returned her to his sister's side. With a smile and a lazy flick of one finger to Bella's cheek, and a polite inclination of his head in Georgiana's direction, he withdrew.

On the other side of the ballroom, Elaine Changley

shut her ivory fan with a snap. Her cold blue eyes remained fixed upon a head of gold curls just visible through the throng. Surely Dominic hadn't left her for a schoolgirl? Impossible!

The intervening bodies shifted, and Lady Changley was afforded a full view of Georgiana Hartley, slim and elegant at Bella Winsmere's side. The blue eyes narrowed. Her ladyship had not reached her present position without learning to sum up the opposition's good points. There was no doubt the girl had a certain something. But the idea of the charms of a delicate and virginal schoolgirl competing with her own experienced voluptuousness was too ridiculous to contemplate.

Lady Changley's rouged lips set in a hard line. The thought of what her so-called friends would say if, after all her crowing, she was to lose a prize like Dominic Ridgeley to a chit of a girl fresh from the schoolroom was entirely too galling to bear. Perhaps a little reminder of what she could offer was due.

IT WAS PAST midnight when Georgiana slipped on to the terrace outside the ballroom. The last dance before supper was in progress, and the terrace was vacant except for the moonbeams that danced along its length. As the chill of the evening bit through her thin gown, she wrapped her arms about her and fell to pacing the stone flags, drawing in deep breaths of the refreshing night air.

She had yet to become fully acclimatised to the stuffy atmosphere of *tonnish* ballrooms. Feeling the heat closing in on her, she had very nearly suggested to her cavalier of the moment, Lord Wishpoole, that they retire to the terrace. Luckily, a mental vision of his lordship's face expressing his likely reaction to such an invitation had stopped her from uttering the words, and doubtless saved her from the embarrassment of extricating herself from his lordship's unnecessary and very likely scandalous company. Wary of giving Bella any further reason to view her with concern, she had pleaded a slight headache to Lord Wishpoole and headed for the withdrawing-room. Once out of his lordship's sight, she had changed direction. The long windows of the ballroom had been left ajar, but the weather had turned and few guests had availed themselves of the opportunity to stroll on the long terrace.

Georgiana leant against the low balustrade and wished she was not alone. The idea of strolling beside Lord Alton, conversing easily while they took the air, was enticing. Only, of course, there was no possibility of Lord Alton wishing to stroll with her. Unfortunately, reality and dreams did not merge in that way.

The sound of footsteps approaching one of the doors at the far end of the terrace brought her upright. Someone pulled a set of doors wide, and light spilled forth. Startled, Georgiana looked around for a hiding-place. A tall cypress in a tub stood against the wall. Without further thought, she squeezed herself between the balustrade and the tree.

Through the scraggly branches of the tree she watched as a tall woman glided on to the terrace. The moonlight, resurrected now the doors were again shut, silvered her blonde hair. As she turned and looked towards the cypress, Georgiana caught a glimpse of diamonds glittering around an alabaster throat. The lady's silk dress clung revealingly to a ripe figure; her long, graceful arms were quite bare.

Again light flooded the terrace and was abruptly cut off. Georgiana's eyes grew round.

Dominic Ridgeley's blue eyes were hard as they rested on Elaine Changley. His brows rose. "To what do I owe the pleasure of this meeting, my lady?"

Inwardly, Elaine Changley winced at his tone. *My lady?* Clearly she had lost more than a little ground. But not a suspicion of her emotions showed on her sculpted face as she moved forward to place one slim hand on the Viscount's lapel. "Dominic, darling. Why so cold?" she purred.

To her surprise and real consternation, Lady Changley sensed an instinctive rejection, immediately suppressed, but undeniable. Shock drove her to make a grab, however unwise, for her dreams. Allowing her lids to veil her eyes, she moved seductively closer. "Surely, my love, what lies between us cannot be ended with a simple 'Goodbye'?"

Lady Changley was a tall woman. In one smooth movement, she pressed herself to Dominic's chest, reaching up to place her lips against his.

Automatically, Dominic's hands came to her waist, initially to hold her from him. But as he felt her silken form between his hands he stopped and quite coldly considered the situation.

He had come to the terrace in response to Elaine's note, intending to make it quite clear that his "Goodbye" had meant just that. The problem he was having with Georgiana Hartley, or, rather, with making sense of his feelings towards a schoolroom chit, was his major and only concern. He had almost succeeded in convincing himself that it was merely a passing aberration, that the reason he no longer desired the company, let alone the favours, of the delectable Lady Changley was no more than a function of the natural passage of time and had nothing whatever to do with a slim form in green silk gauze. Almost, but not quite.

And now here was Elaine, providing him with a perfect chance to test the veracity of his conclusions. The acid test. Surely, if he were to kiss her now, a woman he had recently known so well, he would feel something?

On the thought, his hands moved to draw her more firmly against him. Then his arms closed around her and his head angled over hers as he took possession of her lips and then her mouth. He felt the ripple of relief that travelled through her long limbs. Warning bells sounded in his brain. He felt nothing—no glimmer of desire, no flicker of flame. The coals were long dead.

Abruptly he brought the kiss to an end and, lifting his head, put Elaine Changley from him. "And that, my dear, is very definitely the end. Adieu and goodbye." With a terse bow, he spun on his heel.

Before he could leave, Elaine, desperate, stretched out one white hand to his sleeve. "You can't just walk away from me, Dominic. There's too much between us."

The chill of his very blue eyes as they turned on her froze Elaine Changley's blood. But, when he spoke, Dominic's voice was soft—soft and, to Elaine Changley, quite deadly. "I suspect, my dear, that you'll find you're mistaken. I should perhaps point out that any embarrassment you might suffer upon our separation will be entirely your own fault. And, furthermore, any attempt on your part to talk more into the relationship than was ever present will only result in your further embarrassment. So—" Dominic smiled—a singularly humourless smile—and lifted her hand from his sleeve, and thence, mockingly, to his lips "—I will, for the last time, bid you adieu."

Elaine Changley made no attempt to detain him as he strode from the terrace. She was shivering, though not from the cold. Far too experienced to run after her ex-lover, Lady Changley forced herself to stand still until her composure returned. Only then did she follow Lord Alton back into the ballroom.

Georgiana let out a long breath. She emerged from behind the tub, automatically brushing her skirt free of small sticks and needles. She felt as if she had hardly breathed since scuttling behind the tree. That, of course, was the reason she was feeling light-headed. Nothing to do with the revelation that Bella's brother was quite clearly and indisputably in love with Lady Changley. Why else would he have kissed her like that? She had been too far away to overhear their conversation, or to see their expressions, but the evidence of her eyes had been plain enough. Lady Changley had melted into Lord Alton's arms. And he had welcomed her and kissed her as if he intended to passionately devour her.

She knew her love for him was hopeless. Had always known it.

Georgiana shivered. Slowly she looked around the terrace. Her innocent daydream seemed more distant than ever, elusive as the mist which wreathed the treetops. With a deep sigh, she pulled open one of the ballroom doors and re-entered the heated room. She finally located Bella amid a knot of their friends. Pushing through the throng, she made her way to her side, rehearsing her request to leave early on the grounds of a headache which she could now quite truthfully claim.

CHAPTER FIVE

DURING THE NEXT WEEK, Georgiana had plenty of opportunity to develop her tactics for dealing socially with Viscount Alton. Contrary to her expectations, his lordship graced all the functions she and Bella attended. He was politely attentive. There was nothing in his behaviour to feed the flame she was valiantly trying to dampen. To her irration, she found that fact depressing. More than ever aware of the disparity of their stations, she doggedly reminded herself that a thick skin could only be obtained through exposure. Consequently, she did not shrink from contact with Lord Alton. Instead, whenever he asked her to dance—which he invariably did at least once, and, on one memorable occasion, twice—she endeavoured to amuse him with her observations on life in the *ton*. To her surprise, he seemed genuinely entertained by her comments. Indeed, he went out of his way to encourage her to air her opinions. Doubtless, she thought, it ensured he was not overcome with boredom in her otherwise unenlivening company.

Her own motive in maintaining a steady flow of conversation lay in distracting his lordship from the other peculiar responses he awoke in her. Breathlessness, often occurring with a unnerving sense of exhilaration, was the least of these. Sometimes she believed the thudding of her heart would be plainly audible if she weren't covering the noise with her chatter. Thankfully, he had not yet noticed the tremors that ran through her at his slightest touch. She had hoped these would ease with time, with familiarity, as it were. Unfortunately, they were becoming more acute with each passing day; she went in dread of his remarking them.

Absorbed as she was with dealing with his lordship, by the time they climbed into their carriage each night to return to Green Street she was thoroughly worn out. Gradually, the strain grew, until, in order to preserve her defences for the evenings, she found herself forced to forgo the pleasures of the day. When she excused herself from the afternoon's promenade for the second day in a row, Bella's concern became overt.

"Georgie, I simply cannot bear to see you so pulled down." Bella plumped herself down on the *chaise-longue* beside her friend. Georgiana was listlessly plying her needle, setting the occasional stitch in a piece of fine embroidery. Bella glanced anxiously into her face. "You aren't going into a decline, are you?"

Despite her tiredness, Georgiana grinned. "Of course not." After a moment she added, "I assure you I've no intention of pining away. It's just that I find the…the tension of the evening entertainments draining."

Born and bred to such things, Bella could not readily imagine being drained by a ball. However, she was not without sympathy. She frowned as she mulled over the matter. "We could cut down a trifle, perhaps. The Minchintons' ball is on Friday—we need not go to that, I suppose."

But curtailing Bella's activities because of her own weakness was further than Georgiana was prepared to go. She was supposed to be Bella's companion, not an inhibiting influence. "Don't be a goose," she replied, her tone affectionate but firm. "I'm only feeling a bit low, that's all. I dare say if I make a special effort I'll be fine by this evening." She paused. "On second thoughts, perhaps some fresh air would help. If you'll wait, I'll get my bonnet and come with you."

"Of course." Bella smiled encouragingly.

But as soon as Georgiana disappeared through the door, the frown return to Bella's face. Far from reassuring her, Georgiana's rapid about-face convinced her that her friend was endeavouring, however unsuccessfully, to conceal the true effect of her hopeless love. Who knew to what depths of misery Georgie descended when no one was by? Bella fretted over the problem, rendered more acute by the restraint she felt in confiding in anyone. Arthur was her long-time mentor, but in this case Bella felt she would need Georgiana's permission before revealing her friend's state to him.

Georgiana's footsteps sounded in the hall. With a sigh, Bella rose and picked up her discarded bonnet, absent-mindedly swinging it by its long aqua ribbons. She sorely needed advice. Then, in one instant of blinding clarity, she saw the answer. Dominic. He knew all of Georgiana's background. And, after all, Georgiana herself had seen fit, at the very outset, to confide in him.

When Georgiana stuck her head around the door, Bella grinned widely. "Yes, I'm coming," she called and, feeling much more light-hearted, all but tripped from the room.

"PLEASE, DOMINIC. I really *must* talk to you. Privately." Bella put every ounce of sisterly need into her gaze as it rested on her brother's handsome face. But his habitually bored mask showed no evidence of lifting. In fact, she noted, he regarded her even more dubiously than he had before her plea.

"I warn you, Bella, I need no lectures from you."

Far from striking fear into her heart and stifling her request as intended, his precise tones made her relax and give a dismissive smile.

"Not about that! I want to talk to you about Georgiana."

"Oh!" Dominic followed her gaze to the object of their discussion, twirling gaily about the dance-floor in Harry Edgcombe's arms. Then the piercingly blue eyes swung back to Bella. "What about Miss Hartley?"

Bella looked at the knots of people surrounding them. "Not here." She glanced impishly up at him. "Don't you know of an alcove where we might be alone?"

The blue eyes glinted down at her. "Don't be impudent." He caught her hand and drew it through his arm. "As it happens," he said, leading her through the crowd, "I do. But I can't spare too many minutes. I'm engaged to dance with Miss Hartley myself, two dances hence."

"It won't take long," Bella promised.

The small ante-room Dominic led her to was thankfully empty. She sank on to a well padded sofa. Dominic elected to stand, leaning one blue-silk-clad arm along the mantelpiece. "Perceive me all ears, dear sister."

Bella eyed him suspiciously, but could detect no hint of the sarcasm he frequently employed when irritated. "As I said, it's about Georgiana." Now she came to it, she found herself short of the necessary words.

"Has she discovered Arthur's little deception and become difficult?"

"No, no. Nothing like that." Bella frowned, then, sensing Dominic's growing impatience, she abandoned her efforts to find the best phrasing and blurted out, "She's fallen in love."

For a moment, she wondered whether he had heard. His face showed no reaction to her words; he seemed frozen, petrified. Then his black brows rose. "I see." He turned aside, resettling the fine lace on his cuff. "It is, after all, not an uncommon happening. Who is the lucky man?"

"That's just it. She won't say."

Dominic's eyes rested thoughtfully on his sister's dark head. "And you imagine, as she won't divulge his name, he must therefore be in some way unsuitable."

"No, that's not it either." Bella glanced up to find her brother's eyes full on her, irritation fermenting in their blue depths. She hastened to explain. "He's not unsuitable in the way you mean. But it seems she's fallen *irrevocably* in love with a man who's about to offer for another. She says he doesn't know she's in love with him. I've tried to get her to confide in me, but she won't. She says I know him so it wouldn't be fair."

Dominic digested this information in silence. Then, abruptly, he pushed away from the mantelpiece and paced across the room. Returning, he looked again at his sister. "How, then, am I supposed to help? I do take it I'm supposed to help?"

Bella smiled, a trifle warily. "Yes, of course. I wouldn't have told you if I didn't think you could help. I want you to find out who Georgie's gentleman is."

Dominic's brows flew. "That all?"

At his tone, Bella's face fell. "But you must be able to guess. Who is it whom I know is about to marry? Or at least offer for someone. You men always know such titbits before it's common knowledge."

Pacing once more, Dominic considered his acquaintance. He knew all the gentlemen his sister was on speaking terms with, and would very likely know if any were contemplating matrimony. "Unfortunately, to my knowledge, no one fits the bill."

Twisting her fingers anxiously, Bella ventured, "I had wondered whether it was Lord Edgcombe."

"Harry?" Dominic paused, then shook his head. "Not likely. He does have to marry in the not overly distant future or risk his family hauling him to the altar themselves. But he must marry money, and I doubt Miss Hartley's prospects fit his bill."

"But couldn't she have fallen in love with him anyway? He's certainly personable enough."

Again, Dominic gave the matter his consideration. Again, he shook his head. "Harry has no plans to marry yet awhile. I doubt he'd even mention the possibility to a young lady circumstanced as Miss Hartley is. And, certainly, he would not have suggested he's about to do the deed." He uttered a short laugh. "Not even to escape a snare would Harry bring up the subject of marriage."

Bella sighed. "So you can't guess either." Disheartened, she stood and shook out her skirts.

Dominic hadn't moved from his stance in the middle of the floor. Now he looked shrewdly at Bella. "What prompted you to ask for help?"

Bella shrugged. "It's just that Georgie's so wan and listless nowadays."

"Listless?" her brother echoed, the vision of Miss Hartley as he had last seen her vivid in his mind. "I've rarely seen anyone *less* listless."

"Oh, not in the evenings. She seems quite lively then. But during the day she's drawn and quiet. Her looks will suffer if she goes on as she is. If *only* she would accept Mr Havelock."

"Havelock? Has he offered for her?"

Bella frowned at the odd note in her brother's voice. It was not like Dominic to be so insultingly disbelieving. "Yes," she averred. "Not only Mr Havelock, but Lord Danby and Viscount Molesworth. *And* Lord Ellsmere, too!"

For once, she had the satisfaction of knowing she had stunned her brother. Dominic's brows rose to astronomical heights. "Good lord!"

After a moment, his puzzled gaze swung back to her face. "And she refused them all? Even Julian?"

Bella nodded decisively. "Even Lord Ellsmere." She looked down at her hands, clasped schoolgirl fashion before her. "I don't know what I'm to do, for there's bound to be more offers. They can't seem to help themselves."

She looked up to see her brother's shoulders shaking. Bella glared. "It's not funny!"

Dominic waved one white hand placatingly. "Oh, Bella! Would that all women had a sense of humour like Miss Hartley's. I assure you she would see the oddity in such a situation."

Bella was puzzled by her brother's far-away smile. But before she drummed up enough courage to ask what prospect it was that so fascinated him, he came back to earth. "And, speaking of Miss Hartley, we must, I'm afraid, return to the ballroom."

Falling into step beside him, Bella tucked her hand in his arm. "You will try to discover who he is, won't you?"

Dominic's eyes glinted steely blue. "Fear not, Bella mine. I'll give it my most earnest consideration."

And with that Bella had perforce to be content.

IT WAS WELL AFTER midnight when Dominic returned to Grosvenor Square. He let himself in with his latchkey. In the large tiled hall, shadows danced about a single candle burning in a brass holder on the central table. He had long ago broken his staff of their preferred habit of lying in wait for him to return from his evening entertainments. Picking up the candle, he stood at the foot of the stairs, contemplating the broad upward sweep. Then he turned aside and made for a polished door to one side of the hall.

The fire in the library was a glowing mass of coals. He lit the candles in the large candelabrum on the mantelpiece before crouching to carefully balance a fresh log on the embers. After a little encouragement, the flames started to lick along the dry wood.

Standing, he stretched, then crossed to the sideboard. A balloon of fine brandy in one hand, he returned to the wing-chair by the fireplace and settled his cold feet on the fender.

Georgiana Hartley. Undoubtedly the most beguiling female he had met in over a decade on the town. And she was in love with another man. Furthermore, she was in love with a man who didn't even have the good sense to love her. Ridiculous!

Dominic stared into the flames. For what felt like the six hundreth time, he tried to make himself believe that his interest in Miss Hartley didn't exist. But he had travelled that road before and had given up weeks ago. What he had yet to discover was what his interest in Georgiana Hartley portended.

He couldn't believe it was love. Not after all these years. His experience of the opposite sex was as extensive as hers was negligible. And he had never felt the slightest inclination to succumb to any of the proffered lures. Why on earth should he suddenly wish to entangle himself with a young woman barely free of the schoolroom?

Yet he could not get her out of his mind. Her heart-shaped face and honey-gold eyes inhabited his thoughts to the exclusion of almost everything else. He had underestimated the strength of his distraction when he had returned from Candlewick to Brighton. The chit had unexpected depths. Her eyes, like a siren's song, beckoned with a promise he found difficult to resist. Luckily he had realised his state before Elaine had precipitated any renewal of their intimacy. She had, predictably, reacted badly to his withdrawal.

Light from the flames gilded the spines of the leather-covered tomes on the shelves which stretched away into darkness on either side of the fireplace. Dominic took a sip of his brandy, then sank his chin into his cravat, cradling the glass between his hands. He had no regrets about Elaine. In truth, his desire for her had waned before the advent of Georgiana Hartley had banished all thought of illicit dalliance from his mind. A smile of gentle malice touched his lips. Doubtless Elaine would suffer due embarrassment as a result of her posturing.

It had been her plan to use public knowledge of their relationship to pressure him into making her aspirations come true. She had been most indiscreet. Lionel, Lord Worthington, his guardian prior to his attaining his majority, had even been moved to post to Candlewick to dissuade him from contracting a *mésalliance,* on account of the bluster of a trollop's long tongue. No, he had no sympathy for such as Elaine Changley.

The fire crackled and hissed as the fresh log settled. With a sensation akin to relief, he turned his mind from the past to contemplate the nebulous future. What did his feelings for Georgiana Hartley mean? Did they amount to anything more than infatuation, regrettable but harmless and, most importantly, transient? Would the lovely Georgiana fade from his mind in six months' time, as Elaine Changley had? These were the questions that tormented him. They had forced him to return to London, to assuage a need he did not wish to acknowledge. Yet, after a week in the capital, he was no nearer the answers.

The only truth he had uncovered was that his normally even temperament was now somehow dependent on Miss Georgiana Hartley's smile.

He dropped his head back against the deeply padded leather. He had tried to tell himself she was too young, little more than a schoolgirl. Any liaison between them would be virtually cradle-snatching. But, whenever he thought along such lines, Arthur's and Bella's happiness would rise up to mock him. And, even worse, Georgiana no longer *looked* like a schoolgirl. Every time they met, Fancon's gowns, or, rather, the delectable shape they displayed, shredded his well rehearsed rationalisations.

But enough was enough. According to Bella,

Georgiana was making herself ill over some no-hoper. He had no right to intervene. Not, that was, unless he wished to take their interaction further, to make some positive move in her direction. And that, he was not yet prepared to do.

If Bella, or anyone else, got a whiff of his possible intentions, there would be no chance of wooing her in private. Their every meeting would be watched over by dozens of gimlet eyes. Every word, every expression would be duly noted and analysed. He couldn't subject her to that, not when he wasn't sure what he wanted of her.

Experience, however, was on his side. If he wished, he did not doubt he could create the necessary opportunities to advance his cause, without alerting every gossip-monger in the *ton*. He smiled. There was an undeniable challenge in such an enterprise. The snag was, he was not yet sure. Not sure of what he felt for her. Not sure of what he would do once he was certain the odd feeling in his chest was more than infatuation.

It had taken him three weeks to reach his present state of acknowledged indecision. He had no intention of enduring the situation for much longer, particularly if Georgiana threatened to pine away before his very eyes. Still, how did one test an infatuation? Never having suffered such an emotion before, he had no real idea how to proceed.

The clock in the corner ticked ponderously, marking his heartbeats. His eyes grew unfocused as he stared at the flames slowly dying around the charred log. Finally he stirred. He drained his glass, then rose to return it to the tray. He relighted his bedroom candle at the candelabrum, then snuffed the five long candles it held.

In the soft flickering light of the single flame, he made his way to the door.

If he wanted to burn out his obsession with Georgiana Hartley, there was only one way to go about it. He needed to meet with her often, in every possible context, to see all her faults and blemishes, the little incompatibilities which would reduce her status in his mind to one of a mere acquaintance. That was the only way forward.

And, if it proved to be more than infatuation, it was high time he faced up to the truth. And acted.

"I TOLD YOU everyone would be here." Bella stopped on the lawn below the terrace. Tucking her furled parasol under one arm, she retied the strings of her new bonnet in a jaunty bow beneath one ear. "Lady Jersey's entertainments are always well attended, particularly when they're held here."

"Here" was Osterley Park, and the entertainment in question was an alfresco luncheon. To Georgiana, standing patiently by her friend's side, it seemed as if the entire *ton* was gathered on the manicured lawns sloping gently away from the Palladian mansion to the shrubberies and parkland beyond. "Lady Lyncombe is nodding to us. Over there on the left."

Bella turned and bowed politely to the portly matron, who had three gangling girls in tow. "Poor dear. Freckle-faced, the lot of them. She'll never get them off her hands."

Georgiana stifled a giggle. "Surely it can't be that bad. They might be quite nice young girls."

"They can be as nice as they please, but they'll need something more to recommend them to the eligible gentlemen." Bella sighed, in keeping with her worldly-wise pose.

Strolling by her side, Georgiana wondered what it was that recommended her to the gentlemen. Certainly not her looks, for, in her estimation, these were only passing fair. And her fortune was, she suspected, so small as to be negligible. Yet she had received four offers. Despite the fact that she had wished to avoid each one, the very existence of four eligible offers was no small fillip to her confidence.

Smiling and bowing to acquaintances, they strolled the length of the lawn to where three gaily striped marquees had been erected. One housed the beverages; one protected the food. The third was a withdrawing-room of sorts, where ladies feeling the effects of the sun could rest before rejoining the crush.

And it certainly was a crush. The broad expanses were filled with swirling muslins and starchy cambrics, parasols and elegantly cut morning coats dotting the colourful scene. It was difficult to see more than ten feet in any direction. Registering this fact, Georgiana turned to Bella to point out the advisability of staying close together. Too late.

"If you're looking for Bella, she's fallen victim to Lady Molesworth."

Georgiana looked up into Viscount Alton's blue eyes. He was smiling, and she noted the set of small lines radiating from the corners of his eyes. Such a handsome face. Entranced, she forgot her role of sister's companion and smiled warmly back.

Dominic expertly captured her hand and conveyed it to his lips. He caught his breath when she smiled with such guileless joy. For one instant, he could almost believe…

A sudden intentness in Lord Alton's gaze brought Georgiana to her senses. "Oh! Er—where exactly?" She flustered and blushed, and turned away as if looking for Bella, to cover her confusion.

"No, no. This way." Dominic's voice was gentle, softened by an emotion he couldn't quite define.

Georgiana looked where he indicated—to the right— and found Bella deep in discussion with Lord Moles-worth's mother—she who had decreed Georgiana could not do other than marry her son.

Dominic recalled Bella's mention of the luckless Viscount. His grin grew. "Perhaps," he said, "as Bella is so absorbed, I could escort you on a ramble by the lake. It's really much more pleasant than being packed amid all this crowd. Unless you're famished?" One black brow rose interrogatively.

"Oh, no," Georgiana disclaimed. She bit her lip. The prospect of a stroll in less cramped surroundings was very tempting. But could she weather such an excursion with Lord Alton? Were her nerves up to it? She glanced up at him and found him regarding her quizzically, as if trying to read her mind. As she watched, a faintly satirical gleam entered the very blue eyes, and his brows rose slightly, as if in challenge. Puzzled, she put aside her misgivings. "If it wouldn't be too boring for you."

With a laugh, Dominic offered her his arm. When she laid one small hand on his sleeve, he covered it with his other hand. "My dear Miss Hartley—or can I call you Georgiana?" He felt the hand under his quiver. His brows rose again. He looked down into her golden eyes.

"Oh, yes. Surely, in the circumstances, I can claim that privilege?"

Georgiana had no idea how she should answer. But her nerves were already a-tingle, and she didn't have the capacity to cope with distractions. So she merely inclined her head in assent. "If it pleases you, my lord."

Oh, it pleased him. In fact Dominic felt inordinately pleased with that small success. "As I was saying, my dear Georgiana," he continued, deftly steering her clear of Lord Harrow, another of her present encumbrances, "your company is forever entertaining. Tell me, which of your suitors do you favour?"

Now what on earth was she to answer to that? Georgiana thought quickly, then assumed a bored air. "Why, in truth, I'd not given the matter much thought, my lord." She heard a deep chuckle. "It's all so fatiguing, this marriage game." Lassitude dripped from her every syllable.

Laughing, he countered, "Very neat, my dear. But don't let any of the *grandes dames* hear you espousing such controversial standards. You'll be driven forth, cast out from the bosom of the *ton*."

Georgiana smiled, dropping her pose. "In all honesty, I'm not sure I'm suited to this life."

To mock her words would be the easy way out. Instead Dominic answered seriously. "My dear, it's such as you who keep the *ton* alive."

Her eyes flew to his face.

Reading the question in the golden-lit depths, he explained, "If we did not have people with different ideas, people brought up to different ideas, such as yourself, join us now and then, to refresh our tired fashions, then the *ton* would be an excessively boring and stale

society. Instead, if you look about you carefully, you'll
see the *ton* encompasses a wide spectrum of tastes and
types." He smiled down at her. "Don't worry. You'll fit
in. You'll eventually find your place, that niche that has
your name engraved on it."

Shyly Georgiana returned his smile.

They strolled on in companionable silence, around
the shrubberies and on to the shore of the lake. A cool
breeze lifted off the expanse of grey-green water, flicking little wavelets across the surface. Beeches lined an
avenue that followed the bank, golden leaves a carpet
beneath the still canopied crowns. There were other
guests enjoying the peace, but none intruded on their
privacy.

While enjoying the early autumn colours, Georgiana
pondered the cause of his earlier satirical look. As she
noted the giggling and sighing of more than one damsel
they passed, it suddenly occurred to her that Lord Alton
might have thought she was questioning the propriety of
walking alone with him. Inwardly, she sighed. If only
that were her trouble. But she was abysmally aware she
was in no danger of receiving any amorous attentions
from Bella's brother. Rather, she was more afraid of
boring him witless. She cast about in her mind for a
suitable topic of conversation.

Far from being bored, Dominic was revelling in the
unusual pleasure of strolling in relative peace in a glorious setting with a beautiful woman who was blessedly
silent. The only itch to his contentment was the realisation of how deeply contented he in fact was. That, and
the strength of his desire to preserve the moment at
whatever cost. That unnerved him.

"Do you spend much time with the Prince Regent? What's he like?"

Georgiana's questions broke his train of thought. Dominic paused, considering, before he answered. "My family have for the past few generations been close to the throne." He smiled down at her. "In the present case, the Regent."

"But…" Georgie hesitated. She had taken in enough of the discussion between Lord Alton and Arthur over Bella's dinner-table to realise the Viscount was more deeply involved in politicking than one might suppose from his pose of arrogantly bored aristocrat. Carefully choosing her words, she ventured, "You discuss politics with His Highness, don't you? Not just…well, social matters."

Inwardly cursing Arthur for his lapse from their normal secretiveness, Dominic attempted to turn her far too perceptive query aside. He laughed lightly. "I assure you, my dear, that—er—social matters are generally dominant with the Regent."

The teasing look he sent her along with his words should have had her blushing. Instead, he saw her beautiful eyes narrow slightly, and knew his diversion had failed. Damn it! She was younger than Bella. She should accept his word without question. And since when did young ladies institute probing inquisitions into a man's politics? She deserved a set-down. Instead, Dominic heard himself say, "However, you're quite right. I do act as a sort of…conduit—a channel of communication, if you like—between certain factions of the Parliament and the Regent." He paused to help her step over a large tree root distorting the even surface of the path. Settling her hand once more in the crook of his arm, he continued, "Despite appearances, Prinny is not entirely insensitive to the problems of the realm. And, while he has limited powers as far as actual law-making goes, his influence can go a long way to seeing changes made where they are desperately needed."

"And you explain these things to him?"

Dominic laughed. "Oh, no! I merely act as a form of Greek messenger."

Georgiana looked her question. Smiling, he explained. "My task is merely to bring up the subject, to introduce the problem, whatever it might be, to His Highness's notice." He grinned. "That's why I'm back from Brighton with leisure to enjoy your company."

Georgiana frowned, puzzling this out. "He didn't like your last problem?"

Her companion's gaze had shifted to the distance, but he was still smiling.

"Not in the least. I'm presently in disgrace, although, of course, that's not general knowledge."

It seemed to Georgiana that there was quite a deal about the fascinating Viscount that was not general knowledge. But before she could frame any further questions, they emerged from the beech walk and were joined by a gaggle of young ladies and their escorts. Viscount Molesworth was there; so too was Lord Ellsmere. Georgiana caught a look of surprise on Lord Ellsmere's handsome face, followed swiftly by an expression she could only interpret as consideration. However, he said nothing to her, beyond a polite greeting, and fell into step on the other side of Lord Alton, engaging the Viscount in a low-voiced conversation which seemed to have a distinctly pugilistic flavour. In a laughing, chattering group, they made their way back to the marquees.

Bella met them there. To Georgiana's disappointment, she got no further chance to converse alone with Lord Alton.

TWO NIGHTS LATER, a masked ball was to be held at Hattringham House. Bella was thrilled. "It's quite fun, really. Most people know who you are, of course, but the masks allow everyone to pretend they don't."

It was the afternoon of the big event, and Bella was lolling on Georgiana's bed.

Georgiana was frowningly considering her wardrobe. The one evening dress she had yet to wear was the topaz silk. For some reason, she had resisted temptation, saving it for some undefined purpose. She rather thought the time for wearing it had come. Why she should feel so she had no idea. She simply did. She drew it forth and held it to her.

"Oooh, yes!" said Bella. "I'd forgotten about that one. It's perfect."

"You don't think it's a little too…?" Georgiana gestured vaguely.

"Heavens, no! A 'little too…' is exactly what one wants for a masked ball."

"Do you have a mask I can borrow?"

"Heaps! They're in a drawer in my room." Bella sat up and jumped off the bed. "Come, let's go and look. Bring the dress."

Five minutes later they had found the mask. A bronzed affair with elaborate upswept wings, it fitted snugly across Georgiana's upper face from forehead to upper cheeks. Her hazel eyes glittered from the darkened depths of the slanted eye holes. There was no debate on the matter; it was perfect.

When they descended the stairs that evening to twirl joyfully about Arthur in the hall, his face told them they were both visions of delight. "You won't be able to move for all the beaux at your feet," he said, taking one hand of each fair maid and gallantly bestowing a kiss on them both.

As he escorted his two charges to their carriage, Arthur smiled in fond anticipation. He was accompanying them ostensibly because the Hattringham House ball was one of the major events of the Season. In reality, he cared little for the social swim but intended to keep a watchful eye on his youthful wife. Bella too often forgot that what she intended as innocent play might be reciprocated by actions far from innocent. As he rarely had time to devote solely to his wife, Arthur was looking forward to enjoying the evening. He knew Dominic would be there and was quite sure he could leave his brother-in-law to look after Georgiana. In fact, he thought, as his gaze rested on the alluring figure clad in topaz silk seated opposite, he doubted his brother-in-law, in his present state, would have eyes for anyone else.

Georgiana travelled the miles to Hattringham House in an unusual state of nervous anticipation. Nervous anticipation of itself was no surprise—she was accustomed to feeling it grow every time she appraoched the moment she would meet Bella's brother. But tonight the tension was heightened. It was the fault of the dress. If she had known how it would affect her, she would never have worn it. Far from decreasing her anxiety, the realisation tightened the knots in her stomach. Inwardly quivering with trepidation, she accepted Arthur's hand to descend from the carriage to the torchlit steps of

Hattringham House. With assumed calm, she glided beside Bella as they made their way through the hall and into the ballroom beyond.

There was no footman to announce anyone, of course. The guests merely entered and joined the shifting throng. Already the rooms were crowded. Glittering jewels winked under the chandeliers. Gay silks and satins swirled, fans fluttered in flirtation, curls bobbed teasingly about artful faces. A hubbub of conversation rose to swamp them; warm air redolent with a heady mix of perfumes and flower scents wrapped them about.

"Phew! What a crush!" exclaimed Bella. "And it's not even ten."

A tall, dark-haired gentleman materialised at Georgiana's side. He bowed elegantly over her hand. "Could I beg the favour of this dance, fair maid?"

Behind the dark mask, Georgiana descried the features of Lord Ellsmere. "I would be honoured, my lord," she replied, rising from her curtsy.

"Now how do you know if I'm a lord or not?" her partner asked as he whirled them on to the floor.

"Given that at least half the gentlemen present must be titled, it seemed a reasonable assumption," Georgiana glibly explained. "And besides, even if wrong, the mistake could only flatter, whereas, if it were the other way about, I could be stepping on toes."

His lordship laughed. "You never step on my toes, my dear."

Abruptly Georgiana wondered whether he had accepted her dismissal of his suit or was, in reality, merely waiting in the expectation that she would change her mind. Held easily within his arm, she was loweringly conscious that she felt nothing—no ripple of excitement, no increase in her heartbeat to betray her emotions. His nearness touched her not at all.

The dance ended and they whirled to a halt. Immediately they were mobbed by a crowd of gentlemen, all wishful of securing a dance with the exciting newcomer. Not everyone recognised her; of that Georgiana was certain. But before she could make sense of all their requests and determine whom it was safe for her to accept, a deep voice spoke from just beside her.

"My claim is first, I think."

Georgiana glanced up, her breath trapped, as usual, somewhere between her lungs and her throat. Her eyes took in the tall, broad-shouldered form at her side, exquisitely garbed, dark hair falling in waves about a dark mask. Blue, blue eyes watched her from the depths of the mask. Even if his eyes and voice hadn't informed her clearly who he was, her senses were screaming it.

"Of course, my lord," she said, drawing again on her inner strength, the only way she could weather the storm of emotions his nearness always unleashed within her. She placed her hand on his proffered arm and allowed him to lead her on to the floor, entirely forgetting the rest of her court.

"Well!" expostulated Viscount Molesworth, left standing by Lord Ellsmere. "If that don't beat the Dutch!" He glared at the broad shoulders of the gentleman whose arms now held the lady in topaz silk. His glare turned to a petulant frown. "Who is he, anyway?"

Lord Ellsmere was watching the couple on the dance-floor, a slight smile on his face. He looked down at the Viscount. "Don't you know?"

Lord Molesworth puffed indignantly. "Wouldn't ask if I did. Stands to reason."

Julian Ellsmere continued to watch the dancers, then, shaking his head in wonderment, left Lord Molesworth without his answer.

Georgiana was struggling to subdue her senses, running riot as usual. As they reached the end of their first circuit, she felt almost in control again. If Lord Ellsmere left her cold, Lord Alton did exactly the opposite. She felt flushed—all over. And the peculiar sensation of weakness she had suffered during their more recent meetings seemed tonight to be intensified. Perhaps it was because he was holding her rather more closely than was the norm. Still, at least her brain seemed to be functioning again.

If she had been more experienced, Georgiana might have wondered at her partner's silence. But, engrossed in her inner struggle, she did not question what it was that kept Lord Alton speechless for the better part of the waltz. Dominic was, in fact, dealing with a revelation of his own. When he had seen Georgiana enter the ballroom at Bella's side her beauty had stunned him to immobility. In his eyes, she was the most ravishing female in the room. A goddess, all gold and bronze. A golden angel, from the topmost gold curl to the tip of her tiny gold slippers. A prize beyond price. He had watched as she circled the floor in Julian's arms, dazedly waiting until he could approach her. He no longer questioned the effect she had on him; it was now too marked to ignore. But, as he had deftly extricated her from her other admirers, for the first time his full attention had been focused on her. What he saw had effectively knocked him back on his heels. He was far too experienced not to recognise the signs. In all their previous meetings, his mind had been fully occupied in analysing his responses to her, not her responses to him. Now, all his well honed expertise on alert, he let his senses feel for her, and convey back to him her state. Every little move she made was now registered—every indrawn breath, every flicker of an eyelid. The information came in and was automatically assessed, allowing him to respond to her smoothly, easily, encouraging her, heightening her awareness of him, learning her reactions to his attentions. His instinctive conclusions hammered at his conscious mind. When had it happened? In truth, he didn't care. All that now concerned him was how to capture what was there, how to foster and nurture her feelings, to make them grow to what he desired them to be. And all his experience told him that wouldn't be difficult.

So, with gentle patience, he waited until she had herself in hand once more and could cope with his, "And what might your name be, fair one?"

Georgiana blinked. Surely he recognised her? But then, she reflected, she wasn't sure the others had either. Maybe it wasn't that obvious. She thought quickly, then replied, "I really don't think the purpose of her ladyship's entertainment would be furthered if I answered that question, my lord."

Inwardly, Dominic grinned, but outwardly he was all dejection. "But what, then, should I call you, sweetheart?"

It was a struggle to keep her tone even. "'Sweetheart' will do very nicely, my lord."

Great heavens! Had she really said that? Georgiana glanced up from under her long lashes and blushed when she encountered her partner's blue gaze. But he merely smiled, slowly, and said, "Sweetheart it is, then, my dear."

His deep voice sent tingling shivers down her spine. What on earth was she doing? What on earth was he doing?

The music ceased, and Georgiana turned towards the other end of the ballroom, where she had left Bella. Her partner detained her by the simple expedient of tightening the arm that still lay about her waist. "Oh, no, sweetheart," he said on a soft laugh. "Hasn't anyone told you?" At her enquiring look, he explained, "One of the main—if not the primary—purposes of a *balle masquée* is to permit those who wish to…further their acquaintance to do so without attracting the notice of the tattle-mongers." His voice had dropped to a mesmerising tone. His breath wafted the curls about her ear as he bent closer to add, "And I find I very definitely want to further my acquaintance with you."

Georgiana gasped. There was no doubting the subtle invitation couched in those otherwise innocuous words. Involuntarily, her eyes sought his in the darkened recesses of his mask. The glow she saw in the blue depths merely served to tighten the iron band that had clamped around her chest, threating to suspend her breathing. "My lord!"

Despite her panic, her words came out in a seductive whisper, quite contrary to her intention. It was as if something stronger than her will was impelling her to accept the challenge she saw in his eyes.

He laughed, softly, his eyes on hers, and Georgiana's bones felt weak. Then he put the challenge into words.

"Surely, sweetheart, you're not afraid of what you might learn?"

His head was bent close to hers, his large body overwhelmingly near. His breath felt warm against her cheek; his hands came up to surreptitiously stroke her arms where they were bare above her elbow-length gloves. Georgiana could not repress the shiver of pure delight that coursed through her at his touch.

What on earth was he doing? Dominic mentally sat at a distance and marvelled at himself. He knew—none better—that this was no way to behave towards a gently reared young lady. To experienced courtesans, to the likes of Elaine Changley, his attentions would be perfectly in order. But delicate virgins were apt to flee for cover, to faint or screech if treated to such subtle but strong tactics. Certainly, they wouldn't know how to respond to them. The trouble was, Georgiana Hartley's responses had more in common with those of a courtesan than of the virgin he knew her to be. Fascinated, he waited for her reaction.

Georgiana had no thought of fleeing, fainting or screeching. Her conscious mind was entirely taken up with a fight against her desire to learn what it was his lordship proposed to teach her. Desire won, hands down. She'd deal with reality later.

"Afraid?" she echoed, buying time. "Hardly that. But I do wonder at the wisdom of being seen too much together. Surely our friends, if no one else, will recognise us and think it odd?"

Dominic understood the hidden meaning in her words, but chose to ignore it. He was in no hurry to confirm or deny his recognition of her. "In this mêlée?

I doubt any of our friends can even see us. Can you see any of your party?"

He had already seen Bella and Arthur move into one of the adjoining salons, so was not surprised when, after a quick survey of the room, Georgiana shook her head. "I can't see anyone I know."

Smiling, Dominic tucked her hand into his arm. "You see? A *balle masquée* is a time to have fun. So come and enjoy yourself with me." As he steered her in the direction of the terrace, he added for her ears only, "I assure you I have every intention of enjoying myself with you."

To Georgiana's delight, the evening proved to be one of unalloyed pleasure. Initially, she was wary, convinced Lord Alton had not recognised her, and on tenterhooks lest he, not knowing who she was, overstepped the line. Instead, while he certainly drifted very close to the invisible limit of acceptable conduct, he never once gave her cause to rue her deception. For deception it certainly was. What on earth would he think if he ever learnt it was his sister's little protégée on whom he was lavishing his attentions?

To be the object of his attentions was a most sinful pleasure. Georgiana sparkled, animated as she had not been since her father's death. For one blissful evening she forgot her situation, forgot her cousin, forgot everything beyond the dancing lights in a pair of cerulean blue eyes. They walked through the salons and he pointed out numerous well known identities hidden behind their masks, elaborating on their idiosyncrasies, regaling her with gossip and the latest *on dits,* making her laugh, making her blush. When she confessed to hunger, they found the supper-room and helped themselves to heaps of lobster patties. She had her first taste of champagne, and giggled as it fizzled down her throat. They danced again, waltzing with effortless grace. Georgiana felt as if she were floating, held to earth by the strong clasp of his arm about her waist, drawn to heaven by the warmth in his eyes. Later they strolled on the terrace. She stood at the balustrade and he stood behind her, pointing out the features of the famous topiary gardens, thrown into silvered relief by the moonlight. His breath wafted the curls by her ear; his lips gently grazed her temple. Gently, so gently that she had no strength to resist, his hands lifted to her bare shoulders in a practised caress, skimming down over her bare arms. Ripples of delight shivered through her. He drew her around to face him, lifting one gloved hand and raising it to his lips.

"The evening is gone, sweetheart." His eyes lingered on hers, then dropped to her lips. For one instant, Georgiana wondered if he would kiss her. She hovered, poised on the brink of returning such an embrace, and felt oddly deflated when, in a voice curiously devoid of emotion, he remarked, "Come. Let me take you to find your party."

It was some minutes before Georgiana spied Arthur, Bella by his side, just inside the door to the main salon. She turned to the gentleman beside her, only to find he had disappeared, melting into the still considerable crowd. Suppressing a smile at his tactics, Georgiana went forward to Bella's side.

"Good heavens, Georgie! I was starting to wonder if you'd been spirited away." Bella looked closely at Georgiana, then asked, "Where have you been?"

"Oh, just here and there," replied Georgiana, smiling beatifically. She couldn't help her smile, even though it was making Bella suspicious. Still, with Arthur present, she doubted her friend would seek to interrogate her tonight. And she would handle tomorrow's queries when they came.

Ten minutes later, the Winsmere carriage rolled out along the road back to London.

Dominic Ridgeley watched it go. Pulling on his gloves, he nodded to a waiting footman, who promptly departed to summon the Viscount's carriage. Once comfortably ensconced in soft leather, the excellent springs ironing out the inevitable bumps and jolts, Dominic allowed his mind to coolly assess his involvement with Georgiana Hartley. He placed due emphasis on the "cool"; there had been more than one moment during the evening just past when, for all his experience, he had felt anything but cool. She was an enigma, his golden angel, an innocent who responded with delicious abandon to every practised caress he bestowed on her, who promised to respond with even greater passion to those caresses he had yet to expose her to. A golden angel who had already captured his hardened rake's heart, but, unless he mistook the matter, had yet to realise that fact. A fascinating proposition.

He treated the darkness to a smile of pure delight. Who would ever have believed it?

As the miles fell beneath his horses' hoofs, he relived the evening in his mind. She had accepted at face value his intimation that he hadn't recognised her. Would she still believe that tomorrow? And, if she did, what would she then make of his attentions to an unknown lady? Dominic grimaced. He would have to take the earliest opportunity to disabuse her mind of the idea he had not known who she was. Silly child. He would have known her instantly even if she had worn a full domino. Still, she did not have the experience to know she affected him as much as he affected her. More, if anything. The memory of how hard he had had to fight to refrain from kissing her on the terrace made him groan.

No more anonymous wooing. From now on, he resolved, he would openly court her. Doubtless, eyebrows would be raised. Too bad. His friends were sure to have recognised him tonight anyway. Julian Ellsmere certainly had. And Julian had known which lady he had spent the evening with. Thank heavens she had already refused Julian. The last thing he needed was to have a resurgence of the old story. God knew why the gossip-mongers had never realised that Julian himself bore him no ill will over the affair of Miss Amelia Kerslake. His black brows rose cynically. Truth, of course, was never of great interest to the gossips.

With a deep sigh, Dominic leant back against the squabs and shut his eyes. Without the slightest difficulty, he conjured up the vision of a pair of big hazel eyes, so brilliant that they seemed to flash with gold fire. His doubts were gone. All considerations of age and station had long since fallen away, discarded as irrelevant in the face of his desire. He wanted Georgiana Hartley. And he intended to have her.

CHAPTER SIX

THE HATTRINGHAM HOUSE masked ball proved a revelation to others as well. While Georgiana waltzed and laughed on the arm of her cavalier, faded blue eyes, pale and washed out, watched her from the anonymity of the side of the room. Under his breath, Charles Hartley cursed. It didn't look promising.

Two weeks he had spent, searching the countryside for his little cousin. Finally he had been forced to conclude that the minx had somehow found her way to London. He had closed up the Place—had been forced to do so. Dismissing the Pringates had been an ugly affair, from which he was thankful to have escaped with a whole skin. But paying them off had severely depleted his reserves. He had hastened to town, reduced to finding lodgings in a mean and dingy street beyond the fashionable areas. Once installed, he had suddenly found himself at *point non plus*. Where would Georgie have gone?

That question had worried him until he was nearly crazed. Luckily, the recollection that her servants had disappeared with her surfaced to lead him from the brink of despair. From what he had seen of them, they would never have countenanced Georgiana doing anything that would bring her into danger. Or ill repute.

Hence, they must have found lodgings in an acceptable quarter.

Days of trudging the streets had followed, calling surreptitiously at the fashionable hotels, hours of drinking in the taverns favoured by the servants of the gentry. Gradually he had been forced to consider the more *tonnish* areas. Finally, his luck had turned. He had seen her in Bond Street.

She had been dressed in the height of fashion, a parasol shading her delicate features, and he had almost missed her. The effect her appearance had had on him, leaving him gaping, had, by sheer luck, saved him from prematurely revealing his presence.

Before he had gathered his wits, she was joined by another female, likewise fashionably elegant. A nagging sense of the familiar had finally crystallised. Little Bella Ridgeley! He had barely made her out, rigged up to the nines as she was, but she was still the little girl he had teased so unmercifully whenever her big brother had not been around.

His eyes had narrowed. So Georgiana had sought refuge at Candlewick Hall—the one place he had not considered looking. Smart of her—or was it pure luck? He had decided on luck, for there was no way Georgiana could have known, and was about to step forward and accost the fair pair, when they were helped into a waiting carriage by a burly footman.

Balked of his prey, the wisdom of reconnoitring the lie of the land was brought home to him. Bella had married a Lord Winsmere. A powerful man. If the Winsmeres were Georgiana's friends, he had better be sure of his strategy before he approached her.

He had followed the carriage through the bustling

streets and had seen the ladies set down outside the house in Green Street. They had entered, and he had found an alley close by, from which he could keep the door in view. Georgiana had not re-emerged until the evening, when she had left in the carriage with Bella, both gorgeously arrayed in evening gowns. The sight of those gowns had sent a spasm of sheer fury through him. They had swanned off to a ball while he, half perished with cold, was forced to slink off to his miserable lodgings, with no prospect of a decent meal in sight. He had consoled himself with the thought that at least he now knew where his pigeon had come to roost.

But how to best approach the matter of getting his hands on her once more? With his limited resources, joining the social whirl was a near impossibility. His clothes alone would mark him as pecuniarily embarrassed. The cent per centers were too fly to be taken in by a glib tale; they would advance him nothing. Thanks to the restrictions his father's failings had placed on him, he had no friends among the swells. How to break into the glittering circle?

He had cudgelled his brains for hours. Eventually he had found a young tailor operating on the outskirts of the fashionable districts, one too inexperienced to quibble about his offer of a small down payment with the remainder of the costs to be sent on account. With his most immediate need assuaged, he had turned his mind to gaining an entrée to the balls and parties his cousin frequented.

The Hattringham House masked ball had presented itself, ready-made for his needs. For the cost of a mask and a deal of studied self-confidence, he had been able to enter the ballroom as a guest, to wander slowly through the salons, carefully studying the female forms present. He had not even had to be covert about this enterprise; most of the young bucks were similarly engaged.

As it transpired, he had not recognised her. It was her voice, gaily answering some sally, which had identified her for him.

Now, as he watched her dance for the third time with the handsome dark-haired man who had monopolised her company for the entire evening, he ground his teeth. He stood no chance of competing honourably with the likes of her present cavalier. And, even from the obscurity of the sidelines, he could sense the rapport which existed between the pair. Damn her! She'd escaped him, only to fall victim to some other aspiring scoundrel. He brushed aside the thought that none but he knew her worth.

Seething, muttering imprecations beneath his breath, he watched helplessly as the dashing cavalier waltzed past, his cousin held securely in strong arms, mesmerised by a smile too experienced for any young damsel to resist.

"Soon," said Charles, entirely to himself. "I'll have to move soon." Having seen quite enough of his cousin and her consort to despair of parting them that night, he left Hattringham House, his brain awash with half-formed schemes.

IT WAS THE NEXT afternoon before Georgiana had leisure to thoroughly examine the events of the Hattringham House ball. Viewed in the calm light of day, she wasn't entirely sure what to make of them. Had he really not recognised her?

Over the weeks, by dint of subtle questioning, she had

learnt a great deal more of Bella's brother. For instance, a quiet afternoon spent in the back parlour the previous week had yielded the tale of the initial incident that had given rise to Lord Alton's reputation of being dangerous company for young ladies.

"It happened during the Season immediately following Papa's death. Dominic had missed the beginning of the Season, still tied up with settling the estate." Bella had laid aside her embroidery and stared in concentration at the opposite wall. "I wasn't there, of course, but I've heard the tale umpteen times. Apparently Lord Ellsmere—he's a particular friend of Dominic's, you know—fell desperately in love with a scheming miss from somewhere up north. I forget her name—something like Kertlake. She and her mama had come to town determined to catch the biggest matrimonial prize." Bella turned to Georgiana. "Well, you know how eligible Julian Ellsmere is."

Georgiana had had the grace to look sheepish.

"Well," her preceptress had continued, "Julian fell very heavily, and no one could make him see what she was really like. Apparently she was an out-and-out schemer, flirting with every man, but carefully checking their assets at the same time. Lots of people tried to dissuade him, but he went ahead and proposed and was accepted. Then Dominic returned to town. He saw through Miss Whatever-her-name-was and decided something had to be done. It was too late for Julian to draw back with honour, so the lady had to be made to withdraw." Bella had paused, eyeing Georgiana carefully. Georgiana had raised her brows in question. Bella had grimaced.

"You know what men are. And you've seen what

Dominic's like. So I don't suppose you'll find it hard to believe that he swept the lady off her feet. He's a bigger catch than Julian. So the lady broke off her engagement with Julian, who by now had his eyes well open. Dominic had managed it so she did it in the expectation of him offering for her, but he never made any formal declaration or anything like that. And, of course, as soon as Julian was publicly free, Dominic just dumped the girl. The trouble was, not everyone was in the know. A lot of gossips just saw Dominic entrapping a beautiful girl and then ruthlessly discarding her. That's what started it all. And, needless to say, Dominic doesn't give a damn what people think of him. Naturally, all his friends know the truth."

At this point, Bella had picked up her embroidery again. Then she had paused, to add matter-of-factly, "Of course, later, when he went around seducing all the bored wives and beautiful widows—the Lady Changleys of the world, you understand—they simply painted his reputation blacker."

Smothering a choking laugh, Georgiana had bent her head once more over her own embroidery, her thoughts far removed from *petit point*.

"Mind you," Bella had added, waving her needle in the air to give her point emphasis, "despite all, he's never particularly enamoured of them—the women he seduces, I mean." She had frowned, totally absorbed in her subject and no longer conscious of her audience. "I suspect it's because it's all so easy." She had shrugged. "Just like me, getting bored with the Season—it's all too easy without some purpose behind it."

They had fallen silent after that, each busy with their own thoughts.

Now Georgiana sat alone in the back parlour, having seen Bella off on a visit to her old nurse. Her thoughts revolved incessantly, driven by an unnerving juxtaposition of longing and uncertainty. The breathtaking thrill of basking in the warmth of his smouldering blue gaze… All the subtle attentions he had paid her throughout the long night of the masked ball… She'd already lost her heart to Lord Alton. Now he seemed intent on leading her on to more dangerous ground. But had he known it was her he was leading? Surely not. Her mind rebelled at the thought. If he had known, then that would mean… No. He couldn't be seriously pursuing her. What on earth could he mean by it, if he was? And what on earth was she to do about it?

She puzzled and worried at her questions, but when Johnson knocked and entered the room two hours later she had still not found any answer.

"There's a gentleman to see you, miss. A Mr Charles Hartley."

The butler's words effectively banished Georgiana's dreams. Charles? Here? How on earth had he traced her? And why?

The soft clearing of Johnson's throat recalled her scattered wits. She had enough unanswerable questions without Charles adding to the score. And, secure and safe in Winsmere House, she had no reason to fear her cousin. Johnson, she felt sure, would hover protectively near the door. "My cousin?" It was hard to believe.

Johnson bowed. "The gentleman did mention the connection, miss."

From the butler's stiff tone, Georgiana surmised her cousin had failed to find favour in his shrewd eyes.

The observation gave her confidence. "I'll see him in here."

"Very good, miss." Johnson made for the door, but paused with his hand on the knob. "I'll be just outside the door, miss, in case you should need anything."

Georgiana smiled her gratitude as Johnson withdrew.

A minute later, the door opened once more to allow Charles Hartley to enter. In the light streaming in through the long windows, Georgiana studied her cousin as he crossed the room towards her. His appearance had improved considerably since last they had met. She suppressed a grin at the memory. He had been drunk. Now he was clearly quite sober. His clothes were not as elegant as those she had grown used to seeing, but were clean and, unless she much mistook the matter, new. His cravat was tied neatly, if not with flair. A great improvement over the stained and ill-fitting togs he had worn at the Place. He was neither tall nor short, neither corpulent nor lanky. Yet his figure was unimpressive compared to the other in her mind. His colouring was much paler and less vibrant than her own. Lank fair hair hung across pallid skin; pale reptilian eyes regarded her with little evidence of emotion. Repressing her instinctive shrinking, she extended her hand as he drew near. "Charles."

As he took her hand and bowed over it, Charles was conscious that his little cousin had somehow changed. The young girl who had fled to her chamber to escape his lovemaking had grown even more lovely. And more confident. But she would never be a match for him. He smiled, struggling to keep his thoughts from showing. She had blossomed into a more delectable piece than he would have predicted. The figure outlined by the bronze silk dress she had worn at the ball was quite real, albeit now garbed in sober grey. Perhaps he would enjoy the role of her husband rather more than he had anticipated.

At his continued scrutiny, Georgiana allowed her brows to rise haughtily.

Recalled to his purpose, Charles assumed a serious face. "Georgiana, I've come to beg your pardon."

Now Georgiana's brows flew upwards in surprise.

Charles smiled tentatively and pressed his advantage. "For my boorish behaviour at the Place. I... Well—" he shrugged and smiled self-deprecatingly "—I was swept away with desire, my dear. I should have told you, of course, of the arrangements that had been made. But I had a hope you would love me for myself and it would not be necessary. I see now I should have explained it to you at the start. You see, my father and your father wanted us to marry." At her instinctive recoil, Charles raised a placating hand. "Oh, at first I felt as you. You can imagine my dismay, a young man being told his marriage was already arranged. I ranted and raved, but in the end I agreed to do my duty to the family. So I waited for the day your father would send you home. As things fell out, he died before he had brought himself to tell you and send you away from him." Pale eyes carefully scrutinised Georgiana's face. "I can imagine how attached he was to you, and doubtless he sought to keep you by him for as long as possible." Charles smiled meaningfully into Georgiana's eyes. "I can understand his feelings."

To his consternation, Charles could detect no response to his revelations, other than a slight widening of the huge hazel eyes.

"In the circumstances, you can imagine my surprise when I first saw you, first learned of your beauty."

Another smile accompanied this piece of flattery, but evoked no hint of feminine preening.

Charles frowned. Was the child paying attention? He turned the frown to good effect as he continued, "I'm afraid my behaviour was rather wild. I can only ask you to excuse my excesses on the grounds of my incredible relief that, now you were finally here, everything was going to be all right."

Still Georgiana gave no sign of reaction to his tale.

Mentally groping in the dark, Charles put on a humble face and asked, "Georgiana, can you possibly forgive me?"

At the start of her cousin's tale, Georgiana had schooled her features to impassivity. As his story unfurled, she was thankful for the iron control, polished over the weeks of social gadding, that held her silent. She had no doubt that the existence of a long-standing, family-arranged betrothal between them was a fabrication. Her father had always shown particular concern for her eventual state. He had not expected to die suddenly, it was true. But that he had died forgetting to tell her she was formally betrothed was impossible. She resisted the impulse to laugh scornfully, and forced her voice to a cool and even tone. "I suggest your behaviour at the Place is best forgotten."

At his too ready smile, she assumed her most regal manner and forged on. "However, as to this other matter you have raised, of us being betrothed, I'm afraid I must insist that such a betrothal never occurred. Certainly my father never told me of it. Nor were there any documents among his effects to support such a notion. I'm afraid, if your father led you to suppose there was an agreement, then he misled you."

Charles's frown was quite genuine. So much for that idea. He would have to try his second string. He turned slightly and moved away from his cousin, taking a few steps away, then pacing back. His features obediently fell into a look of downcast dismay. He looked straight at Georgiana, an expression of wordless misery on his face. Then he gestured eloquently and turned aside. "Georgiana. My dear, what can I say to convince you?"

If she had not been so sensitive on the subject, Georgiana would have found his histrionics quite entertaining. As it was, she felt no inclination to smile, let alone laugh.

From the corner of his eye, Charles watched her stony countenance. Intuition told him an avowal of love would fall on barren soil. Instead, he opted for a more avuncular line. "I would do everything possible to make you happy. Your father's death has left you alone in the world. Please, I beg you, allow me to take on the task of caring for you."

Georgiana barely managed to keep from laughing in his face. He, to talk of caring for her! He had threatened her—more than threatened her—and under his own roof! She could manage quite well, she felt, without his sort of protection. With perfect composure she replied, "Please say no more. My mind is quite unalterable on this point. I will not marry you, Charles."

Yet another proposal, she thought with a wry inward grin. Even less welcome than the others.

Charles sighed dramatically and turned so she could no longer see his face. All in all, he was just as well suited with her decision. It was hardly a great surprise. At least now he had a clear path to follow. After a pained moment, he turned back to her and smiled bravely. "I knew it was no use. But, you see, I felt I had to try. If I could just ask that we remain friends?"

Georgiana blinked. Friends? Well, it couldn't hurt to make that concession. It meant so little. She smiled gently, somewhat relieved that the episode seemed set to conclude on a much more reasonable note than she had anticipated. She held out her hand, a friendly enough gesture, but still a clear dismissal. "Friends, then, if you wish it."

Charles took her hand and bowed over it. As he straightened, his face cleared as if reminded of a pleasant event. "Ah, I nearly forgot." His eyes sought Georgiana's. "Those paintings you were looking for. At the Place."

Georgiana's heart leapt.

Sensing her response, Charles inwardly smirked. So much for her impenetrable shell.

"Yes?" Georgiana prompted, not bothering to conceal her eagerness.

Charles smiled. "I don't want to get your hopes up, but the Pringates were clearing out the attics when I left. They sent me a message two days ago that they had found some pictures, among other things. I wrote back to ask who had painted them. If they are the ones you seek..." He let his voice trail away.

Breathlessly Georgiana seized the proffered moment to issue the invitation Charles was angling for. "You'll let me know at once? Please, Charles?"

Genuinely pleased, he allowed his smile to broaden. "I'll let you know at once."

Deeming it wise to leave well enough alone, he merely bowed over her hand and smiled encouragingly as she crossed to the bell-pull to summon the butler.

NATURALLY, after she had considered the matter from all angles, Georgiana sought Bella's opinion of Charles's visit and his declaration.

"Friends?" The incredulity in Bella's voice left little doubt of her opinion of Charles. She snorted. "He's a bounder. Always was, always will be."

Georgiana shrugged. "Well, that's neither here nor there." She bent her head over her stitchery. It was the day after Charles's visit and they were in the back parlour, as was their habit of a morning.

Bella stifled a yawn. "Ye gods! I declare I'm infected with your illness."

Georgiana raised an enquiring eyebrow.

"Finding the evenings over-tiring," Bella explained. "I would never have thought a musical supper would be so positively exhausting."

"I rather think that depends on the music," put in Georgiana, with a smile for her hostess. "Besides, from what I saw, you were half asleep through most of the recital."

Bella waved a hand airily. "It's fashionable to nod off. All the best people do it."

With a gurgle of laughter, Georgiana set her work aside. "Seriously, though, do you think Charles will give me my father's paintings back?"

"Don't get too carried away. They might not be your father's at all."

A discreet knock heralded Johnson's entry. "A note for you, miss. There's a messenger waiting for your reply."

Georgiana lifted the simple note from Johnson's salver. It was sealed with a nondescript lump of wax.

Dismissing her butler with a nod, Bella turned to find her friend regarding the missive in her hand with some nervousness. "Well? Open it!"

With a small sigh, Georgiana broke the seal and spread out the single sheet. "It's from Charles," she told the waiting Bella. After a moment, her face brightened. "He's found them! Oh, Bella! They were there after all!"

Seeing the sunshine in Georgiana's face, Bella relaxed and grinned back. "How lovely for you. Is he sending them over?"

Georgiana was reading on. A small frown clouded her brow, then lifted. "Yes and no. He hasn't actually got them yet. He says he's sent to Pringate to bring them to the Hart and Hounds—that's the posting inn, the last before London on the road to Candlewick. I remember stopping there on our way here."

Bella nodded absent-mindedly. "Yes, but why? Why not just bring them to London?"

Georgiana, engrossed in deciphering Charles's scrawl, shrugged aside the quibble. "Charles says he's going to meet Pringate this afternoon to pick up the pictures, and asks if I would like to come too. Oh, Bella! Just think! By this afternoon I'll have them."

"Mmm." Bella eyed her friend with a frown. It would be of no use to tell Georgiana that Charles was not to be trusted. From her face it was clear nothing on earth would stop her from going to fetch her paintings. With a definite feeling of misgiving, Bella held her peace.

While Georgiana penned an enthusiastic reply to Charles's invitation, Bella sat and worriedly chewed her lip. But, by the time Johnson departed to give Georgiana's note to the messenger, she had perked up and was able to listen to Georgiana's excited ramblings with an indulgent smile. It was obvious really. To protect Georgiana from Charles's machinations, all she had to do was precisely what she had always done whenever Charles had threatened. She would tell Dominic.

When Charles called for Georgiana at three, Bella played least in sight. Charles was high on her list of unfavourite people. She had already surreptitiously dispatched a note to her brother, summoning him to her instant aid. As she watched Charles's small phaeton carry Georgiana away, she struggled to subdue a disturbing sense of disquiet.

Impatiently, she waited for Dominic to call.

ENSCONCED in the comfort of well padded leather, Dominic Ridgeley, Lord Ridgeley, Viscount Alton, man of the world and political intriguer, was deep in consideration of the beauties of nature. Or, more specifically, one particular golden-haired, golden-eyed beauty. The silence of the reading room of White's was punctuated by the occasional snore and snuffle and the crackle of turning pages. Otherwise, there was no sound to distract him from his reverie. The daily news-sheet was held open before his face, but he would have been hard pressed to recall the headlines, let alone the substance of any of the articles. This morning Georgiana Hartley occupied his mind to the exclusion of all else.

He had not seen her for over twenty-four hours. Which fact, he felt, was more than ample excuse for his preoccupation. A political dinner had prevented him from attending Lady Overington's musical supper—a mixed blessing, he was sure. Hence, he had to be content with reliving the events of the masked ball. A slow grin twisted his lips as he recalled his angel's response to some of his more outrageous sallies. He would have to make certain he disabused her mind of her apparent belief that he had not known her identity. The point niggled, like a burr caught under his collar. It had been a strategic error, to allow her to leave him still thinking he was showering his attentions on a damsel unknown to him. An error he was more than experienced enough to recognise. Still, he would ensure the matter was rectified at their next meeting—tonight, at the Pevenseys' gala. Consideration of her likely reactions to his revelations kept him entertained for some minutes. The sight of her face when the penny finally dropped, her innocent confusion, all unknowingly reflected in her glorious eyes, would afford him untold pleasure.

A soft smile of pure anticipation curved his fine lips.

Seeing it, Lord Ellsmere paused, before clearing his throat meaningfully.

At the sound so close by his ear, Dominic jumped. His eyes met those of his friend in pained surprise.

Julian Ellsmere grinned. "Interesting thoughts, old man?"

Dominic struggled up out of the depths of his chair. "Damn you, Julian! I was just—"

"Shhhh!" came hissing from all corners of the room.

"Come into the smoking-room," whispered Lord

Ellsmere. "I've got some news I think you should hear."

They had been at Eton, then Oxford, together, had shared all the larks and adventures of well heeled young men. And had remained close friends to the present. Which, when they'd found a secluded corner of the smoking-room, allowed Lord Ellsmere to say, "Don't know how deep your interest goes with your sister's protégée, but I just saw her being driven out of town by a rather rum customer. Tow-headed, pasty-faced bounder."

The sudden hardening of the lines of his friend's face told Lord Ellsmere more clearly than words just how deeply Dominic Ridgeley's interest in Georgiana Hartley went.

"When?"

"'Bout twenty minutes. Up the North Road."

Dominic's eyes had narrowed. "Tow-headed?" When Julian Ellsmere nodded, he continued, "Medium height and build? Fair skin?"

"That's the man. Know him?"

But Dominic was muttering curses under his breath and heading for the door. When Julian caught him up in the hall, where the porter was scurrying to find his cane and gloves, Dominic turned to him and said, "My thanks."

Lord Ellsmere waved one languid hand. "Oh, think nothing of it. As I recall, I owe you one." He smiled, then sobered to ask, "You'll go after her?"

"Most assuredly. The silly chit should have known better. I'd go bail that's her cousin she's with. And between Charles Hartley and a viper there's not much difference."

The porter returned, and Dominic pulled on his gloves. As he took his cane from the man, Lord Ellsmere, frowning, added, "One other thing. Might be significant. This tow-headed chap… Saw him leaving Hattringham House t'other night."

The chill in Dominic's eyes was pronounced. "You're sure?"

Julian Ellsmere nodded. "Quite certain." After a moment he asked, "Need any help?"

At that, Dominic smiled in a way that made Julian Ellsmere feel almost sorry for Charles Hartley. "No. I've dealt with Charles before. It'll be a particular pleasure to make it clear to him that Miss Hartley is very definitely out of bounds."

Lord Ellsmere nodded and clapped his friend on the shoulder.

With a fleeting smile, Dominic was gone.

A brisk walk saw him entering Alton House. Immediately the door shut behind him, he issued a string of commands which had his groom and coachman running to the mews and his valet pounding up the stairs in search of his greatcoat.

Dominic waited in the hall, frowning, his cane, still in his hand, tapping impatiently against one booted foot. Julian had said he had seen them. That meant an open carriage. Surely Charles wasn't proposing to drive her all the way to Buckinghamshire in an open carriage? No. When dusk fell, the cold would be intense. Presumably the open carriage was just part of his scheme, whatever that was.

Timms's cough interrupted his thoughts. "I don't know as this is the most opportune moment, m'lord, but this note came some time ago from Lady Winsmere."

Dominic's frown lifted. He took the note and broke it open. The sound of his carriage drawing up in the street coincided with his man's precipitate descent with his coat. An instant later, garbed in his many caped greatcoat and clutching his sister's missive in his hand, Viscount Alton climbed into his carriage.

"Winsmere House. Quickly!"

"OH, DOMINIC! Thank God you've come. I've been so worried." Bella's plaintive wail greeted Dominic as he crossed the threshold of her parlour.

"Don't fly into a pucker, Bella. Julian Ellsmere has just told me he saw Georgiana leaving town with a man who sounds like Charles. Has she?"

"Yes!" Bella was wringing her hands in agitation. "She was so set on it, I knew I couldn't stop her. But I don't trust Charles one inch. That's why I sent for you."

Taking note of his sister's unusually pale face, Dominic replied with far greater calmness than he felt. "Quite right." He swallowed his impatience and smiled reassuringly. "Why don't we sit down and you can tell me all about it?"

Haltingly, prodded by gentle questions, the tale of Charles's visit and the subsquent events was retold. By the end of the tale, Dominic was confident he saw the light. He leant forward to pat Bella's hand. "Don't worry. I'll fetch her back."

Bella blinked up at him as he stood. "You'll go straight away?"

"I was setting out when Timms gave me your note. Just as well. At least now I can go directly to the Hare and Hounds." Dominic's blue eyes critically surveyed his sister. At his insistence she reclined on the *chaise*. Her face was too pale and her agitation was too marked, even given the cause. Shrewdly he drew his own conclusions. He had been going to suggest she come with him, to lend propriety to their return to Green Street. But in her present condition he rather thought any further excitement was to be assiduously avoided. And, if truth be known, he would much rather be alone with Georgiana on the drive back to town. He had every intention of reading her a lecture on the subject of herself—care of. Afterwards, he felt sure he would enjoy her attempts to be conciliatory, not to mention grateful. And it would give him a heaven-sent opportunity to correct her mistaken assumption regarding his conduct at the masked ball. Yes, he was definitely looking forward to the return journey. Propriety, in this instance, could go hang.

He smiled again at his sister. "Don't fret. Arthur will be home shortly. You can tell him all about it. I suspect we won't make it back until late, so you'd best send your regrets to the Pevenseys."

"Lord, yes! I couldn't face a party on top of all this."

Dominic grinned, then bent to bestow a kiss on one pale cheek. "Take care, my dear. You burn the candle with a vengeance."

She grimaced at him but refused to rise to the bait.

Dominic crossed the room, but turned at the door to consider the listless figure on the *chaise*. Had she realised yet herself? One dark brow rose. With a last affectionate smile, he left.

CHAPTER SEVEN

JOYFUL ANTICIPATION of seeing her mother's face again carried Georgiana through the streets of London, unaware of the man beside her. However, as the phaeton turned northwards and the more populated streets fell behind, a tingling sense of premonition awoke in her mind.

The afternoon remained fine, a brisk breeze whipping at her cloak and bonnet, promising hard frosts for the morning. As the buildings thinned, the air became perceptibly chillier. Charles's conversation, uninspiring though it had been, had disappeared along with the fashionable dwellings. He seemed to be concentrating on driving the carriage at a slow but steady pace.

Georgiana stared ahead, willing the comforting bulk of the Hare and Hounds to loom on the horizon. But, from Green Street, it would take at least an hour to reach the comfort of the posting inn. A frown drew the golden arches of her brows together. Charles had called for her at three, which, now she came to think more clearly, was surely a little late for an expedition of such distance. It would be dark by the time they returned to Winsmere House. Still, there was little she could do about it now, beyond praying that the plodding nag drawing the phaeton would find its second wind. With a discontented grimace, she gave her attention to their surroundings. She refused to give further consideration to the doubt nagging from the deepest recesses of her mind, the little voice which warned that something was amiss.

Ten minutes later, a surreptitious movement beside her had her turning her head in time to see Charles replace his fob watch in his pocket.

He smiled at her. "Not long now."

Georgiana knew the smile was meant to reassure. It missed its mark. Odd how she had forgotten how Charles's smiles so rarely reached his eyes. Her suspicions, unspecified but now fully awakened, took possession of her mind. The horse's plodding hoofs beat a slow accompaniment to her increasingly trepidatious heartbeat as she reviewed the potential threats she might all too soon have to face.

In the end, she was so preoccupied with her imaginary dragons that she missed the sight of the Hare and Hounds. Only when Charles turned the phaeton under the arch of the innyard did she shake off her reverie to look about her.

She had stopped here on her way to London. But that time she had been travelling in the luxury of Lord Alton's coach, with attentive servants to guard her. Now, as Charles handed her down from the open carriage, she glanced about to see the yard full of people. Ostlers hurried fresh horses out of the stables beyond the yard, while others led weary equines freed of the traces to rest. Stableboys rushed hither and yon, under everyone's feet, helping with the harness and carrying baggage back and forth from the inn. Inn servants stood with jugs of steaming ale and mulled wine, ready to refresh the passengers of the coaches pulled up for the change of horses. At the centre of the commotion stood the southbound accommodation coach, a huge, ponderous vehicle, settled like a dull black bullfrog on the cobbles. The passengers were alighting for their evening meal. Georgiana found herself the object of not a few staring eyes. She was about to turn away when one gentleman raised his high-crowned beaver and bowed.

With a start, Georgiana recognised a distant acquaintance of Bella's and Arthur's. She had been introduced to him at one of the balls. With a small smile, she acknowledged the bow, wondering at the hard-lipped, cold-eyed look the man gave her.

Accepting Charles's arm over the uneven surface, more from necessity than inclination, she was about to ascend the two steps to the inn's main door when a sudden commotion on the coach's roof claimed all eyes. Three well dressed youths—roof passengers—were laughingly struggling with each other. At the coachman's loud "Hoi!", they desisted and, shamefacedly realising they were the centre of attention, sought to descend to less exalted positions. Waiting for his companions to climb down the rungs before him, one of the young men looked about the yard and caught sight of Georgiana. Her eyes met his with a jolt of recognition. He was the younger brother of one of the débutantes being presented that Season. She had danced with him at his sister's come-out. His open-mouth stare told Georgiana quite clearly that something was severely wrong.

She had barely time to smile at the young man before Charles tugged her through the inn door. To her surprise, she found that Charles had hired a private parlour for their use. Distracted by the memory of the stares of the two gentlemen in the yard, she paid scant attention to this discovery. As she meekly followed the innkeeper up the wooden staircase, the reason for the stares occurred. Of course! She and Charles shared no more than a fleeting family resemblance. The gentlemen thought she was here, alone, with a man who was no relation. She blushed slightly. There was, of course, nothing wrong with being escorted somewhere by one's cousin. She knew that. It was often the case in Italy, where families were large. She had not thought there was any impropriety attached to her going to an inn with Charles. Surely, if there had been, Bella would have raised some demur? But the disapprobation on the older man's face, and the sheer stunned disbelief in the younger's, stayed with her, banishing all ease.

So, when she heard the click from the parlour door as the latch fell into place behind the burly innkeeper, it was with a heightened sense of suspicion that she surveyed the neat parlour. It was empty. No Pringates. No paintings. Georgiana's heart plummeted. Drawing a steadying breath, she turned to face Charles. "Where are the Pringates?"

Her cousin stood, leaning against the door, watching her with a shrewdly calculating gaze. After a moment, he pushed away from the solid oak panels and strolled towards her. "Doubtless they've been delayed. Let me take your cloak."

Automatically surrendering her cloak, Georgiana forcibly repressed a shudder as Charles's fingers inadvertently brushed her shoulders in removing it. Inadvertently? She risked a quick glance up at his face. What she saw there did nothing for her peace of mind.

Quelling the panic rising within, she forced herself to act ingenuously. "Are we going to wait for them?"

Charles straightened from laying her cloak over a chair. Again she was subjected to a careful scrutiny. Georgiana struggled to quieten the hammering of her nerves and face him calmly. Apparently Charles was satisfied with what he saw.

"Having come this far, we might as well wait for a while." His eyes raked her face again. "Perhaps a tea tray would fill in the time?"

Eager to have something to occupy them ostensibly while she considered the ramifications of her latest impulsive start, Georgiana forced a smile of agreement to her lips.

The innkeeper was summoned and, in short order, a buxom young serving girl bustled in with a tray loaded with teapot, scones and all necessary appurtenances. Charles dismissed her with a nod and a coin, holding the door for her.

Under cover of wielding the teapot, Georgiana watched Charles close the door. She almost sighed audibly when she saw he did not bother to lock it.

With renewed confidence, fragile though she suspected it was, she gave her mind over to plotting her moves. The first imperative was to learn what Charles had in mind. And, she supposed, there was always the possibility that she was inventing horrors where none existed. A slim hope, she felt, with her nerves jangling in insistent warning.

Taking a sip of strong tea to help steady herself, she asked, "There are no paintings, are there?"

Her question coincided with Charles taking a sip from his own cup. He choked but recovered swiftly. His faded blue gaze lifted and fixed on her face, and she had her answer. He smiled, not pleasantly. Georgiana felt her muscles tense.

"How perceptive of you, sweet cousin."

His congratulatory tone purred sarcastically in her ears. For the first time since leaving the Place, Georgiana knew she was face-to-face with the real Charles Hartley. She fought down a wild desire to rush to the door. Charles might not be large, but he was a great deal larger than she was. Besides, she needed to know more. She was sick of mysteries. "Why? Why all this elaborate charade? What do you hope to gain?"

Charles laughed mirthlessly, his eyes never leaving her face. "What I want. Your hand in marriage." Then his gaze slid slowly over her. "Among other things."

His tone made Georgiana feel physically ill. She forced herself to sip her tea calmly, drawing what strength she could from the strong black brew. Her mind wandered frantically amid the pieces of the puzzle but could not make out the picture.

"Not worked it out yet?"

Charles's taunt broke into her mental meanderings. She looked at him coldly.

He smiled, enjoying her obvious discomfort. He leant back in his chair, balancing it on its back legs. "I'll spell it out for you, if you like."

Georgiana decided that, however distressful, knowing his plans had to be her primary aim. So she allowed a look of patent interest to infuse her features.

Charles's lips twisted in a gloating grin. "My plan is quite simple. We arrived here just as the accommodation coach was unloading. You were seen entering this inn with me by at least two people who know you. That, in itself, will cause only minor comment. However, when we leave here tomorrow morning, while the northbound accommodation coach passengers are breakfasting in the main room downstairs, I feel certain the sight of you leaving at such an early hour with me, without the benefit of maid or baggage, is going to raise quite a few brows."

Georgiana's heart sank as she pictured the scene. He was right, of course. Even she knew what a scandal such a sighting would provoke, regardless of the truth of the matter.

"So, you see, after that you'll have little choice but to accept my proposal." Charles's grin turned decidedly wicked.

Georgiana had had enough. Carefully replacing her cup on the tray, she wiped her hands on the napkin and then, laying the cloth aside, fixed her cousin with a determined stare. "Charles, I have no idea why you are so set on marrying me. You don't even like me."

At that, he laughed. Hand over heart, he bowed from the waist mockingly. "I assure you, sweet Georgie, I'll manage to drum up enough enthusiasm to convince all and sundry of what took place here."

Georgiana shook her head slowly. "It won't work, you know. I won't marry you. There's no reason why I should."

The cynical twist of Charles's lips told her she had not heard all of his plan. "I hesitate to correct you, fair cousin, but, unless you want the Winsmeres mired in scandal, you'll most certainly marry me. It won't have escaped the notice of the gossip-mongers that you're supposedly in their care."

Involuntarily, Georgiana's lip curled. "You really are despicable, you know."

To her surprise, her tone was perfectly controlled. In fact she felt strangely calm. The lack of expression in Charles's cold eyes sent shivers up and down her spine. But now her own, usually latent temper was on the rise. It had been one thing when he had threatened *her;* to threaten her friends was another matter entirely. She folded her hands and met his gaze unflinchingly. "Be that as it may, I repeat, I will not marry you. Unless things have changed rather dramatically in England, I suspect you still need me to speak my vows. That being so, if you persist in your plan to ruin my reputation, then, when I leave here, I will stop at Green Street only long enough to pick up my luggage and servants. I'll return to Ravello." Summoning a disaffected shrug, she lifted her chin and added, "I always meant to go back eventually. And, with me gone, no scandal of any magnitude will touch Bella and Arthur."

For one long moment, Charles stared at her, eyes quite blank. It had never occurred to him, when he had planned this little campaign, that his prey would simply refuse to co-operate. Having seen her riding high in the social whirl, the threat of a catastrophic fall from grace had seemed an unbeatable card. Now, looking into hazel eyes that held far too much calmness, Charles knew he was facing defeat. Typically, he chose to counter with the usual threat of a bully. With a low growl, he rose menacingly, his chair falling back with a clatter on the floor.

Georgiana's eyes widened in dismay. She felt trapped, unable to move, caught and transfixed by the animosity which poured from Charles's eyes. Not until then had she realised just how much he disliked—nay, hated—her. She stopped breathing.

Charles was poised to come around the table, muscles tensed to lay ungentle hands on her, when the unlikely sound of quiet applause broke across Georgiana's strained senses. She turned towards the door.

Deafened by his anger, Charles only turned after seeing her attention distracted.

The sight that met their eyes was, to Georgiana, as welcome as it was unbelievable. The door lay open. Absorbed in their mutual revelations, neither had heard the click of the latch. Leaning against the door-frame, his greatcoat open and negligently thrown over his shoulders to reveal the elegance of his attire, Lord Alton surveyed the room. Having successfully gained the attention of both its occupants, he smiled at Georgiana and, pushing away from the door, strolled towards her.

In a daze, Georgiana stood and held out her hand, bemused by the sudden turn of events. Blue eyes met hers, conveying warming reassurance and something else—something very like irritation. Bewildered, Georgiana blinked.

Dominic took her hand and bowed over it, then placed it on his arm and covered it comfortingly with his own large hand. "Miss Hartley. I am here, as arranged, to convey you back to town."

Georgiana's eyes flew to his and read the silent message there. The warmth of his hand banished her fears. She had complete confidence in him.

With an encouraging smile, Dominic turned and, seeing her cloak, released her to fetch it.

The action broke the spell which had held Charles immobile. His normal pasty complexion had paled at the sight of his childhood nemesis. Now his face flooded with unbecoming colour. "You're out of order, Ridgeley," he ground out through clenched teeth. "My cousin is in my care. And she's not returning to London."

Settling Georgiana's cloak about her shoulders, Dominic raised his brows in fascinated contemplation of the thinly veiled threat. His gaze met Charles's squarely, then wandered insultingly over the younger man's frame. Dominic Ridgeley was a man in his prime, a noted Corinthian, five years older, three inches taller and two stone of sheer muscle heavier than Charles Hartley. And Charles knew it.

To Georgiana's intense relief, he dropped his eyes, blanching, then flushing again. Bella's brother tucked her hand in the crook of his arm and patted it comfortingly.

"Come, my dear. My carriage is waiting."

By some magical machination, Georgiana found herself escorted gently but firmly out of the inn by a route which exposed her to no one other than the innkeeper, bowing obsequiously as they passed. Handed into the same luxuriously appointed coach that she had used on her previous visit to the inn, she sank back against the fine leather with a small sigh of relief tinged with disillusionment. The search for her mother's portrait had nearly ended in nightmare.

The evening was closing in. Georgiana glanced up to see Lord Alton's large frame silhouetted by the light thrown by the flares in the innyard. He paused, one foot on the carriage step, and gazed back at the inn, an expression she could not define on his face. Then, abruptly, he stepped back. "Your pardon, my dear. Unfinished business." He frowned and added, "I won't keep you more than a minute."

He shut the carriage door, and Georgiana heard him call up to the coachman to watch over her. Peering out of the window, she saw him stride purposefully through the main door of the inn.

As the minutes ticked by, the conviction grew that Lord Alton's "unfinished business" lay with Charles. Georgiana fretted, frustrated by her helplessness. She had almost reached the point of sending the coachman in search of his master when Lord Alton appeared on the inn steps. As he strode across the yard, Georgiana scanned his person. He was undeniably intact. His greatcoat swung, impeccable as ever, from his broad shoulders. She expelled a little sigh of pent-up breath and hurriedly moved farther along the seat to make room for her rescuer. Then he was in the carriage and they were moving.

To her consternation, Georgiana found travelling in a closed carriage with Bella's brother was almost as much an ordeal as being in the inn parlour with Charles. But, while with Charles she'd had to subdue her disgust, with Lord Alton it was an entirely different emotion she fought to control. At one level, she revelled in his nearness, in the delicate wafts of sandalwood and leather that subtly teased her senses. Occasionally a deep rut jolted her shoulder against his arm. But the feelings which rose up inside her were too dangerous, too damning. Ruthlessly, she fought to quell them, forcing her breathing to slow and her mind to function.

"Did Bella send you?"

Dominic had been waiting, with what patience he could muster, for her to recover. He frowned into the gathering gloom and turned towards her. "Both Bella *and* Julian Ellsmere."

"Lord Ellsmere?"

"The same. He saw you leaving London with Charles—a 'tow-headed bounder' was his description."

His clipped tones destroyed any impulse Georgiana had to laugh.

"Then Bella sent around a note and told me where to look for you." Dominic studied his angel's face in the faint glow of light cast back from the carriage lamps. He could see no sign that she understood the danger she had been in, no comprehension of the fear and worry her impulsive start had visited on him. His tone became noticeably drier. "I find it hard to understand why, knowing Charles as you do, you consented to this ill advised junket."

At the clear censure in his voice, Georgiana stiffened. She swallowed the peculiar lump in her throat to say in a small, tight voice, "I'm sorry if I've caused you any inconvenience."

Inwardly Dominic cursed. This interlude was not progressing as planned. He was having the devil of a time holding on to his temper, rubbed raw by the troubled speculation of the hour and more it had taken to reach the inn. The impulse to shake her was strong. Yet, in his present mood, he doubted the wisdom of laying hands on her. And, wise in the ways of young ladies, he knew his angel, far from being adoringly penitent, was close to taking snuff. If he gave in to temptation and read her the lecture burning the tip of his tongue, she might well treat him to a deplorable display of feminine weakness. For once, he wasn't sure of his ability to withstand such a scene. With a "Humph!", he folded his arms across his chest and stared moodily out of the window.

For her part, Georgiana kept her gaze firmly fixed on the passing shadows, concentrating on subduing her quivering lips and blinking away the sudden moisture in her large eyes. It was really too much! First he had taken charge of her, like a guardian, just because she had asked for help. Then he had not had the sense to recognise her at the masked ball and had made her lose her heart with his wickedly sophisticated ways. Now he was treating her like a child again, upbraiding her, blaming *her* instead of Charles!

Trying not to sniff, Georgiana determinedly dragged her mind away from its preoccupation with the gentleman beside her and turned it to consideration of something—anything—else.

Lord Ellsmere's actions, for instance. Why had he gone to Lord Alton, rather than directly to Bella? That Bella should have summoned her brother was no surprise, but why had Lord Ellsmere done so? No answer occurred to her. Giving up on that issue, she wondered how to acceptably ask what he had done when he had re-entered the inn. She felt she had a right to know; it might prove important in any future disputation with Charles. Surreptitiously, she glanced at him.

In the light thrown by the lamps of a passing carriage, she saw a bloody scratch across the knuckles of his right hand.

"Oh! You've hurt yourself!" Without a thought for propriety or the consequences, Georgiana captured his hand in hers, holding it closer to examine the wound in the dim light. "You've been...been milling with Charles!" Settling the large hand firmly in her lap, she whipped out her small handkerchief and wrapped it tightly over the cut, tying a small knot in the lace edging to keep it in place. "There was no need, I assure you."

A deep sigh greeted her protestations. "Oh, there was every need. Charles needed to be taught a lesson. No gentleman goes about scheming to ruin a lady's reputation."

"What did you do to him?"

His head back against the squabs, Dominic tried to read her expression. "Don't worry, he still lives." When she continued to wait patiently, he grimaced and added, "He was unwise enough to make a number of suggestions I found distinctly ungentlemanly. I took great delight in making him eat his words."

"But you might have been hurt! You *were* hurt." Georgiana looked again at the hand which still lay in her skirts, gently cradled between hers. Suddenly recalling the impropriety of holding a gentleman's hand in her lap, she reluctantly released it, thankful the dim light hid her blushes.

His lips twisting in a smile he knew she could not see, Dominic equally reluctantly withdrew his hand from where it lay, stilling the all but automatic impulse to reverse the situation and capture her hand in his. He had initially been stunned into immobility by her impulsive actions. When his wits returned, he had seen no reason to shorten a moment which had touched him strangely. Now, sensing her unease, he sought for some comment to distract her.

"Anyway, I doubt you'll be troubled by Charles again."

Georgiana heard and nodded, but, suddenly feeling ridiculously weak, sought refuge in silence. Too many emotions swirled in her breast, conflicting with all the accepted precepts, and his nearness only compounded her confusion. She fixed her gaze on the scene beyond the window, the shadows of trees merging into the darkness. Yet her mind remained centred on the man beside her.

Perceptive enough to sense her turmoil, Dominic smiled into the darkness and, smothering a small sigh of frustration, put aside his plans for furthering his suit. She was nervous and on edge. Doubtless, her recent brush with the despicable Charles had contributed its mite to her state. In fact, now he came to think on it, it was wonderful that she hadn't treated him to the vapours. Most young women would undoubtedly be weeping all over him by this juncture, not concerning themselves with his minor hurts. In the dark, his fingers found the lace edging of her handkerchief wrapped tightly about his hand.

The moment was not right, either, for bringing up the subject of the masked ball. He was far too experienced even to contemplate making love to her now, while she was so touchy. There was, after all, tomorrow. And the day after tomorrow. And all the days after that. For, if nothing else had been settled this evening, he had definitely decided that Georgiana Hartley was not going to be allowed to slip out of his life. Whether she realised it or not, she was there to stay.

He paused in his mental ramblings to glance down at the slight figure beside him. She sat absorbed in her thoughts, her hands tightly clasped in her lap. Another half-hour would see them in Green Street. With another smile for the darkness, Dominic settled his head comfortably against the well stuffed squabs and closed his eyes, the better to indulge his fantasies.

Georgiana sat silently, taking herself to task for her forward behaviour. A lecture on the unwisdom of allowing her fanciful dreams to lead her to read more into Lord Alton's actions than was intended followed. He was very fond of Bella. She should remember that he had come to find her in response to Bella's request—brotherly devotion was the emotion which drove him to protect her, nothing else. Her stern admonitions made her flinch inwardly but did little to ease the tightness around her heart.

Gradually, without conscious direction, her tired mind drifted to consideration of its main preoccupation. Of course he had no interest in her. If he had known who she was at the masked ball, he would have mentioned the fact by now. She knew little of the ways of gentleman rakes, but felt sure a coach trip, together alone, must rate as one of those opportunities too good to let slip. Yet the man beside her remained silent. She stole a glance at him from beneath her lashes. His eyes were closed. Emboldened, she allowed her gaze to skim the contours of his face, the wide forehead and squared chin, his firm, well shaped lips... Finding her mind frolicking in fantasies of how those lips would feel against hers, Georgiana forcibly withdrew her gaze and returned it to contemplation of the darkness beyond the window.

Ravello. The image of the villa there, now hers, materialised in her mind's eye. She seized on it. And was suddenly struck by the obvious solution to her troubles. Charles was a bully and totally unscrupulous. He would continue to threaten her peace of mind while she remained in England. And Bella's brother, too, disturbed her rest and reduced her ability to cope with the daily round of fashionable life. Yet she was not particularly enamoured of the social whirl; it would cause her no great pain to eschew the life completely. It was a pleasant diversion, nothing more.

With sudden conviction, she made up her mind. She would see out the Season with Bella, as she had promised Arthur she would. Then she would return to Ravello, a great deal older and a great deal wiser. She stifled a small sigh and forced herself to promise— when winter set in, she would be in Ravello.

The increasing light coming from street-lamps as they entered the capital made it worth while for Dominic to desert his imaginings in favour of the real thing. He had been watching Georgiana for some minutes, wondering what it was that kept her so serious, when a point which had thus far eluded him surfaced as a question. "Georgiana, do you have any idea why Charles wants to marry you?"

As he said the words, he realised they were hardly flattering. Still, he had a high enough opinion of Georgiana Hartley to be sure she was not the sort of flighty young woman who believed all men who wished to marry her were smitten by her beauty. The memory of her numerous suitors, all of whom were most definitely smitten, himself included, brought a wry smile to his lips.

In the flickering, shifting light, Georgiana saw the smile, and her heart turned to lead and dropped to her slippers. To ask a question like that and then smile condescendingly! Well, if anything was needed to convince her Lord Alton had no romantic interest in her it was that. Doggedly, she forced her mind to concentrate on his query. Frowning with the effort, she shook her head and answered truthfully, "I have no idea."

"It was the same while you were at the Place?"

Georgiana nodded. "Exactly the same." She paused, then decided she might as well tell Lord Alton the whole of it. He knew so much already. Choosing her words carefully, she explained Charles's claim of a long-standing betrothal.

"And you're certain such an arrangement never existed?"

"Quite sure." Georgiana paused, then added in explanation, "My father and I were...very close. He would never have done such a thing and not told me. Not for any reason."

Lord Alton seemed to accept her assurance. He sat silently beside her as the coach rumbled along the cobbles towards Green Street.

Dominic had no doubt that Georgiana's beliefs were true. He only wished he had known of Charles's claim before he had returned to the inn parlour. The tenseness he had felt but not recognised on his drive to the Hare and Hounds had converted to anger once he had got Georgiana safely away—anger that had demanded some outlet. So he had returned to the parlour, to be quite unnecessarily provoked by Charles's animadversions on his cousin. In the end he had administered a thoroughly deserved thrashing. He knew Charles was close to financial ruin—was, in fact, technically bankrupt. Georgiana's small fortune would not come close to meeting his mounting debts. After suggesting Charles would be wise never to approach his lovely cousin again, he had repeated his offer to buy the Place. The sum he named was far more than Charles would ever get from any other, with the Place situated as it was. Charles had only attempted a sneer through swollen and cracked lips.

Dominic contemplated a late-night return to the Hare and Hounds, to pursue further the reason for Charles's apparent fixation with marrying his cousin. Even less than Georgiana did he believe Charles would act for the good of the family. There was something in all this that he was missing, some vital clue which would make all clear. But Charles would almost certainly have left before he could return to the inn.

He turned the anomalies of Charles's behaviour, both with respect to Georgiana and to the sale of the Place, over and over in his mind. Suddenly, the two connected. Dominic straightened in his seat.

"Georgiana, have you been to see your father's English solicitors yet?"

Dragged from the depths of a series of most melancholy thoughts, Georgiana shook her head. "No. I suppose I should, but there doesn't really seem much point."

"But…" Dominic paused, then decided he was going to interfere even though he theoretically had no right. Right be damned. He was going to marry the chit, wasn't he? "Correct me if I'm wrong, but I seem to recall you left Italy before notification of your father's death was acknowledged by your English solicitors. Is that right?"

"You mean," said Georgiana, brow wrinkling in an effort to get the question straight, "before they wrote back after they got the letter from the Italian solicitors?" At Dominic's nod, she agreed. "Yes, that's right."

"And you haven't seen your father's will?"

"No...no. That was left with the English solicitors. But I always knew I would inherit all Papa's money. And the villa at Ravello." She paused, puzzled by his line of questioning, not sure of what possibilities he saw. "But surely if there had been anything more, or anything unexpected, someone would have told me by now?"

"Who are your solicitors here?"

"Whitworth and Whitworth, in Lincoln's Inn."

"Good. I'll take you to see them tomorrow."

Georgiana turned to look at him in amazement. She had not previously had much exposure to the autocratic side of Lord Alton's temperament. She surveyed the satisfied expression on his face with misgiving. "But... why?"

He smiled at her, and she almost forgot her question.

"Because, my dear Georgiana," he said as he captured her hand and raised it to his lips, "Charles, despite all evidence to the contrary, is not a complete gudgeon. His attempts to coerce you into marriage must have some motive behind them. And, as your kinship with him is the only connection between you, I suggest we start looking for the answer with your father's solicitors."

Despite the clear impression that Lord Alton had a stronger motive for insisting she visit her solicitors, Georgiana got no further chance to question him. He had barely ceased speaking when the carriage pulled up outside Green Street. In the ensuing hullabaloo there was no opportunity to do more than thank him prettily for his rescue and meekly accept his instruction to be ready the next morning at eleven.

GEORGIANA RETURNED Arthur's reassuring smile as the Alton town carriage drew up at the entrance to Lincoln's

Inn. Both she and her host had been taken up by an irresistible force at eleven that morning, their objective being the office of her father's solicitors. Despite her belief that nothing new would be learned from Whitworths, Georgiana was enjoying her first view of an area of London she had not previously had cause to visit.

Lord Alton, sitting beside her, had leant forward to speak to the porter. As he leant back, the carriage lurched forward again, over the cobbles and through the large gate of the Inn. The cobbled yard was surrounded by buildings entirely given over to solicitors and clerks. By each doorway leading on to a stairwell hung the bronze plaques of the practitioners within. The carriage drew up before one such door. Lord Alton jumped down and gave her his hand.

Their destination lay on the first floor. A desiccated clerk of indeterminate years, dressed in sombre grey and sporting a tie wig of decades gone by, bade them seat themselves in the small outer office, "While I enquire if Mr Whitworth will see you." He left Georgiana with the definite impression that to be permitted to see the Mr Whitworths was tantamount to being granted an audience with the Regent.

Minutes later he was back, oozing spurious concern. A Mr Whitworth—the elder, as they later learned—followed close on his heels. A portly man of late middle age, he glanced down at the card he held in his hand, given to the clerk by Lord Alton.

Mr Whitworth looked at the two elegant and eminently respectable gentlemen filling his antechamber and became slightly flustered. "My lord...?"

Dominic took pity on him. "I am Lord Alton," he explained smoothly, "and this is Miss Georgiana Hartley, one of your clients. She is presently in the care of my sister, Lady Winsmere. Lord Winsmere," he added, indicating Arthur for the solicitor's edification, "and I have escorted her here in the hope you can clarify a number of points concerning Miss Hartley's inheritance."

It was doubtful if Mr Whitworth heard the latter half of this speech. His eyes had become transfixed on Georgiana, sitting patiently on a chair between her two protectors. Despite the fact she was now used to being stared at, and knew she looked her best in a soft dove-coloured merino gown with a delicate lace tippet, Georgiana found his gaze unnerving. As Lord Alton finished speaking, and the man continued to stare, she raised her brows haughtily.

Mr Whitworth started. "Miss Georgiana Hartley— Mr James Hartley's daughter?" he asked breathlessly.

Georgiana looked puzzled. "Yes," she confirmed, wondering who else had her name.

"My dear young lady!" exclaimed the solicitor, grasping her hand and bowing elaborately over it. "My dear Miss Georgiana! Well, it's a relief to see you at last! We've been searching for you for months!" Once he had started, it seemed the man hardly paused for breath. "Almost, we had begun to fear foul play. When we couldn't contact you and all our letters were returned unopened and no one seemed to know where you had disappeared to…" Suddenly he paused and seemed to recollect himself. He waved plump hands in sudden agitation. "But what am I thinking of? Please come into my office, Miss Hartley, my lords, and we will sort this matter out at once."

He ushered them into a large office which bore little resemblance to the spartan outer chamber. Here all was air and light, with a rich red Turkey carpet covering mellow polished boards. Through the windows, the branches of the trees in the small lawn in the middle of the yard could be seen, the last yellow leaves tenaciously defying the brisk autumn breeze.

As they entered, a thin, soberly clad gentleman rose from behind one of two large desks. Mr Whitworth, holding the door, proclaimed, "Alfred, Miss Hartley is here!"

The second Whitworth—for, from the similarity of facial features, there was little doubt of who he was— looked startled. He pulled his gold-rimmed pince-nez off his nose, polished the glass, then returned it to its perch the better to view Georgiana. After a moment of rapt contemplation, he sighed. "Thank God!"

Both Whitworths bustled about, arranging chairs for their guests. They set these in front of the large desks which, side by side, faced the room. Once their visitors were seated, they subsided, each behind his own desk.

"Now!" said Whitworth the elder, chins flapping as he settled, hands folded before him. "As you can see, we're delighted to see you, Miss Hartley. We have been trying to contact you since we learned of your father's death, with respect to the matter of your inheritance." He beamed at Georgiana.

"If we might speak frankly…?" enquired Whitworth the younger, his flat tone a contrast to his brother's jovial accents.

Turning to face him, it took a moment before Georgiana understood his query. "Oh, please," she said quickly when light finally dawned, "Lord Alton and

Lord Winsmere are my friends. I will be relying on their advice."

"Good, good," said Whitworth the elder, causing Georgiana to swivel again. "Not wise for a young lady so well dowered as you are to be alone in the world."

"Quite," his younger brother concurred drily.

"Now, where to begin?"

"Perhaps at your father's bequests?"

"There weren't many—nothing that interfered with the bulk of the estate."

"A few minor legacies to old servants—the usual sort of thing."

"But the major estate remains intact." Whitworth the elder paused to beam again at Georgiana.

Stifling the impulse to put a hand to her whirling head, Georgiana took the opportunity to quell her impending dizziness. It was like watching a tennis game, the conversational ball passing from brother to brother and back again, before their audience of three. Then his last words registered. "Major estate?"

"Why, yes."

"As the major beneficiary of your father's will, you inherit the majority of his estate."

"Which is to say," Whitworth the elder took up the tale smoothly, "the estate known as the Place in the county of Buckinghamshire…"

"His invested capital," intoned Whitworth the younger. "The house in town…"

"And all his paintings not previously sold."

A pause ensued. Georgiana stared at the elder Mr Whitworth, he who had last spoken. Lord Winsmere, having given up the unequal task of allowing his eyes to follow the conversation, stared out of the window, his lips pursed. Lord Alton, even less enthralled by the vision of the Whitworths, had shifted his gaze long since to the young woman beside him. He showed no surprise at the solicitor's news.

"The Place? But… There must be some mistake!" Georgiana could not believe her ears. "My cousin Charles owns the Place."

"Oh, dear me, no!" said the younger Whitworth. "Mr Charles Hartley is not a client of ours."

"And has no claim whatever on the Place. The estate was not entailed."

"It generally passed through the eldest male…"

"But your grandfather divided his estate equally between his two sons…"

"Your father and his brother, your uncle Ernest."

"Both were given an estate—in your father's case, the Place."

"Unfortunately, Ernest Hartley was a gambler."

"Quite ran through his patrimony, as the saying goes."

"He eventually lost everything and turned to your father for aid."

"Your father was enjoying a great success in London at that time. He had married your mother and was much in demand. Dear me, his fees! Well, quite astronomical, they seemed." Mr Whitworth the elder paused for breath.

This time Georgiana could not restrain her need to put a hand to her brow. The world was whirling.

"If we could condense this history, gentlemen?" Viscount Alton's precise tones jerked both Whitworths out of their rut.

"Er—yes. Well," said Mr Whitworth, with a careful

eye on his lordship, "the long and the short of it is, your father and mother wished to spend some time in Italy. So your father installed your uncle as steward of the Place, put his ready capital in the funds, leased the house in London, and left the country. I believe you were a child at the time."

Georgiana nodded absent-mindedly. The Place was hers. It had never been Charles's property, and he had known it.

"When we heard of your father's death," broke in the younger Whitworth, warily eyeing the Viscount, "we wrote immediately to you at the villa in Ravello. The letter was returned by your Italian man of business, stating you had returned to England before learning of your uncle's demise and had planned to stay at the Place."

Whitworth the elder opened his mouth to respond to his cue, but caught the Viscount's eye and fell silent, leaving it to his sibling to continue, "We wrote to you there, but the letters were returned without explanation. In the end we sent one of our most trusted clerks to see you. He reported that the house was shut up and deserted."

The elder Whitworth could restrain himself no longer. "No one seemed to know where you'd gone or even if you'd arrived from the Continent."

Following the tale with difficulty, Georgiana saw what must have occurred. Questions hammered at her brain, but most were not for the solicitors' ears. She fastened on the one aspect that held greatest importance to her. "You mentioned pictures?"

"Oh, yes. Your father left quite a tidy stack of canvases—some unclaimed portraits, and others—in

England. He always claimed they were a sound invest-ment." The dead tones of the younger solicitor left no doubt of his opinion on the matter.

"But where are they stored?" asked Georgiana.

"Stored?" The elder Whitworth stared at her word-lessly, then turned to his brother for help. But the younger Whitworth had clearly decided this was one cue he would do well to miss. "Er..." said Mr Whitworth, chasing inspiration, "I rather suspect he must have left them at the Place."

"Are you certain they haven't been sold?" Lord Wins-mere bought into the conversation. "From what you say, Ernest Hartley sounds the type to hock his grand-mother's spectacles. Excuse me, m'dear," he added in an aside to Georgiana.

But the elder Whitworth waved his hands in a nega-tive gesture. "A reformed character, I assure you. After his—er—brush with the Navy, he was so thankful to be pulled free that he was quite devoted to his brother and his interests."

"Devoted?" echoed Lord Alton incredulously. "Have you seen the Place?"

"Unfortunately, Mr Hartley was unsuited to the task of managing the estate, although he tried his best." The younger Whitworth drew his lordship's fire. "We would seriously doubt he would have sold any of his brother's paintings. He lived quite retired at the Place until his death, you know."

"So," said Georgiana, struggling to take it all in, "the most likely place for my father's pictures—the ones he left in England—is the Place. But they aren't there. I looked."

Both Whitworths shifted uncomfortably but could throw no further light on the matter.

Eventually Mr Whitworth the elder broke the silence. "Are there any instructions you wish to give us, my dear, concerning your property?"

Georgiana blinked, then slowly shook her head. "I'm afraid I'll need a little time to think things through. It's all been rather a surprise."

"Yes, of course. No rush at all," said the elder Mr Whitworth, resuming his genial state. "Mr Charles Hartley will of course be given due notice to quit."

Then, as there seemed nothing further to say, Georgiana rose, bringing the men to their feet.

"One moment, my dear," came Lord Winsmere's voice. "It's as well to know all the facts." He smiled at Georgiana and then turned to ask, "You mentioned capital placed in the funds. What is the current balance?"

The elder Mr Whitworth beamed. The figure he named sent Lord Alton's black brows flying.

An enigmatic smile played on Lord Winsmere's lips as he turned to a stunned Georgiana. "Well, my dear, I'm afraid you'll have more than your earnest suitors to repel once that piece of news gets around."

ARTHUR'S REACTION was echoed by Bella when, over the luncheon table, she was regaled with the entirety of Georgiana's fortune. Arthur told the story; Dominic had declined an invitation to join them, pleading the press of other engagements.

"There's no point in thinking you can hide it, Georgie," Bella said once she had recovered enough to speak. "You're an *heiress*. Even if the Place is all to pieces."

Georgiana was still trying to recover her equilibrium.

"But surely, if we don't tell anyone, no one will know."

Bella felt like screaming. What other young lady of quality, with her way to make in the world, when informed she was a considerable heiress, would act so? Inwardly, Bella railed again at the unknown who had stolen her friend's heart. Dominic had not yet found him; that much was clear. After his successful rescue of Georgiana the evening before, he had stayed to partake of a cold supper. She could well imagine what he had done to Charles, even without the tell-tale handkerchief she had seen him quickly remove from his hand and stuff into his pocket before he thought anyone had noticed. She was more than ready to believe his assertion that Charles would not trouble Georgiana again, and would in all probability not remain over long in England. But, after arranging for Arthur to accompany Georgiana and himself to her solicitors' this morning, her brother had merely bestowed a fond pat on her cheek and left…left her to struggle with the herculean task of convincing Georgiana to forget her hopeless love and choose between her lovesick beaux.

Sudden inspiration blossomed in Bella's mind. "Georgie, my love, we will really have to think very carefully about how you should go on." Bella paused, carefully choosing her words. "Once it becomes known you're an heiress, you'll be swamped. Perhaps it would be better to make your choice now."

Georgiana's gaze rose from her plate to settle on her friend's face. Bella's attempted manipulation was unwelcome, but, seeing the wistful expression in the blue eyes watching her, and knowing that she only meant to help, Georgiana could not suppress a small smile. But, "Really, Bella!" was all she said.

Abashed, Bella retreated, but rapidly came about. "Yes, but seriously, Georgie, what do you plan to do?"

"I'm afraid, my dear," put in Arthur, "that for once Bella is quite right." Bella grimaced at his phrasing. "Once it becomes common knowledge that you have such a fortune, you'll be besieged."

With a sigh, Georgiana pushed her plate away. They had sent the servants from the room to give free rein to their discussion. She rose to fetch the teapot from the side-table. Slipping once more into her chair, she busied herself with pouring cups for both Arthur and Bella before helping herself. Only then did she answer Bella. "I don't know. But please promise me you'll say nothing to anyone about my inheritance?"

Arthur bowed his acquiescence. "Whatever you wish, my dear." His stern eye rested on his wife.

Bella pouted, but, under her husband's prompting, she gave in. "Oh, very well. But it won't help, you know. Such news *always* gets around."

CHAPTER EIGHT

THE ACCURACY of Bella's prediction was brought home to Georgiana before the week was out. Shrewd assessing glances, condescending and calculating stares—the oppressive, smothering interest of the *ton* made itself felt in a dozen different ways. She could only conclude that the clerks in Mr Whitworth's office, or, perhaps, the Mr Whitworths themselves, were less discreet than she, in her naïveté, had supposed.

Bella, of course, behaved as if all the attention was only her due. Her friend continued to hope she would succumb to the blandishments of one or other of her insistent suitors. In fact, thought Georgiana crossly, the entire charade was enough to put anyone off marriage for life. How could she ever hope to convince herself any gentleman was in earnest, that he truly loved her for herself, rather than for the financial comfort she would bring him, when everyone behaved as if her new-found fortune was of the first importance?

With a disgusted little snort, she turned over on the coverlet of her bed, kicking her legs to free her skirts from under her. She had retreated to her room to rest before dressing for dinner and the Massinghams' rout. For the first time since Georgiana had come to Green Street, Bella had also retired for a late-afternoon nap. While she studied the details of the pink-silk-draped canopy, Georgiana considered her friend. Bella certainly seemed more tired these days, though the bloom on her skin showed none of the subtle signs of fatigue. Still, Georgiana couldn't understand how she kept up. Or why. For her own part, the glamour of the balls and parties was rapidly fading, their thrills too meaninglessly repetitive to hold her interest. Now she had no difficulty in understanding Bella's plea of boredom with the fashionable round.

Her eyes drifted to the wardrobe, wherein resided all her beautiful gowns. Bella was always so thrilled when she wore her latest acquisitions. They were worth every last penny just for that. Georgiana grinned. She could hardly deny Bella such a small pleasure when all her friend's energies were directed towards securing her, Georgiana's, future. Nothing seemly likely to turn Bella from her purpose. Her beloved Georgie must marry into the *ton*.

As an errant ray of sunshine drifted over the gilded cords drawing back the curtains of her bed, Georgiana wondered again at the oddity of having a virtual foster-sister. She was fast learning that receiving care and concern laid a reciprocal responsibility on the recipient. But, despite Bella's yearnings, this was one aspect of her life on which she was determined to hold firm. She would marry for love, or not at all.

Just the thought of love, the very concept, brought a darkly handsome face swimming into her consciousness. Vibrant blue eyes laughed at her through a mask, then turned smoky and dark. Resolutely she banished the unnerving image. Dreams were for children.

In truth, if it had not been for Lord Alton's support, she might well have turned tail and fled back to Italy the first day after their discovery at Lincoln's Inn. The puzzle of Charles and his machinations was now clear. Fiend that he was, devoid of all proper feeling, he had decided to marry her before she found out she owned the Place. That way, Dominic had explained, she would likely never have known the extent of her fortune; as her husband, Charles would have assumed full rights over her property.

Dominic. She must stop thinking of him like that, in such a personal way. If she was to preserve her secret, she must learn to treat him with becoming distance. Unfortunately, this grew daily more difficult.

When he had appeared before her at the Walfords' ball the evening after their momentous visit to the Whitworths', she had offered him welcome far in excess of what might reasonably be excused on the grounds that he was her patroness's brother. She hoped he had put it down to a gush of girlish gratitude, no matter how the very thought irked her. But the warmth in his blue eyes had left her with an uncomfortable feeling of no longer being in control, as if some hand more powerful than hers was directing her affairs.

Dominic—*Lord Alton!*—continued to rescue her from the worst of her importunate court. In fact he was now so often by her side that the rest of her admirers tended to fade into the background, at least in her eyes. Georgiana frowned at the wandering sunbeam which had moved to light the bedpost. Now she came to consider the matter, it was almost as if Lord Alton himself was paying court to her.

Another unladylike snort ruffled the serenity of the afternoon. Ridiculous idea! He was merely being kind, giving her what protection he could from the fortune-hunters, knowing she did not like her prominence one little bit. He was her patroness's brother, that was all.

Nothing more.

THE HUM of a hundred conversations eddied about Georgiana, enclosing her within the cocoon of the Massinghams' rout party. The bright lights of the chandeliers winked from thousands of facets, none more brilliant than the sparkling eyes of the débutantes as they dipped and swayed through the first cotillion. Laughter tinkled and ran like a silver ribbon through the crowd. It was a glittering occasion; all present were pleased to be seen to be pleased. The ballroom was bedecked with tubs of hothouse blooms, vying with the ladies' dresses in splashes of glorious colour, perfuming the warm air with subtle scents. A small orchestra added its mite to the din, striving valiantly to be heard above the busy chatter.

Newly entered on the scene, Georgiana had taken no more than three steps before being surrounded by her intrepid admirers, all clamouring for the honour of setting their name in her dance card. With a charm none the less successful for being automatic, she set about her regular task of ordering her evening.

"My dear Miss Hartley, if you would allow me the supper waltz I should be greatly honoured."

Georgiana glanced up and found the serious face of Mr Swinson, one of her earnest suitors, who had become even more earnest over the last few days, hovering beside her. All her instincts cautioned her to refuse his request. The supper waltz, with the implied intention of going into supper on the gentleman's arm at the conclusion of the measure, was the most highly prized of the dances at such a gathering. Whenever possible, Georgiana strove to grant that dance to one or other of her refused suitors, so as not to raise any false hopes among others of her court. But what excuse could she give, so early in the evening? A lie? Resolute, she opened her mouth to deny Mr Swinson, hoping he would accept her refusal without excuse, but was forestalled by a deep voice, speaking from behind her left ear.

"I believe the supper waltz is mine, Swinson."

Swaying slightly with the dizziness his nearness always induced, Georgiana struggled to keep her expression within the limits of the acceptable, and knew she failed dismally. Her eyes were alight, her nerves tingling. She turned and gave her hand to Lord Alton. She didn't even notice Mr Swinson huffily withdraw, eyeing the elegant person of the Viscount with marked disfavour.

Lord Alton bowed low over her hand. "Fairest Georgiana."

His words were a seductive murmur, rippling across her senses. Then, knowing it was unwise, but utterly incapable of resisting the compulsion, Georgiana met his eyes, and the warmth she saw there spread through her, leaving dizzy happiness in its wake.

"My lord."

She retained just enough wit to return his greeting, dropping her eyes from his in a flurry of shyness.

With a gentle smile, Viscount Alton tucked the hand he was still holding into the crook of his arm, thereby making life exceedingly difficult for the numerous other gentlemen waiting to pay court to this most desirable of young ladies. Lord Ellsmere, by his friend's side, grinned. Taking pity on Georgiana, he engaged her in light-hearted conversation.

Georgiana's hand burned where it lay on Lord Alton's silk sleeve. Why was he behaving so? Under cover of paying polite attention to Lord Ellsmere as he related the latest *on dit,* she glanced up to find the Viscount's blue eyes regarding her, an expression she dared not place lighting their depths. Another glance around showed her frustrated court dwindling, leaving only those gentlemen she regarded more as friends than suitors. Unlike those whose interest was primarily pecuniary, none of these gentlemen seemed to find Lord Alton's possessive attitude any impediment to conversing with her.

Possessive? Georgiana's thoughts froze. Then, inwardly, she shrugged. If the shoe fitted… And really there was no other way to describe the way he was behaving. This was the third night in a row he had appeared by her side almost immediately she had entered a room. By his mere presence he eased the crush about her, bringing relief which would doubtless be acute if she could feel anything through the sheer exhilaration of having him so near.

With an effort Georgiana forced herself to attend to the conversation, grateful for the distraction of Mr Havelock, who now joined them. By imperceptible degrees, the circle about them grew as more acquaintances stopped to talk. Gradually the sense of being, in some strange way, identifiably his receded, leaving only a subtle feeling of security.

When Lord Aylesham approached to claim the next dance, Lord Alton relinquished her with no more than a warm smile and a whispered reminder of their later appointment.

Released from the mesmerising effect of the Viscount at close quarters, Georgiana determinedly devoted a large part of her mind to a detailed analysis of his actions and motives. None of her partners noticed anything amiss; she was now too thoroughly practised in the arts of dancing, conversing and general entertaining to need to assign more than a small portion of her attention to these endeavours.

Of all the questions revolving in her head, the most insistent was, *Why?* Why was he doing all the things he was? Why was he behaving as he was? Again and again, only one answer came. It was impossible to attribute his actions to any other cause. *He was making her the object of his attentions.* Delicious shivers ran up her spine when she finally allowed her mind to enunciate that fact. Mr Sherry, whose arms she graced at the time, looked at her askance. Georgiana smiled dazzlingly upon him, completely stunning the poor man.

The next instant her sky clouded again. How could she believe such a magnificent man, with all the advantages of birth, position and fortune, would seriously look in her direction? That he was contemplating anything other than the acceptable was unthinkable. But perhaps he wasn't contemplating anything at all. Maybe she was just an amusing aside, his sister's protégée who needed looking after. Was she simply a naïve foreigner, reading far more into the situation than was intended? Georgiana forgot to suppress her sigh, and was forced to spend the rest of the dance soothing a ruffled Mr Sherry.

While Georgiana struggled with question and answer, alternating between cloud nine and prosaic despondency, the object of her thoughts strolled about the rooms, stopping here and there to chat as the mood seized him. Dominic was in a state of pleasurable anticipation. To his mind, his course was clear. While it was not one he had followed previously, he did not doubt his ability to carry the thing off. The major problem was time—or, rather, the patience required to see the campaign through.

The necessity for taking things slowly was self-evident. This time the object of his desires was not an experienced woman, capable of playing the game with a facility on a par with his. This time he wanted a green girl, an innocent, an angel whose conquest meant more to him than all the others combined. She needed gentle wooing. So the habits of the last ten years were set aside in favour of the strict dictates of propriety. With a wry grin at no one in particular, Dominic wondered how long he could harness the coiled tension that was growing, day by day, beneath the surface of his suave urbanity.

"Dominic! What ho, lad! Up from the princely delights of Brighton?"

Dominic swung to face the speaker, a smile lighting his face. "My lord." He nodded to Lord Moreton, one of his late father's contemporaries. "As you say, sir, the amenities of Brighton palled."

"Palled before the attractions of the young ladies, eh?"

Unperturbed by the close scrutiny of a pair of sharp grey eyes overhung by bushy brows, Dominic smiled in his usual benign way and agreed. "Oh, Prinny's no competition, I assure you."

Lord Moreton guffawed. Slapping Dominic on the

back, he resumed his peregrination through the crowd, allowing Dominic to do likewise.

It was, Dominic supposed, inevitable that people would start to speculate. The very fact that he was here, attending all the balls and parties of the Little Season, rather than pursuing a very different course, in very different company, positively invited the attention of the gabble-mongers. No one was as yet sufficiently bold to put their speculation into circulation, but doubtless that, too, would come. For his part, he didn't give a damn what the gossips said. He'd weathered far worse. But he would need to be vigilant to ensure no disturbing whispers reached his Georgiana's ears. In truth, he was not sure how she might respond. But, with first-hand knowledge of the spitefulness of some among society's civilised hordes, he was not prepared to take any chances.

For the first time, at the ripe old age of thirty-two, he was seriously wooing a young lady. The pace grated. The slowly compounding returns, when set against the constantly high expense in time and restraint, were hard to bear, particularly for one to whom instant gratification of the smallest whim, however fleeting, had become the norm. And unusual abstinence only aggravated his state.

Still, there was at least one shining beacon on the horizon, holding the promise of safe haven in the end. He was too experienced not to be able to read the signs. Her response to him was gratifying, even at thirty-two. Who would have imagined he would be so susceptible to such flattery? Dominic allowed a slow grin to twist his lips. The pull he sensed between them—that magnetic attraction that drew man to woman and bound them together with silken strands of desire—was so strong that he felt sufficently confident to leave her, essentially unwatched, for half the evening. The other half, of course, would be his. At least this way the gossip-mongers would have to wait a little longer for their *on dit*.

"What on earth are you grinning at?"

Startled, Dominic turned to find Bella at his side. His slow smile surfaced. "Pleasant thoughts, my dear." His eyes scanned her face, noting the pallor she had attempted to hide with rouge. "How goes it with you?"

A small frown worried at Bella's arched brows. "Oh, so-so." she paused, then went on in a rush, "If I wasn't so concerned about Georgie, I declare I would have stayed at home with Arthur. These affairs are becoming a dreadful bore."

The quavering note in her voice alerted Dominic to her state. He drew her hand comfortingly through his arm, stroking it soothingly, a small gesture he had used since she was a child. It had the desired effect. While his sister regained her composure, it occurred to him that time, his present arbiter, was about to place a limit on his courtship. The Season had only two more weeks to run. Then the *ton* would retire to their estates for Christmas and the worst of the winter. He was unsure if Bella had yet recognised her condition. Typically she was not one to coddle herself and could be relied on to fail to consider such possibilities until they became too obvious to ignore. But Arthur was not so sanguine. He would undoubtedly wish to remove from London as soon as the Season ended. Which raised the question of Georgiana's future plans.

On impulse, Dominic turned to his sister. "Incidentally, what are you planning for Christmas?"

Diverted, Bella gave him a clear blue stare. "Christmas?" Then, recovering from her surprise, "I haven't given it much thought." She shrugged. "I suppose we'll go down to Winsmere, as usual."

"Why not come to Candlewick? You haven't spent Christmas there since you married. I want to open the house up—just us, but the place needs warming."

Bella was taken aback by the invitation, but the more she considered it, the more value she could see in the suggestion. While she was very comfortable at Winsmere Lodge, it couldn't compare with the graciousness of Candlewick. Nothing could. "I'm sure Arthur wouldn't mind. I'll speak to him tomorrow."

Dominic nodded. "What about Georgiana?"

Bella's brow clouded again. "I've already asked, but she seems set on returning to Italy. I've tried to talk her out of it, but she's so stubborn!"

His suspicions confirmed, Dominic, repressing a grin at his sister's disgruntled tone, said, "Leave it to me. I'll see what my persuasions can do."

Big beseeching blue eyes met his. "Oh, Dominic. If you could only persuade her to stay, I just know she'll make a good match once she gets over this horrible mystery gentleman of hers." Remembering her brother's promise, Bella added, "You haven't found out who he is yet, have you?"

It was Dominic's turn to frown. Amid the delights of wooing Georgiana, he'd forgotten the existence of her "secret love". Now, considering the matter carefully, knowing what he did of that young lady, he was hard put to it to credit the notion. If she had ever in truth had a "secret love", then the man was all but forgotten already. The unwelcome idea that Georgiana's partiality could vacillate like a darting sunbeam, now here, now there, awoke in his mind. Resolutely he quashed it. Quite simply, he had no intention of allowing her the leeway neccesary to vacillate. Seeing the worry etched in Bella's face, he yielded to the impulse to reassure her. "Don't worry your head about your protégée. From all I've seen, she's well on the way to achieving a highly creditable alliance."

The glow in Bella's face brought a smile to Dominic's lips.

"Who? Where…? I haven't noticed any particular gentleman… Oh, Dominic! Don't tease! Who is he?"

But Dominic only shook his head, smiling at her chagrin. "Patience, sister, dear. Don't crowd out the action. Just keep your eyes open and you'll doubtless see it all. But," he said, returning to a sterner tone, "believe me, there's no need for you to worry."

Bella grimaced up at him.

Dominic's brows rose, with that faintly supercilious air that warned Bella he was in earnest. Her rejoinder was destined to remain unuttered as Viscount Molesworth approached to claim her for the cotillion just forming.

Free again, Dominic continued his amble, determined to eschew Georgiana's company until the supper dance provided him with adequate excuse. At the door to the card-room, he was hailed by his brother-in-law.

"Thought you were at home," Dominic said, strolling up and nodding to Lord Green, standing beside Arthur.

"Finished my last box earlier than I'd thought. You've seen Bella?"

Dominic nodded. "She's dancing with Molesworth."

"In that case, come and join us."

"Just a quiet hand," put in Lord Green with a smile, "but at least more life than you're likely to find out here."

The smile on Dominic's face broadened. "Not tonight. I have other fish to fry."

"Ah." Arthur's pensive eye met his brother-in-law's bright blue gaze. "And what a shock that must be to the system."

Dominic's lips twitched, but he responded calmly. "As you say."

"Still," said Arthur, his eyes now on the figure of his wife twirling down the set with Viscount Molesworth, "it's worth it in the end."

With a nod and a smile, Dominic moved on. The cotillion had ended, and the dancers were taking their places, with a great deal of noisy laughter, for a set of country dances. His eyes were drawn to where Georgiana was standing, partnered by Julian Ellsmere. Dominic stood unobtrusively between a sofa occupied by two turbaned dowagers and a potted palm and watched the dancers, anticipation growing keener by the minute.

Suddenly the irritation of being stared at caused him to lift his eyes and look over the dancers' heads. Directly opposite, Elaine Changley stood watching him.

She smiled as their eyes made contact. Then, completely ignoring the ladies beside her, she glided across the ballroom in his direction.

It was a bold move. Under his breath, Dominic

uttered an oath, completely forgetting the proximity of the elderly dowagers. As he watched her progress between the sets, he allowed himself to examine, as if from a distance, her attractions. Other than as a passing diversion, she had failed to activate his interest. He had never encouraged her to believe otherwise. It amazed him that she could confuse the emotion he felt for the lady he would marry with the fleeting passion he had indulged with her.

Elaine Changley was desperate. Just how desperate, she had not known until she had seen the handsome form of Dominic Ridgeley across the room and realised the smile on his face was caused by the sight of his sister's protégée. Her present play was a gamble. By the time she reached his side, she realised how dangerous a gamble it was.

Dominic greeted her with a formal bow and a cold, "Elaine."

Inwardly, Lady Changley winced, but she kept a bright if brittle smile fixed on her lips and attempted to inject some warmth into her habitually cold gaze. "Dominic, darling," she purred, "how pleasant to find you here. Have you come to alleviate the singular boredom of this party?"

Dominic allowed his gaze, which had returned to the dancers immediately after greeting her, to come slowly about to rest on her face—a handsome face, pale and perfectly featured, but devoid of all softness, all womanly feeling.

The music stopped.

Suddenly nervous, Elaine Changley plied her fan, fluttering it delicately just below her eyes.

Curtly Dominic bowed. "If you'll excuse me, my lady, I am engaged for the next dance."

With that, he left her, aware of the avid interest of the dowagers, and of Elaine Changley's eyes, following him.

Paler than ever, Elaine Changley had no move left on the board. She had perforce to remain where she was, her temper in shreds, and bear the sly feminine whispers of the ladies from across the room and the less subdued cackle of the witches on the sofa beside her. Her apparently impetuous approach to Lord Alton had been designed to draw all eyes. His leaving her after no more than a minute made his uninterest as clear as if the town crier had announced it. And he had gone straight to Miss Hartley's side! Seething and impotent, Lady Changley stood rigid as a post, forced to accept the most comprehensive defeat of her varied career with what very little grace she could muster.

A sudden tingling rippling along her nerves told Georgiana, chatting easily with Lord Ellsmere, that her next partner was close. She turned slightly to find her hand taken in a firm grip and placed, equally firmly, on Viscount Alton's arm. Chancing an upward glance, she found his lordship's blue eyes smiling down at her, that curiously warming expression readily discernible.

"Julian, I believe Arthur is looking for a fourth in the card-room."

Lord Ellsmere laughed at the overt dismissal and, with a smiling bow over Georgiana's free hand, he left them.

There was a slight break betwen the country dances and the waltz, while the musicians retuned their instruments. Lord Alton seemed quite content to spend the time staring at her. Unnerved, and knowing she would very likely dissolve entirely if she permitted him such licence, Georgiana strove to find a suitably distracting conversational gambit.

"All the *ton* seem to be attending tonight. The rooms are quite full, don't you think?" Breathless and quivering, it was the best she could manage.

"Are they?" Lord Alton replied, brows rising, but his gaze remaining fixed on her face. "I hadn't noticed."

The expression in his blue eyes and the seductive tenor of his voice infused his words with a meaning far in excess of the obvious. Georgiana blushed.

Dominic smiled. "But you remind me of something I had to ask you."

"Oh?" Georgiana struggled to reduce their interaction to the commonplace. If she could only keep talking, and avoid those soft silences that he used so well to steal her mind and her wits and her very soul, she might just survive. "What was that?"

"Why, only that I wondered what your plans for the winter months were." The music restarted, and Dominic drew her gently into his arms and into the swirling drifts of couples on the floor.

Her feet circling dutifully, Georgiana made a desperate effort to focus her mind on his words. "Ah…" She moistened suddenly dry lips with the tip of her tongue, then tried again. "I… That is to say…" She caught his amused look. A sudden little spurt of anger allowed her to regain her composure. Putting up her chin, she stated calmly, "I expect to be returning to Italy."

A woebegone sigh met her declaration. At her look of surprise Dominic said, "Mrs Landy and Duckett will be so disappointed. I'm sure they would love to see the eminently fashionable young lady you have become, if only to congratulate themselves on their far-sightedness."

Georgiana looked her puzzlement.

Effortlessly guiding her about the turns required to negotiate the end of the room, Dominic waited until they were once more precessing up the length of the ballroom before smiling down into her large eyes. "I have invited Bella and Arthur to spend Christmas at Candlewick. It is my earnest hope you will join us."

Wise in the ways of his Georgiana, Dominic watched her thoughts in her eyes. He waited until the desire to accept his invitation had been overcome by her instinctive fears, and a reluctant refusal was about to leave her lips, before allowing a pained expression to infuse his features. "Before you come to any hasty conclusion, I beg you will consider what a refusal would mean to me, my love."

His evident distress, the unacceptable endearment, combined with her own conflicting emotions, which he had skilfully invoked, left Georgiana's head in a whirl. "What…? Why, what on earth can you mean, my lord?" Her eyes widened. "What did you call me?"

He ignored her last question, and continued in despondent vein, "You must see that it really won't do."

Dizzy, Georgiana made a grab for sanity. She drew a deep breath. "My lord—"

"Dominic."

Georgiana blushed, and was further confounded by his lordship's rising brows and the words, "If I'm to go about calling you 'my love', it's only reasonable for you to use my Christian name."

Georgiana was so flustered that she could think of nothing to say.

"Now where were we?" mused his lordship. "Ah, yes! You were about to accept my invitation to spend Christmas at Candlewick."

Her resolve to flee to the safety of Ravello as soon as she possibly could was melting under the warmth in his sky-blue eyes. "But—"

"No buts," countered Dominic. "Just think of poor Arthur and myself, condemned to a mournful Christmas with Bella all mopey because you've gone off and left her in the dismals again." Glancing down into her sweet face, and seeing that desire was winning his battle, Dominic withheld the news of Bella's condition. He would keep that as an ace up his sleeve, in case of future need. "You couldn't possibly be so cruel."

The music ceased, and for one silent moment they stood, eyes locked. Then, suddenly frightened she would see the strength of his desire in his eyes and be alarmed, Dominic smiled and broke the contact. He raised one long finger to caress a golden curl that hung by her ear. The finger, with a will of its own, moved on to trace the curve of her jaw.

At his touch, Georgiana shivered, pure pleasure tingling along already overstretched nerves.

Dominic's eyes widened slightly. His gaze returned to her eyes, large and luminous under softly arching brows. Instinctively he sought to reassure her. "Besides," he said, his voice no more than a whisper, "there's no reason for you to run away."

Georgiana's tired brain accepted the statement, with all its layered meanings. She understood he knew she had no pressing need to return to Italy, but also, in her heart, heard his vow that she would have no cause to flee him.

"Say you'll come. I promise you Christmas at Candlewick will be everything you could wish." Dominic had not the slightest hesitation in making that vow. He had every intention of seeing it fulfilled.

Entranced, with his darkened eyes demanding only one answer, Georgiana found herself nodding.

A brilliant smile was her reward. Warmed through and through, she allowed him to settle her hand on his arm once more.

The other dancers were leaving the floor, heading for the supper-room. Dominic's appetite had no interest in food, and, from her pensive expression, his Georgiana was not in the mood for lobster patties either. With an imperious gesture he commandeered a footman and sent him on a search for two glasses of champagne.

With the foresight of a man accustomed to success in the field, he had already made arrangments to allow him to appropriate much of the rest of Georgiana's evening without raising any scandalised eyebrows. When the footman returned with their drinks, Dominic handed one to Georgiana and, taking the other himself, steered her away from the crowded supper-room towards the entrance to the ballroom.

With the fizz of champagne tickling her throat, Georgiana held her peace until it became clear he did indeed intend leading her out of the ballroom. Then she raised her face, her eyes meeting his in mute query.

Dominic smiled slowly, allowing just enough time for her to sense his thoughts and blush delightfully, before saying, "I thought you might like to see the Massingham art collection. It's quite impressive, and includes, I'm told, a number of your father's works."

It was, of course, the perfect ploy. Georgiana was all eagerness to view her father's protraits of the last generation of Massinghams. And no one would remark on their absence on such an errand, particularly not when Dominic had had the forethought to request permission from Lord Massingham to show his sister's protégée around the collection, dispersed about the gallery and the large library downstairs.

Delighted with their excursion, Georgiana relaxed entirely in the enjoyment of fine paintings, many of which she, with her tutored eye, could accurately place and appraise. To her surprise, Dominic proved to have a sound knowledge of the painters whose works were displayed. She eventually forced him to admit to an extended Grand Tour, which had included many of the galleries and great houses of Europe.

He did not press her to speak when they stood before one of her father's portraits, but stood back and perceptively left her to her musings.

After long moments of studying again the brush strokes she knew so well, Georgiana sighed and moved on, coming up again level with Dominic, smiling tremulously at his now serious face with its gently questioning look. She allowed him to take her hand. He raised it and, to her surprise, brushed it gently with his lips before returning it to its accustomed place on his sleeve. Strangely comforted, recognising her need only by its relief, Georgiana felt herself curiously but totally at ease by the side of this man who more normally reduced her to quivering mindlessness.

With no need for words, they descended the staircase

and crossed the chequered-tiled entrance hall to the library. The door stood open, glasses and a decanter on a tray bearing witness to the Massinghams' care for their guests, all of whom had apparently succumbed to the lure of the lobster patties. The room was empty. Ushering Georgiana in, Dominic quietly closed the door behind them.

The walls boasted two Tintorettos, a Watteau and one Hartley—a small protrait of one of the sons of the house. It hung between two sets of long windows. Dominic appropriated a three-armed candelabrum from a sidetable and placed it on the sofa table beneath the portrait.

Head on one side, Georgiana studied the small picture. Dominic watched her. The flickering candlelight gleamed on her golden tresses, striking highlights deep in the silken mass, like flames in molten ore. His fingers itched to tangle in those glorious curls, to see her golden eyes widen in surprise, then darken with delight. He could not see the expression in those bewitching eyes, but her lips, warmly tinted and full, were pursed in thought, pouting prettily, all but begging to be kissed. Desperately he sought for some distracting thought. If he continued in this vein, he would never be able to resist the temptation posed by the deserted room.

"It's one of his better works," said Georgiana. She smiled up at her companion, so still and silent beside her. His face was a polite mask, telling her nothing of his thoughts, but his eyes, so intensely blue that they seemed, in the weak light, to be almost black, sent skittering shivers along her sensitised nerves. She found herself wishing she had not donned the latest of Fancon's creations—a sheath of bronze satin which revealed rather more of her charms than she was presently comfortable with. She reminded herself to keep talking. "Papa always said that children were especially hard to do. Their features are so soft—almost unformed—that he claimed it was excessively easy to make them look vacuous."

Dominic, with no interest in anything save the flesh-and-blood woman beside him, asked, "Are there any portraits of you?"

Alerted by the rasping huskiness of his voice, Georgiana moved slightly, ostensibly to gaze out of the uncurtained window, thereby increasing the distance between them. "Of course," she replied, surprised at her even tone. "There are three at the villa in Ravello, and there was supposed to be one, done when I was very young, left in England."

If Georgiana had seen the smile which curved Dominic's lips as she stepped into the window embrasure, she might have recognised the unwisdom of the move. As it was, it was only when, after a moment's silence had further stretched her nerves to tingling awareness, he closed the distance between them, coming to stand behind her, that she realised she was effectively trapped, unable to retreat, her exit blocked by his large body. And he was so close that she dared not turn around.

Dominic's smile was devilish as he moved so that no more than an inch separated them. His hands came up to stroke her upper arms gently, where her ivory skin gleamed bare above her elbow-length gloves. He leant forward so that his lips were close by her ear, and whispered, "In that case, we'll have to make a special effort to locate these mysterious paintings." He grinned at the shiver that ran through her. "Perhaps, now that you own the Place, you should institute a search."

"Mmm-mmm," murmured Georgiana, her mind far from her father's missing paintings. He was so close! Through the thin satin gown, she could feel the radiant heat of him. His breath wafted the soft curls by her ear, sending all sorts of feelings skittering through her body. The caressing hands, drifting so gently over her skin, had ignited a funny warm glow deep inside her, quite unlike any sensation she had previously experienced. She decided she liked it.

Caught up in her novel discoveries, Georgiana was unaware of her instinctive movement, of leaning back against the hard chest at her back, letting her coiffed head rest against one broad shoulder, exposing the long column of her throat and a creamy expanse of shoulders and breasts to the blue gaze of the man behind her.

Dominic stopped breathing. This wasn't how he had planned it. Suddenly the rules of the game seemed to be shifting, leaving him confused, struggling to control a rampant desire which had somehow slipped its leash. His eyes flicked to hers, and found them half closed, heavy-lidded with the first stirrings of passion. Her lips, luscious and ripe, were slightly parted, her breathing swift and shallow. Full understanding of the effect he was having on her hit him with the force of a sledge-hammer.

A muffled groan escaped him, then, unable to resist, he bent his head and touched his lips to where the pulse beat strongly beneath the soft skin of her throat.

Georgiana stiffened at the intimacy, then, as his lips moved over her skin, warm and gentle, yet teasing, so teasing, promising more of the delicious delight, she relaxed fully against him, accepting and wanting to know more as the fires within her grew.

The click of the door-latch brought Dominic's head up.

"This place is nice and quiet. So much noise up there, can't hear yourself think!" The old Duke of Beuccleugh stumped into the room, accompanied by two equally ancient cronies. They headed across the room towards the deep armchairs by the hearth, but pulled up to stare at the couple engaged in rapt contemplation of the picture on the wall between the long windows.

"Very nice brush strokes, don't you agree?" said Viscount Alton, gesturing towards the painting.

Georgiana choked.

Dominic turned, as if just realising they were no longer alone.

The Duke peered at him, then recognition dawned. "Oh, it's you, Alton."

"Your grace." Dominic bowed.

"Admiring the view?" enquired the Duke, hard grey eyes glinting.

With an expression of bland innocence, Dominic explained, "Miss Hartley's father painted the portrait."

"Ah." His Grace's grey gaze switched to Georgiana, curtsying deeply. "Painter chappie, heh? Vaguely recall him, if m'memory don't serve me false." He nodded benignly at Georgiana, then recalled his purpose in the room. "Dancing's started again upstairs."

Dominic took the hint. "In that case, we should perhaps return." He turned to Georgiana and offered his arm. "Miss Hartley?"

Very correctly, Georgiana placed her hand on his sleeve and allowed him to escort her back to the ballroom. She was deeply shaken. Never would she have believed she would enjoy such a scandalous interlude. Yet she had not only enjoyed it; even now, with her eyes wide open, and no longer under his hypnotic spell, she was conscious of how deeply she resented the interruption that had brought a premature end to proceedings. Her concupiscence shocked her.

Unknown to Georgiana, her response had also shocked Dominic although, in his case, the feeling was purely pleasurable. On the stairs he recalled his as yet unfulfilled intention of making clear to the beautiful creature on his arm that he had, most definitely, known who she was at the masked ball the week before. Determined to be rid of this potential source of misunderstanding, he waited until they had reached the upper landing before stopping to glance down at a still flushed Georgiana. Unable to resist a knowing smile, drawing sparks from her huge hazel eyes, he chose what he thought was a simple but effective means of conveying his information. "I most heartily approve of that dress, my love," he said, his voice a sensuous murmur. "It will doubtless vie for prominence in my memory with that topaz silk creation you wore at the masked ball."

Georgiana blushed furiously, completely missing the implication in her thoroughly unnerved state. With an enormous effort, she gathered sufficient control to incline her head graciously and say, "I think perhaps we should return to the ballroom, my lord."

A deep chuckle answered her. "I'm sure you're right, my love. You've had quite enough adventure— for tonight."

There was a wealth of promise in his suggestive tone, none of which was lost on Georgiana. She willed her jittery nerves to compliance and, with the most serene expression she could muster firmly fixed on her face, allowed him to lead her back into the cacophony of the ballroom.

NOT UNTIL she was wrapped in the darkness of the Winsmere carriage on the long drive home from the Massinghams' did Georgiana allow her mind to dwell on the events of the evening. Even in the shielding gloom, she felt herself blush as she recalled those long moments in the library. How could she have been so... so positively *wanton?* Easily, came the damning reply. And now he knew. The thought made her shiver. Drawing her cloak more closely about her, she snuggled into its warmth, feeling the silk lining brush across her bare shoulders. These outrageously fashionable gowns of Fancon's hardly helped. Somehow, scantily clad in satin and silks, she was much more aware of a peculiar need to be held, to be stroked and caressed as she had been that evening. Repressing a little snort of derision, she told herself she could hardly claim it was the dresses which made her feel as she did. They simply made it easier to feel so...abandoned.

Jettisoning that unproductive line of thought, she blushed again as she remembered Dominic's rapid actions when the Duke and his friends had threatened discovery. She had sensed his suppressed laughter and had had to struggle to subdue her own, bubbling up in reply. It was odd, now she came to consider the matter, that she felt no sense of shame, only frustration.

Abruptly refocusing her thoughts once more, she tried to remember what he had said later, before they had gained the ballroom. Her mind promptly supplied the caress in his eyes as they had roamed appreciatively over her face and shoulders before he had complimented her on her gown. What had he said? Something about it being as pretty as her topaz silk.

The carriage jolted over a rut and she slipped sideways on the seat. She resettled herself in her corner, sightlessly watching the house fronts slip past the window.

Then her mind caught hold of the elusive memory, and his words replayed in her head. "It will doubtless vie for prominence in my memory with that topaz silk creation you wore at the masked ball."

Georgiana gasped.

"Georgie? Are you all right?"

Struggling to draw breath, Georgiana managed a reassuring phrase, then, feeling winded, curled up in her corner and gave her full attention to her staggering discovery.

He had known!

Which, as she had long ago worked out, meant… Her mind went completely blank, unable to accept the implication. Yet it was the only explanation possible.

Her heart beating in double time, a host of quivery, fluttery feelings crowding her chest, Georgiana forced her mind to grapple with the unthinkable. He had known, therefore he was… Oh, heavens!

THE NEXT THREE DAYS passed in a haze of happiness. Georgiana hardly dared to believe her deductions, yet, whenever she met Lord Alton, every word, every action, confirmed them. He was paying court to her. Her—little Georgiana Hartley!

Bella seemed quite unaware and, yielding to the

promptings of some sixth sense, Georgiana did not explain the source of her sudden elation to her friend. Bella had, certainly, noticed her glow. Uncharacteristically, she had yet to enquire its cause. But Georgiana was too much in alt to worry about such inconsistencies.

She had artfully managed to drop the information that Dominic had invited her to Candlewick for Christmas and she had accepted. Bella had feigned complete surprise, but Georgiana suspected she had known of her brother's intent. The subtle smugness in her smile suggested as much.

It was Lady Chadwick's gala tonight. She would see Dominic there, she was sure. They had yet to meet outside a ballroom, but it had only taken a moment or two to work out his strategy. Young and naïve as she was, even she knew any overt gesture on his part, any attention which could not be credited to a natural assistance to his sister's protégée, would make them the focus of the most intense speculation. She had no wish to figure in the latest *on dit,* and was grateful for his care of her reputation.

So she had to make do with the caress in his eyes every time they met, the gentle promise of his smile, the touch of his fingers on hers. It was nowhere near enough. She contented herself with the thoughts that, when the time was right, he would surely advance their courtship to the stage where the heady delights he had introduced her to in the library of Massingham House would once again be on their agenda.

Bella had retired to rest before the Chadwick gala. Georgiana had come to her room with a similar intention. But her thoughts denied her sleep. Restless, she jumped off the bed and paced the room in small, swirling steps, then broke into a waltz, spinning about as anticipation took hold. Whirling almost out of control, she did not see the door open, and cannoned into Cruickshank as she entered.

"Oh!" Georgiana put a hand to her whirling head. "Oh, Cruckers! What a start you gave me."

"I gave you?" said her dour maid, righting herself and shutting the door firmly. "Now, Miss Georgie, whatever's got into you? Whirling about like a heathen, indeed!"

Georgiana giggled, but made no other reply. She was in love, but she had no intention of letting anyone into the secret. Anyone other than Dominic.

Cruickshank sniffed. "Well, if you're so wide awake, I'll get your bath-water brought up. We may as well spend the time beautifying you."

Georgiana, thinking of the admiration she would see in a pair of bright blue eyes, gladly agreed.

THERE WAS NO supper waltz at the Chadwicks' gala. Dominic had, instead, claimed both the first and the last waltzes of the evening. Twirling down the long ballroom, under the glare of the chandeliers, Georgiana suddenly realised why it was he always chose a waltz. He was holding her far closer than was the norm. And, when she blushed, all he did was laugh softly and whisper, "As I cannot steal you away, my love, to a place where we might in safety pursue our mutual interest, you can hardly deny this lesser joy." The look that went with the words only made her blush more.

At the end of the dance, the last waltz of the evening, she was breathless and very nearly witless. Laughingly declining a most sensually worded invitation to take the air on the terrace—a highly dangerous undertaking, she had not a doubt—she whisked herself off to the withdrawing-room. A glass of cool water and a few moments of peace and quiet were all the restorative she needed. It would never do to let Bella see her return from a dance with her brother in such a state. There was, she felt sure, a limit to her friend's blindness.

When she entered, the withdrawing-room, a large bedchamber on the first floor, was empty of other guests. While she sipped the cool water an attentive maid brought her, Georgiana strolled to the long windows. The cool night air beckoned; Georgiana stepped out on to the small balcony. Behind her, the door of the withdrawing-room opened and shut, but she paid the newcomers no heed.

Not until the words, "Alton's such a cynical devil. D'you think he means marriage this time?" riveted her attention.

Slowly Georgiana turned to face the room. Standing still and silent in the shadows of the billowing draperies, she was concealed from the occupants, two matrons of considerable years and similar girth. They had dropped into two chairs and were busily fanning themselves while they considered the night's entertainment.

"Oh, I should think so," opined one, the fatter, pushing a wilting ostrich plume from over one eye. "After all, why else would he be dancing attendance as he is?"

"But she's hardly his sort," countered the other, resplendent in blue bombazine. "Just look at Elaine Changley. What I want to know is why an out-and-outer like Alton should suddenly succumb to a sweet young thing whose charms can't possibly compare to those he's become accustomed to."

"But haven't you heard?" The fat matron leaned closer to her companion and lowered her voice in conspiratorial fashion. "It's her land he's after." She sat back in her chair and nodded sagely. "Seems she's inherited a section of land Alton's been chasing for years."

"Oh. Well, that sounds more like it. Couldn't imagine what had come over him." The blue bombazine rustled and shuffled, then stood and stretched. "Come on, Fanny. If we don't get back soon, that boy of yours will catch something you'll wish he hadn't."

Frozen, her senses suspended, Georgiana remained on the balcony while the two ladies fussed over the frills on the gowns before departing for the ballroom.

The Place. Georgiana wished she had never heard of it. And, of course, the words rang all too true. According to Bella, it was an obsession of her brother's. Georgiana's heart turned to ice, a solid chilled lump in her breast. Slowly, hardly aware of what she was doing, she came back into the room, pausing to place the glass she was carrying on a side-table.

Then she looked up and caught sight of herself in the mirror above the dressing-table. Huge haunted eyes stared back at her, stunned and distressed. She couldn't go back to the ballroom looking like that.

Drawing a deep breath, Georgiana shook herself, then straightened her shoulders and blinked several times. Pride was not much comfort, but it was all she had left. Determined to think no more about what she had heard until she had the privacy to indulge her tears, she left the room.

Once back in the crowded ballroom, misery hovered, threatening to engulf Georgiana if she relaxed her superhuman effort to ignore the matrons' words.

She had to survive the rest of the gala. But Bella, seeing the stricken look in her friend's eyes, was immediately concerned.

"No, Georgie! We'll leave right now. There's no reason at all we need stay for the rest of this boring party."

With a determined frown, Bella silenced Georgiana's protests, and, within minutes, they were ensconced in the carriage and on their way to Green Street.

Bella yawned. "One thing about leaving just that little bit early—you can always get your carriage straight away." She stretched and settled herself. "Now, what's the matter?"

But Georgiana had had time to get herself in hand. She had anticipated the question and strove to deflect Bella's interest. "Nothing specific. It's just that I seem to have developed a migraine. I find it hard to go on once it comes on."

"Oh, you poor thing!" exclaimed Bella. "You just lie back quietly. As soon as we're home, I'll get Cruick-shank to brew a tisane for you. I won't speak to you any further. Now try to rest."

Grateful for Bella's silence, Georgiana sank into her corner of the seat and gave herself up to her chaotic thoughts. After several minutes of totally pointless rec-ollection, she forced herself to view the facts calmly. First of these was the relationship she knew existed between Lord Alton and Lady Changley. There was no doubt it was real—not just from the gossip, but from the evidence of her own eyes, on the terrace that fateful night. The memory of the passionate kiss Lord Alton had bestowed on Lady Changley was imprinted indel-ibly on her mind. He had never kissed her—let alone with such ardour. She recalled her early conviction that his attitude to her was merely that of helpful friendship, giving what assistance he could to his sister in her efforts to find a husband for her protégée. And his behaviour at the masked ball? Well, she had always thought he had not known who the lady in the topaz silk was. When had he told her he knew? Only a few days ago, long after he had learned of her inheritance. He could easily have found out what she had worn to the ball—from Bella if no one else. And then, too, Bella's ready acceptance of her sudden happiness could be easily explained if her friend knew her brother was paying court to her.

Georgiana stifled a sob. A few hours ago her world had looked rosy indeed. Now all her hopes lay in ashes about her. She had thought he was different, blessed with all the virtues, strong and steady and protective.. Now it seemed he was no different from the rest. His love for her was superficial, assumed, of no great depth, called forth only by her possession of the Place. His main interest in life was status and wealth, with all the trappings. Why, he was not much better than Charles. And Bella thought nothing of Dominic's marrying her to gain title to the land. In all probability, he planned to keep Lady Changley as his mistress, even after they were married.

Georgiana tried to whip up her anger, her disdain. She must despise him, now she knew of his plans. But, as the miles rolled by, a cold certainty crept into her heart. She loved him far too much to despise him. Surely love wasn't meant to hurt so much?

Disillusioned on every front, she huddled into her corner and wept.

CHAPTER NINE

A SLEEPLESS NIGHT filled with hours of crying was no remedy for Georgiana's ailment. Bella took one look at her in the morning and insisted she spend the day in bed. Georgiana was in no mood to argue. But she winced at Bella's last words, floating in her wake as, having insisted on tucking her in, she tiptoed out of her bedroom. "For don't forget, we've the Mortons' ball tonight, and that's one event we can't miss."

Georgiana closed her eyes and let misery flow in. But she knew Bella's reasons for attending the ball, the Mortons being old family friends, and knew she could not avoid going. She had revised her opinion of Bella's part in her brother's schemes. No one who was as kind as Bella could possibly be party to such cold-blooded manipulation. And there was Arthur, too. Try as she might, it was impossible to cast Bella's husband in the light of a hard-hearted character who would idly watch while a young girl was cajoled into a loveless marriage. No. Neither Bella nor Arthur knew of Dominic's schemes. Not that that made life all that much easier, for she could hardly ask them for advice on such a matter. Still, she was glad she had at least two friends she could count true.

The evening came all too soon. Under the combined ministrations of Cruickshank and the redoubtable Hills, supervised by Bella herself, the ravages of her imaginary migraine were repaired until only her lacklustre eyes and her pallid complexion remained as witness to her inner turmoil.

Those items were sufficient, however, to immediately draw Dominic's attention to her distress. As was his habit, he gravitated to her side immediately she appeared in the ballroom.

"Georgiana?" Dominic bowed slightly over her hand, his eyes searching her face.

Flustered and weak, Georgiana retrieved her hand immediately, not daring to meet his intent gaze. Her heart was thudding uncomfortably, bruised and aching.

Dominic frowned. "My dear…"

At his tone, desperation flooded Georgiana. She raised her head, but still could not meet his eyes. "I'm afraid, my lord, that my dance card is full."

The silence on her left was complete. She had just entered the ballroom—he must know she was lying.

Dominic felt his face drain of expression. His jaw hardened. The impulse to call her bluff was strong. Then he noticed again her pallor, and the brittle tension in her slim frame, and swallowed his anger.

Stiffly, he bowed. With a cold, "My dear," he forced himself to walk away.

Dominic spent the first two dances watching Georgiana from the side of the room, unsure of his feelings, unsure, for what seemed like the first time in his life, of what to do. What the hell was going on? Then, finding himself the object of more than a few curious glances, he took himself off to the card-room.

He was rapidly inveigled into playing a few hands, but his mind was not on the game, and no one demurred when he left the table and returned to drift idly about the ballroom, keeping an unobtrusive eye on Georgiana. He had been careful enough for their association to have passed for mere acquaintance. If he displayed too overt an interest now, it would be tantamount to a declaration. But the impulse to cross the floor and haul her out on to the terrace and demand an explanation for her extraordinary conduct grew.

If she had betrayed the slightest hint of partiality for any other gentleman, he would have done it, and the consequences be damned. Luckily, she seemed unusually subdued, dancing only with those he knew she deemed her friends, refusing all others.

Slowly, his mind calmed and he started to sort through the possibilities in a more methodical fashion. At the Chadwicks' gala, all had been well, until after their last dance. She had gone off to the withdrawing-room, and he, careful of appearances, had gone to make one in the card-room. When he had returned to the ball-room, he had found the Winsmere party had decamped. That had not surprised him at the time, knowing Bella's condition. But perhaps there had been some other reason for their early departure.

Useless to speculate, when he had no idea what might have occurred. But between that last waltz and this evening, something had happened to destroy the carefully nurtured bond between himself and Georgiana.

Feeling very like hitting someone, but having no idea whom, Dominic scowled and strode out on to the balcony. The cool air brought some relief to his fevered brain. This was ridiculous. He was thirty-two, for heaven's sake! The effect Georgiana's withdrawal was having on him was both novel and highly unnerving.

He didn't like it. And he'd be damned if he'd endure it for a minute longer than necessary.

Drawing a deep breath, he frowned direfully at the young couple who, giggling softly, came up out of the secluded garden. Surprised to find him there, arms folded and looking so grim, they fled back to the ballroom. Dominic sighed. If he did not have to be so circumspect, he could have taken Georgiana into the garden and made delicious love to her—

Abruptly he cut off the thought. Right now, it seemed as if she wasn't even speaking to him.

He would have to find out what was upsetting her. From the few comments he had exchanged with his sister, Bella clearly had no idea what had happened— she still had no idea of his interest in Georgiana. He needed to see Georgiana alone. For several moments, he pondered various schemes for attaining this end, finally settling on the one which, although it would not allow the fiction of the avuncular nature of his interest to stand, had the best chance of success.

With his decision made, he left the terrace to lay the necessary groundwork to put his plan into action.

GEORGIANA had no idea how she survived the Mortons' ball. It remained, long afterwards, a dull ache in her memory. She was glad, she kept telling herself, that Lord Alton had accepted her dismissal so readily. It would have been too much to bear if he had insisted she speak with him. Perhaps he had realised she had come to understand his motives and would not be the easy conquest he had expected. Hopefully, he would stay away from her now. Depressed and weary, she slept the sleep of exhaustion, and awoke the next morning, refreshed at least in body, if not in spirit.

Despondent, she trailed into the breakfast-room.

"Georgie! Are you feeling better this morning?"

Bella's solicitude brought Georgiana to her senses. She had no right to wallow in misery and act like a raincloud over her friend. Summoning a wan smile, Georgiana nodded. "Yes. I'm fine."

Bella's face suggested she did not look fine, but, instead of harping on the subject, Bella started chattering about the events that would fill the next week and bring the Little Season to an end. Georgiana listened with half an ear.

As Bella's catalogue ran its course, Georgiana realised she could not just up and flee to Italy tomorrow, much as she might wish to. She had made a bargain with Arthur, who had stood her friend when she had been in need. She could not shrug off her indebtedness. So she would have to see out the rest of the Season with what interest she could muster, trying not to dampen Bella's enjoyment with her own unhappiness.

She apparently returned sufficiently accurate, if monosyllabic, responses to Bella's opinions, for they rose from the breakfast-table in perfect amity.

"Oh, Georgie! I nearly forgot. Dominic noticed you looked a bit peaked last night, so he's coming to take you for a drive this afternoon."

Bella had preceded Georgiana through the door, so did not see the effect her announcement had on her friend.

"It's really a great honour, you know. I can't even remember the last lady Dominic took up for a drive in the park. He doesn't normally do so—says it's too boring. You must wear your new carriage dress; it'll be just the thing."

Reaching the parlour, Bella turned expectantly.

Georgiana had had enough time to school her features to a weak smile. "I really don't know if—"

"Oh, nonsense!" said Bella, dismissing whatever megrim Georgiana had taken into her head. "Some fresh air is just what you need to blow the cobwebs away."

Sinking on to the window seat and taking up her embroidery frame, Georgiana could not think of any reasonable excuse to decline Lord Alton's invitation. At least, not without explaining a great deal more of the situation to Bella. And that she was definitely not up to doing. Quite clearly, Bella was still in the dark regarding the state of affairs between her brother and her protégée.

Throughout the day, Georgiana formulated and discarded a string of plans to avoid the afternoon drive. In the end, her schemes became so wildly far-fetched that her sense of humour came to her rescue. What on earth did she imagine he'd do to her in the sanctity of the park? Besides, she knew him too well to believe he'd do anything scandalous—at least, not with her. She spent a moment in dim regret over that point, then determinedly stiffened her spine. She would go with him and hope to impress on him that she did not wish to see him again. Perhaps, with one major effort, she could avoid having to live with the dread of dancing with him at every evening entertainment, of being held in his arms, with his blue gaze warming her.

With a despairing sigh, she went upstairs to change.

Cruickshank was waiting with the carriage dress laid

out. Having seen the sudden change in her mistress, and having more than a suspicion of the cause, Cruick-shank fretted and snorted over every pleat in the elegant brown velvet dress with its snug-fitting jacket. Georgiana, knowing she could hide little from her maid's sharp eyes, was thankful to escape her chamber without a lecture. As she descended the curving staircase, the villager hat she had chosen dangling by its ribbons from one hand, Georgiana imagined such a scene, and what Cruickshank might actually say. The possibilities brought a smile to her face, the first for the day.

A sudden tingling brought her head up. Her eyes met blue—bright blue. Lord Alton was standing in the hall below, Bella by his side, watching her. For an instant she froze. Then, drawing what courage she could from knowing she looked as well as might be, Georgiana descended to the hall and placed her hand in his, curtsying demurely.

He raised her and carried her hand to his lips, and there was no doubt of the warmth in his gaze. Georgiana blushed vividly; her heart fluttered wildly. She had forgotten how devastatingly charming he could be.

She turned to Bella, who remained rooted to the spot, an arrested look on an otherwise blank face. But before Georgiana could make any comment, Dominic said, "We'll be back in about an hour, Bella." And, with a nod for his sister, he firmly escorted Georgiana outside.

Handed into a curricle of the very latest design, Georgiana quickly tied her hat over her curls. The breeze was brisk, stirring the manes of the two black horses stamping and sidling between the shafts. A small tiger held their heads. Dominic climbed up beside her and, with a flick of the reins, they were off, the tiger scrambling for his perch behind.

As he threaded his team through the traffic, Dominic realised that his supposedly straightforward plan to have an hour's quiet conversation with his love had already run off the tracks. For a start, there were no horses which could be described as docile in his stables. Until the present, this had not proved a problem. The pair he had unthinkingly requested be harnessed to the curricle were Welsh thoroughbreds, perfectly capable of stomping on anyone or anything they took exception to. And they had not been out for days and would willingly run a hundred miles if he would just drop his hands and give them their heads. Stifling a sigh, he gave them his undivided attention.

Once the park gates were reached, he set the horses to a trot, letting them stretch their legs at least that much. They tossed their heads impatiently, but eventually responded to the firm hand on the reins and accepted their lot. Only then did he turn to view his second hurdle. What on earth had possessed her to wear that hat? He knew perfectly well that the outfit she wore—the very latest in carriage wear—should have been completed by a tight-fitting cloche, perhaps with a small feather or cockade on the brim. The temptation to tell her as much burned his tongue, but he left the words unsaid. At the moment, he did not think a demonstration of his familiarity with feminine apparel was likely to further his cause.

"Someone is waving to you."

Dominic looked about and returned the salutation, ignoring the invitation to draw up his carriage by Lady Molesworth's barouche.

Georgiana's fingers were clutching her reticule so tightly that she could feel the thin metal brim twisting. She wished he would say something, or that she could think of a safe topic to discuss. Finally, sheer desperation drove her to say, "I believe the weather is turning more cold…" only to hear her voice clash with his.

They both fell silent.

Dominic glanced down at the top of her hat and grimaced. Without being able to see her face, he felt he was groping in the dark. He dropped his voice to a softer tone. "Georgiana, my dear, what's wrong?"

His experience with his sister, on top of his extensive expertise in related spheres, enabled him to get the tone just right, so that Georgiana felt that if he said another word in such a gentle way she would burst into tears in the middle of the park and shame them both. She waved her small hands in distress. "My lord… Please…" She had no idea what to say. Her mind wouldn't function, and her senses, traitorous things, were too much occupied with manifestations of his presence other than his conversation. "There's nothing wrong," she eventually managed in a very small voice.

Swallowing his frustration, Dominic wondered just what he had expected to achieve with a question like that in the middle of the park. He should have guessed that whatever it was that had upset her would prove too distressing to discuss reasonably in such surroundings. The situation wanted improving, and he would get rid of that hat, too.

Without the least effort, he instituted a conversation on recent events, none of which could be construed as in any way disturbing. Gradually, he won a response from Georgiana.

Grateful for his understanding, and believing the worst was behind her, Georgiana set about recovering her composure, and her wits, eventually contributing her half of the conversation. As they bowled along, the horses' hoofs scattering the autumn leaves, the breeze whisked past her cheeks, bringing crisp colour to hide her pallor. Bella had been right: fresh air was just what she needed. By the time they had completed their first circuit, she was chattering animatedly when, to her surprise, the curricle headed for the gates. They had been out for less than half an hour. "Where are we going?"

"Back to Green Street," came the uncompromising reply. "I want to talk to you."

The ride back to Winsmere House was, not surprisingly, accomplished in silence. Georgiana stole one glance up at Dominic's face, but, as usual, his features told her nothing.

The curricle swayed to a halt. Before she could attempt to climb down, he was there, lifting her effortlessly to the pavement. Breathless, she stood for one moment within the circle of his arms and dared to look up into his face. "There's really no need—"

"There's every need." Dominic's face remained shuttered. His hand at her elbow drew her up the steps.

Georgiana, trembling inwardly with an odd mixture of exhilaration and sheer terror, drew a deep breath and swung to face him. "My lord—"

"Ah, Johnson."

Georgiana turned to find the door open and Bella's butler bowing deferentially. The next instant she was in the hall.

"We'll use the drawing-room, I think."

Borne inexorably over the threshold, Georgiana

gave up all hope of avoiding the coming interview and crossed the room, her fingers fumbling with the ribbons of her hat.

Dominic shut the door and watched with relief as she cast the offending headgear aside. He moved to a side-table and stripped off his driving gloves, dropping them on the polished surface.

"Now—"

The door opened.

"There you are!" Bella came tripping over the threshold, big eyes bright.

Georgiana looked on her with undisguised relief.

Dominic looked on her with undisguised irritation. "Go away, Bella."

Brought up short, Bella turned to stare at him. "Go away? But whatever—?"

"Bella!" The dire warning in his voice was enough to send Bella about and start her for the door. Then she remembered she was in her own house and no longer needed to heed her brother's orders. She stopped, but before she could turn again a large hand in the small of her back propelled her out of the room.

The drawing-room door shut with a sharp click. Stunned, totally bewildered, Bella turned to stare at its uninformative panels.

Inside, Dominic turned to find Georgiana regarding him with distinct trepidation. Wondering how long his patience was going to last, he crossed the room and took her hands in his, covering her cold fingers with his warm ones. "Don't look at me like that. I'm not going to eat you."

Georgiana smiled weakly.

"But you are going to tell me what's wrong."

Glancing wildly up at him, eyes wide, Georgiana drew breath to reiterate that there was nothing wrong, when she caught his sceptical look and fell silent.

"Precisely." Dominic nodded sternly. "I'm not addle-pated enough to swallow any tale you might concoct, so the truth, if you please."

Standing there, her hands warm in his, the temptation to cast herself on his broad chest and sob out all her woes was dreadfully strong. In desperation, Georgiana sought for some way out, some tale he would accept for her not seeing him again. But another upward glance under her lashes convinced her the task was hopeless.

"It's… It's just that our…our association has become sufficiently marked that people might start talking and…" Her voice trailed away altogether.

She looked up to find an oddly amused expression on Dominic's face.

He smiled. "Actually, our association has, until today, been sufficiently well hidden. However, I dare say they will start talking now."

Distracted, Georgiana frowned. "You mean after our drive in the park?"

Still amused, Dominic nodded. "That. And tonight." At Georgiana's puzzled look, he explained, "It's the Rigdons' ball. And as from now, I'm going to be so very attentive to you that even the blindest of the gossips will know my intentions."

"Your intentions?" Georgiana's voice had risen strangely.

Dominic regarded her with some slight annoyance. "My intentions," he repeated. After a moment he sighed and went on, "I know I haven't proposed, but surely, Georgiana, you are not so scatter-brained you don't know I'm in love with you and intend asking you to marry me?"

Georgiana stared at him. Of course she knew he intended to marry her. But that he loved her? No, she knew that wasn't right. Gently, she tried to ease her hands from his, but he would not allow it.

Dominic frowned. "Georgiana, love, what is the matter?"

Becoming more nervous by the minute, Georgiana shook her head, not daring to look up at him. "I can't marry you, my lord." There, she had said it.

"Whyever not?"

The calm question took her breath away. Inwardly Georgiana groaned. She closed her eyes and wished herself anywhere but where she was. Yet when she opened them again, a pair of large, well formed hands were still clasped firmly around hers. She risked a glance upwards. He was calmly waiting for an answer. Nothing in his face or stance suggested he would let her go without one.

Dominic stood silently and hoped she would hurry up. The effort of keeping his hands on hers, rather than sweeping her into his arms and kissing away whatever ridiculous notions she had taken into her head, was draining his resolution. In the end, he repeated his question. "Why can't you marry me?"

Georgiana drew a deep breath, closed her eyes, and said quite clearly, "Because you're in love with Lady Changley and were planning to marry her."

Sheer surprise kept Dominic immobile and slackened his hold on her fingers.

Instantly Georgiana whisked away and, on a broken sob, rushed from the room.

Even after the door closed behind her, Dominic made no move to follow her. How on earth had she come to that marvellous conclusion? How on earth had she learned of Elaine Changley? Feeling remarkably sane for a man who had just had his first ever proposal thrown in his face, before he had uttered it, Dominic strolled to the sofa and sat down, the better to examine his love's strange ideas.

Within a minute a subtle smile was curving his lips. Another minute saw him chuckling. So that was what all this fuss was about. His ex-mistress. It really was absurd. Undoubtedly Elaine would be thrilled if she ever knew she was the cause of such difficulties. And Julian Ellsmere would laugh himself into stitches if he ever heard. He spent a moment wondering which busybody had told Georgiana of Elaine Changley, then dismissed the subject from his mind. There were any number of loose tongues about town.

Standing, Dominic stretched, then relaxed. He would just have to arrange to explain to his love the subtle difference between what a gentleman felt for the woman he made his mistress and the emotions he felt for the woman he would make his wife. It was, as it happened, a point he was supremely well qualified to expound. His smile broadened. He had told her he would see her at the Rigdons' that night. As he recalled, Rigdon House had a most intriguing conservatory, tucked away in a corner of the mansion, unknown to most guests. The perfect place. As for the opportunity, there would be no difficulty arranging that.

Strolling to the door, relieved of his strange burden of not knowing what had gone wrong, Dominic felt on top of the world. Then, out of the blue, two phrases, heard at widely differing times, coalesced in his mind. He froze. Georgiana's secret love was a man she had met during her earliest days in London who she believed was in love with and about to marry another woman. He had searched her acquaintance to no avail—there was no such man. Now she had just admitted that she thought *he* was in love with and had been about to marry Lady Changley. *Ha!*

Dominic's smile as he left Winsmere House could have warmed the world.

IT WAS WITH a strange mixture of trepidation and relief that Georgiana entered the Rigdon House ballroom. She had initially felt devastated and drained after her interview with Lord Alton, but a peaceful hour in her bedchamber had convinced her that it was all for the best. At least he now knew she would not accept an offer from him and why. She told herself her problems were over. Yet, deep down inside, she was far from sure he would accept her dismissal. And buried even deeper was the uncertainty of whether she really wanted him to.

She had not left her chamber until, arrayed for the evening, she had descended for dinner. Arthur's presence would, she had hoped, inhibit Bella's ability to question her closely about her brother's strange behaviour. As it transpired, Bella had evinced not the slightest degree of curiosity, even in the privacy of the carriage on the way to the ball. Dimly Georgiana wondered if Bella's brother often did such outrageous things.

After being presented to Lord Rigdon, whom she had not previously met, she and Bella drifted into the crowds of guests, chattering avidly while they waited for the dancing to begin.

Joining a circle of young ladies, many of whom she now knew, Georgiana went through the usual process of filling in her dance card, allocating the vital supper waltz to Lord Ellsmere. To her surprise, he also requested another waltz, earlier in the evening. She was puzzled, for he had rarely danced twice with her since she had refused his suit. Still, she numbered him among her most trusted cavaliers and gladly bestowed on him the first waltz of the night.

It was while she was circling the ballroom in Lord Ellsmere's arms that she first became aware of a change in her status. A number of dowagers sat on chairs lining the walls. From the direction of their sharp glances and the whisperings behind their fans, she realised with a jolt that she was the subject under discussion. A few minutes later, as the waltz ended and, on Lord Ellsmere's arm, she joined a small group of young people, she surprised a look of what could only be envy on the face of Lady Sabina Matchwick, one of the Season's *incomparables*.

Slowly, it dawned that, as Dominic had prophesised, people were beginning to talk. Finding Bella by her side, and momentarily alone, Georgiana could not help but ask, "Bella, tell me. Is it really so very unusual for your brother to drive a lady in the park?"

Bella's candid blue gaze found her face. "Yes. I told you. Dominic's never taken any lady driving before."

"Oh."

At her stricken face, Bella burst into a trill of laughter. Impulsively, she hugged Georgiana. "Oh, Georgie! I'm so happy!"

The approach of their partners for the next dance put an end to any confidences. Georgiana dipped through the cotillion and barely knew what she did. As dance followed dance, she realised the nods and smiles denoted not scandalised horror, but a sort of envious approval. Heavens! Just by taking her for a drive, Lord Alton had all but publicly declared himself. How on earth was she to rectify the mistaken impression? Then Georgiana reminded herself that in a few short days her Little Season would be over. And she would go back to Ravello and forget all about Lord Alton and his very blue eyes.

It was almost time for the supper waltz. Lord Ellsmere came to claim her. By some subtle manoeuvre, he separated her from her court and proceeded to stroll down the long room with her on his arm.

"My dear Georgiana, I do hope you won't forever hold it against me, but I've a confession to make."

Startled out of her abstraction, Georgiana stared at him. "Confession?" she echoed weakly. Oh, dear. Surely he was not going to start pressing her to marry him, too?

As if sensing her thoughts, he smiled at her. "No, no. Nothing to overset you. At least," he amended, frowning as if suddenly giving the matter due thought, "I hope it won't upset you."

Georgiana could stand no more. "My lord, I pray you'll unburden yourself of this horrendous secret."

He smiled again. "It's really quite simple. I engaged you for this waltz in proxy, as it were."

Her heart was beating an unnerving tattoo. "Who…?" Georgiana didn't bother finishing her question. She knew who. And as if to confirm her suspicions, she felt a familiar tingling sensation start along her nerves, spreading from the bare skin of her shoulders and neck in a southerly direction. No, Lord Alton had not accepted his dismissal.

"Ah, here he is."

With a smile and an elegant bow to her, Lord Ellsmere surrendered her to the suavely elegant gentleman who had come to stand beside her.

Georgiana felt her hand being raised and the warm pressure of his lips on her fingers.

"Georgiana?"

His husky tone rippled across her senses. Despite all her intentions, she could not prevent herself from looking up. And she was lost. His eyes caught hers and held her gaze effortlessly. Somewhere in her unconscious the subtle perfection of his attire registered, along with an appreciation of face, form and figure, all apparently designed with her own prejudices in view. But her conscious mind was only aware of the total mastery he exerted over her senses, the hypnotic tug which drew her, unresisting, into her arms. Before she knew it, they were waltzing.

With an effort, Georgiana managed to free enough wit to realise he was smiling at her in amused appreciation, quite certain of his conquest. Then, as her senses probed the ballroom about them, the enormity of his strategy hit her. They might have been waltzing amid a host of other couples, but every eye in the ballroom was on them. She blushed vividly.

This evidence of her sudden awareness drew a deep chuckle. "Don't worry. You look radiantly lovely. Just think what a handsome couple we make."

Georgiana tried to summon enough anger to glare at him, but her overwhelmed emotions were not up to it.

Dominic looked down at her, her golden eyes and

creamy skin, the glorious riot of her golden curls filling his vision. More than satisfied with her capitulation
thus far, he made a mental note to play on her senses
more often—a subtle torture, at present, but so very
rewarding.

The music drew to a close, Georgiana waited to be
released, but, instead of bowing and escorting her back
to Bella's side, Dominic simply tucked her hand into his
arm and walked out of the ballroom. Entirely unable to
resist, and with a sinking feeling that it would be singularly pointless to try, Georgiana found herself wandering
the corridors on Lord Alton's arm.

Suspecting that the amble had more purpose than was
apparent, Georgiana turned an enquiring gaze upwards,
to be met with a smile of quite dazzling effect.

"I thought, my love, that, given your apparent mis-
conception regarding my feelings towards you, we
should find a quiet spot where I might endeavour to
disabuse your mind of its strange notion."

Georgiana tried, really tried, to come up with some
suitable response, but not a coherent phrase came into
her head. At the end of the long corridor, Dominic
turned right, opening a glass-panelled door and ushering her through.

Vines and species of *ficus* grew out of large tubs artfully arranged to give the impression of a tropical forest.
Cyclamens provided bursts of exotic colour amid the
greenery. A small fountain played a lonely tune in the
middle of a circular tiled courtyard. Of other humans,
there was no sign.

With no real idea of what he meant to say, Georgiana
was caught between a desire to hear his words and a
conviction that it would be unwise to do so. But she was

given no choice in the matter as, smoothly compelling, Dominic led her to a rustic ironwork seat. At his nod, she sat, and he sat beside her, retaining possession of her hand and showing no inclination to release it.

Sensing her skittering nerves, Dominic smiled reassuringly and raised her fingers to his lips, placing a leisurely kiss on each rosy fingertip, his eyes all the while holding hers. He watched as her golden eyes widened and her breathing suspended, then started again, more shallowly and less evenly. Entirely satisfied, he grinned wickedly. "Now where were we, when you so abruptly left the room this afternoon? Ah, yes! You believe I'm in love with Lady Changley and was intending to marry her." He directed a look of patent enquiry at Georgiana, clearly seeking confirmation.

Trapped, in every way, Georgiana coloured.

Smiling again, Dominic continued, his voice light but perfectly serious. "I'm not, I'll have you know, in favour of the idea of a gentleman discussing his paramours with anyone, least of all with his intended bride. Young ladies are not supposed to be cognisant of the sorts of affairs women such as Lady Changley indulge in. However, as you have already heard of her, I'll admit we enjoyed a short liaison, which ended some weeks before I met you."

Dominic paused to allow the full implication of his words to sink in. Georgiana's attention was complete; she was hanging on every word, and he doubted not that she would remember what he said, even should she fail to immediately register its import.

Pensively he began to stroke her fingers with his thumb. "Like all rich and single peers, I am high on the list of prey for such as Lady Changley. She, unwisely, believed I was besotted enough to offer marriage. At no stage did I do so. You'll have to take my word for that, although you will notice no public charges for breach of promise have been levelled at me. That's because she knows no one would believe I would be so lost to all propriety as to offer to make her my Viscountess."

To Georgiana his words were every bit as intoxicating as the sensations produced by the insistent pressure of his thumb over the sensitive backs of her fingers. Then his eyes lost their far-away look and his gaze became intent, capturing her own as if to focus her entire being on him. Georgiana felt herself drowning in blue.

Without releasing her from his spell, deliberately, Dominic raised her hand to his lips, but this time turned it to press a warm kiss to her palm. He smiled at the marked shiver the caress produced, but his eyes were nevertheless perfectly serious as he said, "The feelings I have for you, my love, are far removed from the lust a man feels for his mistress, a fleeting emotion which dissipates, usually in months if not weeks. No man marries his mistress. No man falls in love with his mistress."

Georgiana could not have moved if the ceiling fell. She was mesmerised—by his voice, by his eyes, by him. Drawing a shuddering breath, she waited for what was to come, knowing she could not prevent him from saying the words, knowing that, once said, they would bind her, no matter how hard she struggled, tying her to him, not by his love, but by hers.

Dominic continued to devour her with his eyes, following her reactions. He waited until full awareness returned to her, then said, "What I feel for you is far removed from mere lust. I can hardly deny I know what that is and can readily define it. What I feel for you is not that. I fell in love with you the first moment I saw you, asleep in my armchair by the drawing-room hearth at Candlewick. You belong there." He paused, knowing that his next move was chancy, but, confident he had gauged her responses, and her temperament, accurately, he smoothly continued, "Regardless of what you may say, regardless of how many times you deny it, I know you love me in exactly the same way I love you."

His words, delivered in a low, deliberate, slightly husky tone, sent shivers up and down Georgiana's spine. He was right, of course, at least in defining her love. Oh, what temptation he posed! Still trapped in his gaze, she knew immediately his attention shifted. His eyes were now fixed on a golden ringlet hanging beside her face. One long finger came up to caress the soft curl, then moved on with tantalising slowness to outline the curve of one brow, then the length of her pert nose, and then traced, oh, so lightly, the full bow of her lips. The roaming finger slipped under her chin and tilted her face upwards. Georgiana's eyelids drooped. His lips touched hers in the gentlest of kisses.

When he drew back, she could barely cope with the sense of loss, could barely restrain herself from throwing her arms about his neck and behaving like a wanton. Again, she blushed rosily, not at his actions but at her thoughts.

Entirely satisfied with progress thus far, Dominic sat back and waited patiently until her breathing slowed, watching her through half-closed lids. When she had recovered sufficiently to glance at him once more, he took up his dissertation. "As you've realised, the rest of the *ton* are now *au fait* with my intentions. Our affairs are thus public knowledge, and should, given your age, proceed with all due circumspection."

He smiled, his eyes lighting with a certain devilment that awoke an answering spark in Georgiana. She found herself smiling back in genuine empathy.

"Thus, you will now be wooed in form. I will drive you in the park every afternoon, weather permitting. I will escort you to whichever evening functions it is your desire to attend. The *ton* will be edified by the sight of me at your pretty feet. Therefore, having attained that position, it will be no great difficulty to propose to you at the end of the Season."

Whereat you'll accept me. And thank God there's only a week of the Season to go! Dominic left his last thoughts unsaid, contenting himself with another warm smile. Dropping a last kiss on Georgiana's fingers, he rose.

"Come, my child. We should return you to the ball before the dowagers start having the vapours."

THE INTERLUDE in the conservatory disturbed Georgiana more than she had believed possible. She had never before been exposed to, let alone been called upon to withstand, anyone as compelling as Bella's brother. The magnetic force he wielded was of a magnitude that rendered mere reason impotent. Settled in her corner of the *chaise* on their way home from Rigdon House, she was conscious that the attractions of Ravello and freedom were dimming in the light of the flame Lord Alton was skilfully igniting.

That he meant to do it, she had not a doubt. Deliberate, calculated, he made no effort to hide his tactics.

He wanted the Place. In the darkness of the carriage, Georgiana shivered.

Their discussion had at least relieved her mind of one nagging, guilty worry. He did not and had never loved Lady Changley. Of that, she was certain. She could not decide whether it was the hint of humour that had coloured his voice when he had spoken of his mistress or the coldly unemotional way he had considered her machinations that had convinced her. But convinced she was. Lady Changley might or might not have believed he was in love with her. Whichever way it was, she was only another victim of his lordship's potent charm.

Unfortunately, all that did was prove he had the ability to make women fall deeply in love with him. It hardly proved that he loved her.

The more she considered the matter, the more she doubted the possibility. Why would such a handsome man, so eligible in every way, with all of the last ten years' débutantes to choose from—*incomparables* included—have decided to opt for her? Little Georgiana Hartley, whose head barely topped his shoulder, who knew next to nothing of the fashionable life of England, let alone the political side with which he was so intricately involved. Why had he picked her?

The Place. It was the only answer.

Miserable all over again, Georgiana lay sleepless for a long time after Cruickshank had snuffed her candles. In the dark, she wrestled with demons who all too often had bright blue eyes. He professed love, and she longed to believe him. Yet, when it came down to it, his actions belied his words. Admittedly she had been brought up in Italy, but she couldn't believe national boundaries changed human nature so very much. True love always brought desire in its wake, as was only right and proper. Yet the chaste kiss he had bestowed on her had held no hint of burning passion. And she knew that wasn't how he kissed a woman he desired.

Again and again, her thoughts brought her back to the same depressing conclusion. He was an expert in seduction; she was a novice. Her hand in marriage would secure the Place, so he had calmly set about capturing it. In the world of the *ton,* it would be considered a very fair exchange—her land for the position and wealth he could provide.

As the hours of the night gave way to a grey dawn, Georgiana considered for the first time whether she might be wise to listen to the promptings of her heart, to accept the proposal he had told her was coming, even knowing that her love wasn't shared. She knew he would always treat her well—with respect and affection, if not with the love she craved. She would fill the position of his wife, be able to care for him, bear his children.

A vision of Candlewick swam before her, and she spent some time imagining what might be. But she could not place him in the picture beside her. Instead, he appeared as a nebulous figure, arriving in the dead of night, leaving with the dawn.

With a sob, Georgiana buried her face in her pillow. No. It was impossible. If she couldn't have his love, the rest was meaningless. She would leave for Ravello as soon as the Season ended.

CHAPTER TEN

"HUMPH!"

The loud snort brought Georgiana awake with a start. Cruickshank stood by the bed.

"You'd better wake up and take a look at these."

With a grim look, Cruickshank drew back the bed curtains. The window drapes had already been opened, letting weak morning sunshine bathe the room. For an instant Georgiana stared uncomprehendingly at her maid, then her attention was drawn to the door. It opened to admit a young girl, one of the parlour maids, all but concealed behind a huge stand of cream roses.

The girl peeked at Georgiana around the delicate blooms, then, with a giggle, crossed to deposit the vase on a table by the window.

To Georgiana's astonishment, her place in the doorway was immediately taken by another maid, similarly burdened. When a third maid entered, with yet more cream roses, Georgiana put her hands to her hot cheeks. Cream roses in October!

Hundreds of cream roses.

By the time the procession of maids had transferred all the blooms delivered to the house by the florist's that morning to her bedroom, Georgiana was speechless. She sat and stared. The sheer outrageous extravagance of the gesture numbed her. About her, the delicate perfume of the flowers took hold, flavouring the air with their subtle enchantment.

She needed no card to tell her who had sent them.

At the Rigdons' ball, he had vowed to woo her formally. His public courtship had started that night, when he had returned her to Bella's side but remained possessively beside her, discouraging all her partners but those he approved of simply by being there. The next day he had swooped down on her morning and taken her driving to Richmond, later producing a picnic hamper for lunch and taking her to the Star and Garter for tea. It was impossible to stand firm against the invitation of his smile. He would accept no denials. Powerless to prevent his whirlwind courtship, she had, unwillingly, reluctantly, been swept along, mesmerised by the blue of his eyes. The following evening she had seen the effects of his strategy. As far as the *ton* was concerned, only the ceremony was required to establish her as the Viscountess Alton.

In the four days that had followed, each filled with unsought joy and a hidden despair, he had succeeded in convincing everyone that theirs would be a marriage made in heaven, until it seemed to Georgiana that only she guessed the truth.

Her moods fluctuated wildly, from ecstatic pleasure when he was with her, to blackest despair when he was not. She was counting the days to the end of the Season, to when Bella and Arthur departed for Candlewick and she could flee to Ravello and safety. She had even tried to sound Arthur out on the possibility of leaving before then. But he had looked at her blankly, seeming not to understand her oblique reference. Incapable of being more explicit, she had been forced to let the matter drop.

Cream roses surrounded her. Her consciousness was filled with him to the exclusion of all else. Georgiana sighed.

Only Cruickshank remained in the room, fussing over laying out her clothes, sharp eyes stealing covert glances, trying to assess her reaction.

Shaking free of despondency, Georgiana slipped out of bed. Cruickshank held up a blue morning dress for her approval. Through narrowed eyes, Georgiana studied its clean lines. Then, abruptly, she shook her head. "No, Cruckers. The new green velvet, please."

Cruickshank's eyebrows rose comically, but she made no comment beyond the predictable snort.

Stripping off her nightgown, Georgiana washed her face and donned her soft muslin undergarments while Cruickshank brought out the latest of her purchases from Fancon. If her association with Lord Alton had taught her anything, it was to value the added confidence appearing before him in new and fashionably elegant gowns gave her. Besides, in a few days' time, she would no longer have the pleasure of appearing before him at all. Despite the heaviness of her heart, weighed down by unrequited love, she was determined to live these last few days as fully as she could, to store away the bittersweet memories to warm the long winter days, and nights, in Ravello.

THE EAST WIND was chilly. Grey clouds scudded low across the tops of the trees, skeletal fingers emerging to trap them as the summer cloaks were stripped, leaf by leaf, away. Everywhere summer was in decline, giving way to the gusts of autumn, chill harbingers of year's end.

Perched on the box seat of Viscount Alton's curricle, Georgiana was immune from the cold. Refusing to face her bleak future, she revelled in the warmth of the moment. Her wind-whipped cheeks glowed and her eyes, when she managed to wrench them free of his lordship's steady gaze, sparkled with life and love. She had left her inhibitions in Green Street and was happy.

Beside her, Dominic was host to a range of emotions, some of which were both novel and, to one of his experience, distinctly disturbing. That he loved Georgiana Hartley, in the complete fullness of the term, he no longer doubted. But that she could invoke in him the full gamut of desire, to the point where his mind became prey to salacious imaginings, was not something he had expected. She was a young, innocent, inexperienced, green girl. A golden angel. Yet, no matter how many accurate adjectives he heaped about her name, nothing detracted from the sensual spell she cast over him. She was learning quickly. But she had no idea, he felt sure, of the risks she courted. His well honed skills, all but automatic, were in danger of carrying them away.

There were few people in the park. The cold weather had kept most of the fashionable indoors. They completed one circuit, then went about again, content to prolong their time in such unaccustomed seclusion. Few words were exchanged. Their eyes spoke, and that was enough.

When the gates hove a second time into view, Dominic acknowledged the passing hours and headed his team for the street. His gaze flicked to Georgiana's face, catching her wide-eyed hazel stare, and he knew she had enjoyed their time together as much as he had. In that instant, he made his decision.

He had postponed asking her to marry him, wanting his courtship of her to be a recognised fact before any announcement. Quick betrothals between men such as he and sweet delights such as she had a way of being remembered and whispered about. He wanted no breath of a question to touch her.

But there were only two more days of the Season to go. And there was no doubt of their state. And no reason at all to procrastinate.

As the park gates fell behind, Georgiana was conscious of the day closing in, of a dimming of her joy. For the past hour she had been happy. It was so easy to forget, to imagine instead how things might have been. But always reality eventually intruded, reminding her of the real reason for his interest in her.

By the time Green Street was reached and he lifted her down she was thoroughly depressed once more. He escorted her indoors, and she inwardly shrank at the coming meeting with Bella. Her hostess, to whom she owed so much, was *aux anges* at the prospect of having her for a sister-in-law.

She was shaken out of her dismal thoughts by the words, "The drawing-room, I think, Johnson. You needn't inform your mistress that we've returned."

Before her weary mind had time to do more than register that quite improper order, Dominic had deftly ushered her into the drawing-room and shut the door.

Suddenly conscious of the desirability of putting as much space as possible between them, Georgiana quickly crossed the room. Her heartbeat, which had slowed somewhat since they had left the park, picked up its tempo.

From his stance just inside the door, Dominic viewed her impetuous movement, which had about it the air of flight, and frowned. Then, when he saw the agitated flutter of her small hands, clasping and unclasping before her, a slow smile erased the stern look. She was nervous, no more. A strange rapport existed between them. So she sensed his intention and, true to her age and innocence, was disturbed. His features softened. He crossed to stand beside her.

"Georgiana, my love…"

A small gesture silenced him. Georgiana could stand the strain no more. "Dominic, please," she whispered, infusing every particle of persuasion she could into her tones.

After the briefest of pauses, she continued, "My lord, I am most sensible of the honour you do me, but I cannot marry you."

Dominic suppressed the instinctive retort that he hadn't yet had a chance to ask her and, to his surprise, found himself fascinated, rather than furious. "Why?"

Despite her highly strung state, Georgiana spared a moment to curse silently the incredible evenness in temper that could yield such a mild response. If truth be known, she would infinitely have preferred a more melodramatic reaction. That, she would have known how to deal with. Instead, his deceptively simple question was anything but easy to answer.

In fact, as the minutes stretched, she realised she couldn't answer it at all. In growing panic, she shook her head, dropping her gaze to her nervously clenching fingers.

Dominic sighed. "Georgiana, my love, I should perhaps inform you that I am not one of the school which holds it right and proper that a young lady should refuse her chosen suitor at least three or four times before accepting him, so as not to appear too eager." He waited to see what effect that had, and was not entirely surprised to see her ringlets dance a decided negative.

Allowing silence, so often his ally, to stretch still further, Dominic, close behind her, watched her growing agitation, and chose his moment to murmur, "Sweetheart, I've not got infinite patience."

The gentle tone of his voice cloaked the steel of the words. Georgiana did not miss the implication of either. Her nerves singed by his nearness, she abruptly took a step away, then turned to face him. She had to make him understand the futility of his enterprise.

"My lord, I...must make it plain to you. I will not marry you."

Dominic wasn't really listening. She had not answered his question, which, in itself, was answer enough. He was not in the mood to listen to missish denials, not when her eyes were so soft and her lips, gently parted, just begged to be kissed.

Seeking to impress on him the inevitability of her refusal, Georgiana allowed her eyes to meet his. And, as had happened so often before, in the warm blue of his gaze, she felt their wills collide and hers melt away. Mesmerised, she could barely breathe as he moved closer, one long finger rising to trace the curve of her cheek, stopping at the corner of her mouth. Unable to move, she watched as his eyes fixed on her lips. Unconsciously, her tongue slipped between them to run its moist pink tip along their suddenly dry contours. He smiled. Then, tantalisingly slowly, his head drew nearer, his lips hungry for hers.

As her eyelids drooped, panic seized Georgiana. In desperation, she put her small hands up before her and met the wall of his chest. She turned her head away. She felt him hesitate. In that instant she seized the tattered remnants of her sanity and, on a choked sob, fled the room.

In utter disbelief, Dominic watched her go. As the door shut behind her he uttered one comprehensive oath and, thrusting his hands deep in his breeches pockets, swung about to glare at the window.

After a moment he glanced around, half expecting the door to open and for her to return. When nothing happened, he muttered irritably and ostensibly gave his attention to a minute inspection of Bella's lace draperies. What the devil did Miss Georgiana Hartley think she was playing at? What the devil did she think *he* was playing at?

When the ticking of the mantelpiece clock made it plain any hope of Georgiana's return was forlorn, Dominic let his head fall back. Scowling at the ceiling, he vented his disapproval in one sharp and pungent phrase, then strode purposefully to the door, his face like granite.

Johnson, unperturbed and imperturbable, met him in the hall.

"Dominic!"

In the act of shrugging on his greatcoat, Dominic swung to meet his brother-in-law's sharp gaze.

Arthur stood in the library doorway. Now he took a

step back in clear invitation. "I've some information you might find of interest. If you can spare the time…?"

Even from across the hall Dominic could sense the amusement in the older man's voice. He knew Arthur understood his intentions towards Georgiana. And approved of them. With another shrug, he divested himself once more of his coat and, leaving the heavy garment in Johnson's hands, strolled with as much nonchalance as he could muster past his brother-in-law and into the library.

A delighted chuckle was his reward.

Elegantly disposing his limbs in one of the heavily padded leather chairs, Dominic raised eyes limpid with enquiry to Arthur's face.

Sinking into the chair behind his heavy desk, Arthur met the cool blue glaze with one of unalloyed amusement. "You know, for a man of such vast experience, you're being singularly obtuse in your present campaign."

Dominic's black brows rose haughtily. "Oh?"

"From Georgiana's loss of composure and your own black looks, I assume you've offered for her and been rejected."

From narrowed eyes, Dominic surveyed his brother-in-law. They had always got on well. In truth, there was no one he trusted more. So he dropped his reserve and answered with a languid air, "If you must know, I haven't as yet proposed. I have, however, been refused. Twice."

With an effort that was obvious, Arthur swallowed his laughter. Finally, when he was sure he could command his voice, he said, "Well, that's hardly surprising."

The blue eyes watching him narrowed again. After

a pregnant pause Dominic murmured, "Arthur, if you weren't who you are, I rather think I'd take exception to that comment."

Far from being cowed, Arthur only smiled. "I didn't think you'd seen it."

A world-weary expression of dutifully waiting to be informed of what "it" was infused Dominic's countenance.

"Why, the Place, of course."

"The Place?" echoed Dominic, bewildered.

"The Place," repeated Arthur. "You know, it's that little piece of land you've spent half of the last ten years trying to buy."

"But…" Dominic stopped. It came as a shock to realise that desire for the Place, an obsession nursed and fed for years, had simply been forgotten, displaced, rendered unimportant by his desire for Georgiana. In fact he hadn't thought of the Place with a view to gaining possession for weeks. Not since he had met Georgiana. He frowned.

Arthur sat back and watched his friend's face as the pieces fell into place. It wasn't hard to work out the probabilities once the facts had been pointed out. And, despite Dominic's reputation with the ladies, Arthur, remembering the euphoric daydream that had possessed his own sharp wits in the days he had wooed Bella, found nothing odd in the notion that his brother-in-law had completely mislaid his obsession in the whirl of recent weeks.

Eventually Dominic's features relaxed slightly and he glanced up to meet Arthur's grey gaze. "So she thinks I'm marrying her to get my hands on the Place." It was a statement, not a question.

Arthur shrugged. "It's hardly an uncommon event, for men to marry for property. And I doubt she has any idea of the relative value of the Place and your own estates. But I'd go bail Bella's edified her with the tale of your desire for the land." He paused, but Dominic was frowning at the inkstand on the desk. "Has she given you any other reason for her refusal?"

Without looking up, Dominic shook his head slowly. "Not this time. The reason for her first refusal was quite different." He glanced up with a wry grin. "She'd heard the stories of Elaine Changley and had convinced herself I was in love with Elaine."

"And only wanted to marry her for her dowry?"

Dominic looked struck. "She didn't actually say so," he mused, "but I suppose that must have been in her mind. I didn't think further than disabusing her of the idea that I'd ever been truly enamoured of or considered marrying Elaine Changley."

Arthur said nothing.

Then Dominic shook his head. "No, it won't fit. I started paying court to her at the Hattringhams' ball, before any of us knew she owned the Place."

"The masked ball?" said Arthur, tapping one finger against his lips. "I assume she knew you knew who she was, that night."

Dominic shifted in his chair. "No. But I told her I did know later."

"How later?"

Exasperated, Dominic frowned at his brother-in-law. "At the Massinghams' rout."

"*After* our little visit to Lincoln's Inn."

With a long drawn sigh of frustration, Dominic stretched and crossed his arms behind his head. "You're right." He considered the inkstand again. Then he said, as if talking to himself, "So I'll just have to remove that little obstacle from my path."

Perfectly satisfied with the effects of his interference, Arthur leant back in his chair and watched as his brother-in-law planned his next moves. Finally Dominic looked up.

"There are only two more days left to the Season. How long do you plan to remain in Green Street?"

Arthur smiled. "For as long as it takes you to settle this business."

A quick smile lit Dominic's face. "You are coming to Candlewick, aren't you?"

Arthur nodded. "I've already sent instructions for Jonathon and his nurse to travel direct to Candlewick. The weather's closing in and, as you know, I'm not one to take chances. They should be there by now. I'd thought to send Bella down as soon as she's free of her social activities. Mrs Landy can fuss over her more effectively than anyone else. I'll go to the Lodge and check through business there, then come across before Christmas."

To all this, Dominic nodded. "It'll take a day or two to deal with the Place. But once I've cleared that hurdle from my path, I don't expect any further impediment to our affairs." He paused, then added with a slightly grim smile, "I would be obliged if you would inform Miss Hartley that I have some…pressing business to attend to, but will call on her in two days' time to continue our discussion of her future." He considered his words, then shrugged and rose. "With luck, I'll be able to escort both Bella and Georgiana down a few days after that."

"Good," said Arthur. "The news from the country is

that there'll be early snows. I'd feel happier once Bella's safely installed at Candlewick." He watched as Dominic crossed to the door, waiting until his fingers were on the handle to say, "By the by, do let me know if you feel the need for any further assistance in this matter."

Dominic smiled sweetly. "My friend, I've often thought it was a good thing for England that you were born an Englishman. God only knows what might have happened if Napoleon and his generals had had you as a quartermaster."

Arthur laughed.

With a neat bow, Dominic left, closing the door softly behind him.

TO GEORGIANA'S dismay, relief was not her predominant emotion on waking the next morning to no extravagant gifts, no note requesting her company on a drive, nothing. She sighed. She told herself sternly it was how she wanted things to be. He had at last accepted the fact she would not marry him.

Feeling at one with the gloomy morning, close and grey with drizzle, she dressed without interest and wended her way downstairs, wondering what she could do to fill in the bleak hours.

But she had barely left the breakfast-table to join Bella in the back parlour when Johnson came to summon her.

"A legal gentleman, miss. Name of Whitworth."

Brows rising, Georgiana stood and laid aside her embroidery. "In the drawing-room, Johnson?"

The butler bowed and escorted her to where Mr Whitworth the elder waited patiently, his bright eyes darting curiously about the white and gilt room.

As soon as he had bowed to her, Georgiana waved him to a chair. He looked alarmed when it creaked protestingly under his weight. But Georgiana was too puzzled to waste any time reassuring him. She hadn't sent for him. Why was he here?

Apparently agreeing his presence required immediate explanation, Mr Whitworth made haste to answer her unvoiced query. "My dear Miss Hartley, forgive my calling on you unheralded, but we have received a very generous offer for the Place. The buyer is most urgent to settle, so I took the liberty of calling in person."

Georgiana's immediate reaction was of immense relief. She would be rid of her albatross of an inheritance. If it hadn't been for the Place, she would not now be subject to the most deadening melancholy. And she would certainly never want to return there, as close as it was to Candlewick. But, hard on the heels of relief, came a swift understanding of what it would mean to Dominic—no! Lord Alton—if she sold the Place to another. A sharp stab of empathy brought an impulsive denial to her lips. But she bit the words back and forced herself to consider more carefully.

Dominic wanted the Place…wanted it so badly that he would even marry to get it. But, although she loved him, he didn't love her. She would not, could not, allow him to sacrifice either himself or her to the misery of a one-sided marriage. But she could give him what he wanted.

Mr Whitworth stirred uneasily, then cleared his throat.

Before he could launch into one of his long-winded discourses, Georgiana held up a small hand, commanding silence.

Only a moment's thought was required to convince her Dominic would not accept the Place as a gift from her. But there was nothing to stop her offering to sell it to him. He had tried to buy it from Charles, after all.

"What were the conditions offered by this buyer? And who is he?"

Mr Whitworth was only too happy to answer Georgiana's first question, naming a sum which meant nothing to her, but which, he assured her ponderously, was, "Very generous. Exceedingly so!"

After a moment, he went on, "But the thing that moved me to come here in this manner, my dear Miss Hartley, is that the buyer wishes an answer by this afternoon."

"This afternoon?" echoed Georgiana. She looked at her solicitor. His excited urgency was apparent in the way he almost bobbed in his chair. "Surely, that's rather unusual?"

Mr Whitworth pursed his lips, and she feared she was about to be told every case of rapid sale he had ever heard of, chapter and verse. But instead his breath came out in a little whoosh. "Well, yes," he admitted. "But whoever has that sort of money to throw down can generally call the tune."

"Who is this buyer?"

"Ah," said Mr Whitworth, eyeing her uneasily. "That's another thing. The man who contacted us is an agent, and he won't reveal the name of his principal."

So she could be selling to anyone. Georgiana made up her mind. "I wish to consult with my friends on this matter. I will undertake to send my answer to you this afternoon."

She rose, in a fever to get on with her latest impulsive start.

As if only too keen for her to put the wheels into motion, Mr Whitworth rose too, and rolled forward to take her hand. "Certainly, Miss Hartley. My brother and I will hold ourselves in readiness to act on your behalf as soon as you have communicated your wishes to us."

With that solemn promise, he bowed low and took his leave.

For some moments Georgiana stood, head bowed, eyes on the patterned rug. Then, resolutely straightening her spine, she crossed the room to the small escritoire. Seating herself before it, she pulled forward a pristine sheet of paper and, after examing the nib carefully, dipped it determinedly into the standish. This wasn't going to be easy, but there really was no alternative.

GEORGIANA'S missive brought Dominic to Green Street at noon. As her note had contained little beyond a summons, he used the time while Johnson went in search of her to pace the drawing-room, pondering the possibilities. Avoiding the little tables Bella seemed to have a peculiar penchant for strewing about her rooms, Dominic had arrived for the third time by the fireplace when he heard the door open.

Entering as calmly as she could, Georgiana wished for the tenth time that morning that she did not have to face Dominic—Lord Alton!—over this particular matter. The very thought of the Place rubbed a sore spot in her heart, aggravating its already fragile condition. Thoughts of Lord Alton brought even more pain. But she was determined to go through with it. Unconscious of the worried frown that marred her smooth brow, she pressed her hands together to still their trembling, only to find herself forced, by his outstretched hand, to surrender one into his clasp.

"My lord." Her greeting was little better than a whisper. Pulling herself together with an effort, Georgiana raised her head to look into his eyes, steeling herself for the battle to meet his gaze and remain lucid. To her relief, she found it easier than she had anticipated. He was looking at her with undisguised concern.

"Georgiana, my dear, what's the matter?"

And suddenly it was easy to tell him.

"I've received an offer for the Place. A mystery buyer." She paused, temporarily distracted by the sudden intentness in his gaze, and promptly lost her thread. Luckily her rehearsed phrases came to her rescue. "I remembered how keen you were to buy the property from Charles. I wondered if you still wished to purchase it."

Dominic watched as, gently withdrawing her hand from his, Georgiana subsided into one corner of the sofa, lilac skirts softly sighing, and fixed him with her candid hazel gaze. Outwardly he smiled, warmly, comfortingly. Inwardly he wondered where it was that he had left his usual facility for managing such *affaires de coeur*. He had certainly misplaced it. Ever since Georgiana Hartley had magically appeared in his life, his touch had deserted him. He had told his agent to purchase the Place without revealing his name, purely to spare her any undue embarrassment. Instead, having once again failed to predict her reactions to the events he caused to happen, he had forced her to face the very object he was endeavouring to remove from the relationship.

Capturing her eyes with his, he smiled again. "I'm afraid, my dear, I've a confession to make." He could see from her eyes that she had jumped to the right conclusion, but he confirmed it. "I'm the mystery buyer."

"Oh."

Georgiana's eyes fell. She felt decidedly deflated.

Acutely sensitive where she was concerned, Dominic moved to take her hands in his, and drew her to her feet before him. In his present mood he would not trust himself on the sofa beside her. Standing this close to her, holding her hands so he would not sweep her into his arms, was bad enough, feeling as he did. He looked down on her golden head, bent so he could not see her eyes.

"Georgiana?"

But she would not look up. Her eyes seemed to be fixed on her hands, clasped lightly in his. So, with the patience of one who knew all the moves, Dominic slowly raised her hands, first one, then the other, to his lips. Inevitably, her eyes followed...and were trapped when they met his. He smiled, incapable of entirely hiding his triumph. "Sweetheart, do you know why I want to buy the Place?"

With an effort Georgiana tore her gaze from those fascinating eyes. That blue gaze held untold power over her, giving tantalising glimpses of emotions she did not understand but of which she longed to learn more. But she was returning to Ravello. Forcing a tight smile to her lips, she nodded. "Yes. Bella explained."

"I sincerely doubt Bella could explain." He smiled as she turned to him, hope and uncertainty warring in her big eyes. "Oh, I know Bella told you I've always wanted the Place, to return Candlewick to completeness.

That has, in the past, been something of an obsession with me. Recently that obsession has been eclipsed by a far greater desire. It had, in fact, completely slipped my mind. Until…" Dominic paused, then decided to leave Arthur out of his explanation. "Until I realised you might misconstrue my interest in you for an interest in your property."

If the matter hadn't been so intensely important, so vitally crucial to him, he would have been amused by the sheer intensity of her concentration. Her huge hazel eyes glowed with hope, tinged with disbelief. He had expected that and did not let it worry him. He would convince her he loved her if it was the last thing he did in life. Despite his firm intentions, he felt himself drowning in her honey-gold gaze, felt the inevitable effect of her nearness start to test his restraint.

"My love, I want to buy the Place so it can no longer stand as a point of confusion between us." Dominic dropped a kiss on her knuckles and decided he had better get out of the room with all speed. If he didn't, she would be in his arms and he had no idea where it would end. "If you agree, send a message to Whitworth and he'll settle it with my man of business." He paused, looking deep into the darkened centres of her wide eyes. Smiling, he released one of her hands, carrying the other to his lips in a parting salute. "Once the sale is finalised, I'll call on you and we can discuss our…mutual interest further."

His look dared her to deny him, but Georgiana was too dazed to do anything but stare.

With a gentle chuckle, Dominic lifted a finger to her cheek in a fleeting caress, then bowed elegantly and left her.

CHAPTER ELEVEN

THE SHARP CRACK as the wax seal broke beneath Dominic's long fingers echoed hollowly in the library of Alton House. Outside, Grosvenor Square lay somnolent under a blanket of fog. The weather had turned with a vengeance, and all who could were making hurried preparations to quit the capital before the roads became impassable. Hurriedly scanning his agent's letter, Dominic put it aside and spread the folded parchment the packet had contained. In the warmth and comfort of his library, in the glow of expensive wax candles, Dominic stared at the title-deed of the Place, which he had longed to hold for so long. It was his. Candlewick was whole once more.

Conscious of a mild elation on that score, Dominic grinned wryly. Far stronger was the relief that now Georgiana could have no more doubts of his love for her, no more excuses to deny his suit.

His eyes narrowed. The recollection that he had on more than one occasion underestimated her ability to misread his intentions surfaced. For some reason, she seemed unable to believe he truly loved her. Incomprehensible though that was, it would be unwise to ignore that particular foible. First his ex-mistress, then the Place—what would the next obstacle in this particular course be?

Unbidden, laughter bubbled up. He had never had the slightest trouble making offers before, although admittedly for less exalted positions. However, to date, his particular concern had always been to ensure the women involved never imagined him to be in love with them. He had never had to convince a woman of his love before. And here he was, getting his feet in a tangle at every step, no doubt providing Arthur with untold amusement. All in all, wooing an angel was proving the very devil of a task.

With a self-deprecatory smile, he put the title-deed in the top drawer of his desk, locking it with a small key from his watch chain.

There was only one way forward. His mind refused to entertain the thought of any outcome bar success. He did not doubt he would win her in the end. It was his patience he doubted. Still, at least this time he was forewarned. And if, instead, she fell into his arms without raising any more quibbles, he would be doubly grateful.

Imagining how he would express his gratitude to his beloved, he settled his shoulders more comfortably against the leather and fixed his gaze on the ceiling. A smile of anticipation curved his lips.

Ten minutes later his reverie was interrupted by sounds of altercation in his hall. The library door flew open.

Bella entered. Timms followed close behind, trying to retrieve the bonnet she still wore.

"Dominic! Thank God you're here! You'll have to do something. I never imagined she'd do anything so rash!" Succeeding in tugging her bonnet strings free, she paused only to hand her headgear to Timms before impetuously throwing herself at her brother, who had risen and come forward to meet her. Her small hands grasped his arms. "You must go after her!"

"Yes, of course," Dominic replied, gently detaching her before turning her towards the *chaise*. "And I undoubtedly shall, as soon as you have calmed sufficiently to tell me where and why."

His calm, deliberate tones had the desired effect. Bella plumped down on the *chaise* with relief, her bearing losing the frenetic tenseness of a moment before.

"It's just so unexpected. I had no inkling she might do such a thing."

Dominic forced himself to take the seat facing his sister, reminding himself that any attempt to drag stories out of Bella faster than she was prepared to tell them inevitably took longer than allowing her to proceed at her own pace. Relieved to see her colour improving, and assuming from her words that Georgiana was not in any mortal danger, he contented himself with a bland, "What's happened?"

"I didn't know anything about it until I came downstairs half an hour ago. We were at the Ranleighs' last night—such a crowd! The rooms were so stuffy, I was quite worn out, so I slept late." Bella opened her reticule, hunting through its contents. "I found this on the breakfast-table."

Dominic took the single sheet of delicately tinted paper and smoothed it out. As he scanned its contents, his jaw hardened. Undoubtedly, it was past time someone took Georgiana Hartley in hand. The note blithely informed Bella that its writer had decided to ask the tenants of her father's London property whether they had any idea where his missing pictures might be. As she had ascertained that the house was located in Jermyn Street, she did not imagine she would be away long.

"She told me that when she wrote to Mr Whitworth to instruct him to sell the Place she remembered to ask about the London house. Johnson says she received a letter this morning."

"Jermyn Street!" Dominic stood and paced the room, incapable of remaining still. The words, Doesn't she know better? rang in his brain, but he didn't utter them—he knew the answer. There were times when Georgiana Hartley was too much the impulsive inno- cent for her own good. Over the past ten or more years, Jermyn Street had become the popular address for the well-heeled bachelors of the *ton,* which number included a disproportionate percentage of the most dangerous rakes and roués in England. His gaze returned to Bella's anxious face. "Do you have any idea of the number?"

Bella blushed. Under cover of fossicking in her reti- cule once more, she explained, "In the circumstances, I thought I should see if I could find the letter from the Whitworths. It was on her dresser." She looked up to hand the plain white envelope to her brother.

Dominic received it with undisguised relief and a fleeting smile for Bella's notions of propriety. "Good girl." Then he was reading the fine legal script. "Sev- enteen. Who lives at 17 Jermyn Street?"

Bella shook her head, her gaze on her brother's face. He was clearly going through his acquaintance. Then she saw his expression drain.

"Good God!"

Bella paled. "Who is it?"

"Harry Edgcombe."

"Oh, dear." Bella's wide blue gaze had not left her

brother's face. Recognising from uncomfortable experience the emotions flaring in his eyes, she suddenly wondered whether she would have done better by Georgiana to have tried to find Arthur, instead of flying to Dominic.

Abruptly Dominic headed for the door. "Wait here until I get back."

Seriously alarmed now, Bella half rose. "Don't you think I should come, too?"

Dominic paused, hand on the door-handle. "It would be best if this was done with as little fuss as possible. I'll bring her back here."

And with that grim promise he was gone, leaving Bella with nothing to do but sink back on the *chaise*, wondering if Georgiana was strong enough to weather both Harry Edgcombe's advances *and* Dominic's temper.

DOMINIC DIDN'T bother with his carriage. As the hackney he'd hired pulled up outside 17 Jermyn Street, he reflected that the anonymity of the hack was an added advantage, distinctly preferable to his carriage with his liveried coachman. Instructing the driver to wait for him, he ascended the three steps to the polished oak door and beat a resounding tattoo. Heaven help Harry if he'd gone too far.

The door was opened by a very correct gentleman's gentleman. Recognising the Viscount, he smiled politely. "I'm afraid his lordship is currently engaged, m'lord."

"I know that. I'm here to disengage him."

And with that the astonished retainer was set firmly aside. Dominic closed the door behind him. His gaze swept the hallway and found Cruickshank, seated in a stiff-backed chair in the shadows. Surprised, she came to her feet.

"Where's your mistress?"

Trained to respond to the voice of authority, Cruickshank immediately bobbed a curtsy. "In the drawing-room, m'lord." With a nod, she indicated the door opposite her chair.

Stripping off his gloves and handing them, together with his cane, to Lord Edgcombe's bemused valet, Dominic said, "I suggest you return to Winsmere House. I will be taking your mistress to meet Lady Winsmere. I would imagine they'll return home in a few hours. Should Lord Winsmere enquire, you may inform him they're in my charge."

Bright blue eyes met faded blue. Cruickshank hesitated, then bobbed again in acquiescence. "Very good, m'lord."

With Lord Edgcombe's valet distracted by Cruickshank's departure, Dominic strolled forward and, after a fractional hesitation, opened the drawing-room door.

The sight which met his eyes would have made him laugh if he hadn't been so angry. Georgiana was seated in a chair by the hearth and had clearly been listening with her customary intentness to one of Harry's tales. He was leaning against the mantelpiece, negligently attired in a green smoking jacket, his pose calculated to impress the viewer with his particular brand of assured arrogance. Despite himself, Dominic's lips twitched. The door shut behind him with a sharp click. Both fair heads turned his way.

While most of his attention was centred on Georgiana, Dominic did not miss the relief which showed fleetingly in Harry's eyes. Relieved in turn of its most urgent worry, his mind went on to register the expression in Georgiana's hazel gaze. Total innocence. Then, as he watched, she blushed deliciously and, flustered, looked away.

Inwardly, Dominic smiled. He did not make the mistake of imagining her sudden consciousness was due to delayed guilt on being discovered in such a compromising situation. Oh, no—*he* was the cause of Georgiana's blushes, not Harry. Which fact compensated at least in part for his agony of the past ten minutes.

An interested spectator to Georgiana's reaction, Harry pushed away from the mantelpiece, a smile of real mirth lighting his face. "Ah, Dominic. I wondered how long you'd be."

Acknowledging this greeting, and the information it contained, by shaking Harry's offered hand, Dominic turned to find Georgiana rising to her feet.

"I had no idea… I wasn't expecting…"

"Me to arrive so soon?" suggested Dominic. He advanced upon his love, capturing one delicate hand and raising it to his lips. "I finished my business rather earlier than I had hoped. I take it you've finished yours?"

Georgiana was completely bemused. The last person she had thought to meet this afternoon was Lord Alton. And none of his words, nor Lord Edgcombe's, seemed to make any sense. Entirely at sea, she simply stared into his lordship's blue eyes, traitorously hoping he would take charge.

"No sign of these paintings, I'm afraid," put in Lord Edgcombe, shaking his head. He added in explanation to Dominic, "Moscombe has been with me since

I moved here, and he insists the place was completely empty. Even the attics."

Dominic nodded, and tucked Georgiana's hand into its accustomed place in the crook of his arm. "It was a long shot. Still," he added, blue eyes intent on Harry, "no harm done."

Harry's eyes widened in mock alarm. "None in the least, I assure you." Then a gleam of wicked amusement lit his grey eyes. "Mind you, it did occur to me that Miss Hartley might like to view my art collection."

Dominic's black brows rose. "Your etchings, perhaps?"

Harry grinned. "Just so."

"Etchings?" queried Georgiana.

"Never mind!" said Dominic in the voice of a man goaded. He gazed down into wide hazel eyes and wished they were in his drawing-room rather than Harry's. "Come," he added in gentler tones. "I'll return you to Bella."

Walking beside him to the door, Georgiana struggled to free enough of her mind from its preoccupation with Lord Alton to make sense of what was going on. Emerging into the hall, she looked about for Cruickshank.

"I've sent your maid on." Dominic was beside her, holding her coat.

"Oh," said Georgiana, suddenly aware of a disturbing glint in his lordship's blue eyes. Did that mean she would be travelling in a closed carriage alone with him?

Settling Georgiana's coat over her shoulders, Dominic cast a sharp glance at their host, standing genially beside them. "Harry…?"

Lord Edgcombe's grey eyes met his over Georgiana's head. A slight frown and a shake of the head was all the immediate response Harry made as Georgiana turned to thank him for his trouble. He charmingly disclaimed all effort, bowing with easy grace over her hand. As he straightened, his eyes intercepted Dominic's blue gaze.

"Not a word, I assure you." The grey eyes glinted, amusement in their depths. "You have my heartfelt thanks. Can you doubt it? Any word from me would cook my own goose, after all."

Reassured but puzzled, Dominic raised his brows in question.

Harry grinned and waved an airy hand. "M'sisters are a mite pressed at the moment, it seems. Can you imagine their joy if they learned of—er—what so recently transpired? Why, it would spell the end to my distinguished career." He fixed Dominic with a winning smile. "No, no, m'lad. Rather you than me."

Walking towards the door ahead of the two men, Georgiana, no longer subject to Viscount Alton's mesmerising gaze, tried to follow the gist of their conversation, to no avail. When she turned in the doorway to bid Lord Edgcombe goodbye, it was to see both men cordially shaking hands. Piqued, feeling that something was going on literally over her head, Georgiana tilted her chin a fraction higher and coolly responded to Lord Edgcombe's farewell.

Turning to the street, she majestically descended the steps, but had barely gained the pavement before Lord Alton's long fingers grasped her elbow. A spurt of anger urged her to shake off his hand, but the memory of that odd glint she had seen in his eye undermined her confidence. Before she had time to do more than register the fact that it was into a hackney rather than one of his own carriages he was helping her, she was inside. He followed her, taking the seat beside her. Immediately the driver whistled up his horse and they moved off.

Georgiana strove to quiet her nerves, aquiver with an unnameable emotion. She kept her eyes on the streetscape while she tried to make sense of events. Why had he come to fetch her? Bella? Impulsively, she turned.

"Is Bella all right?"

His face was a mask. At her question, one black brow rose. "As far as I am aware." After a moment he added, "She's waiting at Alton House."

Alerted by the chilled crispness of his tone, Georgiana eyed him warily. "Did she send you for me?"

Suddenly noticing the tension in his long frame, Georgiana tensed too. But his calmly enunciated, "Yes. She sent me," gave her no clue to the cause of what she suspected was his displeasure.

Irritated by his odd behaviour, Georgiana frowned and asked, "Why?"

"Because, having learned that you had taken yourself off to visit a house in Jermyn Street, which, to one who knows London, means almost certainly to call on a bachelor alone, she needed someone to rescue you."

"But I didn't need rescuing," declared Georgiana, turning to face him more fully. "There was nothing the least wrong."

At his strangled laugh she flushed and went on, "I admit it was a relief to find it was Lord Edgcombe who lives there, but that just made it easier. And I made sure I took Cruickshank with me so I wasn't alone."

"When I entered the house, Cruickshank was in the

hall and you were most definitely alone with Harry."
With an effort, Dominic kept his voice even.

Flushing at the censure in his tone, Georgiana swung
her gaze to the street. "Yes, but there wasn't… I was in
no danger of…" Georgiana broke off. Now she thought
it over, she was no longer so sure she hadn't been in
danger. There had been a rather disquieting gleam in
Lord Edgcombe's grey eyes when she had first arrived.
However, the more they had talked, the more she had
become convinced he was merely slightly nervous over
something. Maybe she had misread the signs. Still, he
had done nothing to deserve Lord Alton's suspicions.
"Lord Edgcombe was most truly the gentleman."

"I would imagine Harry would always act the gentleman he undoubtedly is," Dominic retorted, asperity
colouring his words. "But that doesn't mean he isn't a
rake and a gamester, and therefore totally unsuitable as
private company for a young lady. Such as yourself."

There was no mistaking the anger in the clipped
words. Amazed, her own temper flying, Georgiana
turned an incredulous face to him. "But you're a rake
and a gamester, too. Why is it safe for me to be alone
with you but not with him?"

At her question Dominic closed his eyes in exasperation and thought determinedly about his old nurse, about
climbing trees at Candlewick—anything to shut out the
urge to sweep her on to his lap and kiss her witless.
Safe? She was pushing her luck.

Anger growing at his refusal to answer, Georgiana
continued, her long irritation with the oddities of English mores finding sudden outlet. "Why did you send
Cruckers away? Surely it's not acceptable for me to be
riding in a carriage alone with you?"

Forcibly keeping his eyes shut, Dominic answered, "The only reason it's acceptable for you to be alone with me is because we're soon to be married." He waited for her "Oh" of understanding. When no sound came, he slowly opened his eyes.

Georgiana was staring at him in total confusion.

Quickly Dominic closed his eyes. She was definitely not safe.

For long minutes Georgiana could do nothing but stare. But the fact that he had his eyes closed made it easier for her to think. He should have received the deed of the Place that morning. Dominic had said he would visit her once the sale was finalised, *to discuss their mutual interest*. She had no idea what he had meant by that. Now that he owned the Place, she could see no reason why he would still want to marry her.

In real perturbation, Georgiana stared at the handsome face, wishing she could read his motives in the even features. Then, like a beacon on a hill, she saw the light. He had gone too far, too publicly, to draw back now. And that old scandal, the one that had started his rakish career, hung like Damocles' sword, forcing him to offer for her or face the censure of the *ton*.

Which meant she would have to deny him again, one last time. And make it convincing.

She knew he did not love her, not as she understood love. He had shown no fiery passion, uttered no impassioned speeches nor indulged in any melodramatic gestures—all components of love as she knew it. The only time he had kissed her, it had been like a magic caress, so light that she could have dreamt it. But she was in love with him. And, because there seemed to be developing a strange conduit of communication between them, one that did not need words, or even gestures, a sensing that relied on something other than the physical, because of this, she would have to end it now. Or he would know.

And that would be even harder to bear.

Despite his wanting to marry her for her property, something she was honest enough to acknowledge was commonplace in his world, she had always felt safe with him. He had never intentionally done anything to cause her grief. If he ever learned she loved him—not gently, as a well bred young lady should, but to distraction—she doubted he would accept a denial of his suit. He would not cause her pain.

Could he be made to understand that loving him as she did, being married to him, knowing he did not love her in the same way, would cause her even greater pain that if she was never to see him again?

His eyes remained shut. Georgiana could not resist the temptation to study his face, memorising each detail, storing the vision in her heart to last her for a lifetime. She saw his eyelids flicker, then slowly rise. Ill prepared to meet his blue gaze, she straightened and turned slightly away, furiously blinking back the tears which suddenly threatened, pressing her hands tightly together to still their trembling.

Dominic took one look at his love, all but quivering with suppressed emotion, and his anger abruptly vanished.

"Georgiana?"

When she made no answer beyond a small wave of her hand, Dominic drew back, giving her the time she needed to compose herself, ruthlessly stilling the instinctive urge to wrap her in his arms and comfort her.

He didn't dare touch her. Frustrated beyond measure, he felt an insane desire to laugh, to catch her to him and kiss her worries, whatever they were, away. Her silence screamed the fact that she was still labouring under some delusion sufficient to make her balk at the very mention of marriage. Her forlorn countenance showed he had his work very much ahead of him.

His eyes on her guinea-gold curls, Dominic sighed. He wanted her, and he was tired of the roundabout the prescribed methods of courtship had put them on.

He waited until her breathing became less laboured, until the pulse at the base of her throat beat less tumultuously. Then he tried again. "Georgiana, my dear, what is it?"

Georgiana put up one small hand in a gesture he found both imperious and, in her present state, endearing.

"Please, my lord. You must let me speak." Her voice was low, urgent and breathless.

"Of course, my dear." Dominic managed a politely attentive tone. He made no move to take her hand, but continued to sit beside her, the flounce of her skirt brushing his boots, his head inclined to watch her face. She did not look up at him, but fixed her gaze on her clasped hands, tensed in her lap.

Georgiana drew a shuddering breath at his easy acquiescence. If only he would remain so calm, she might manage to accomplish her task. But he was near, so near. Speak—she had to speak or her resolution would crumble. "My lord, you must believe that I most earnestly value your friendship, and the...the proper feeling that lies behind your wish to marry me." She paused, reaching deep to dredge the remainder of her strength, before continuing, "I am aware—have always been aware—that my ownership of the Place was fundamental to your interest in me. Now that you own the Place, there is no reason for any further talk of marriage between us." Resolutely she swallowed the sob that rose in her throat and hurried on. "I realise that, if I were of the *ton* and chose to continue living in London, our association these past weeks might give rise to awkward conjecture. However, as I intend returning to Ravello shortly, I beg you will not let such considerations sway you."

Beside her, Dominic allowed his brows to rise. A smile, soft and gentle, curved his lips.

Georgiana drew a deep breath. "My lord, I hope you will see that, in the circumstances, there is no reason for you to offer for me. Indeed," she said, struggling to subdue her treacherous tears, "I beg you will not renew your offer."

"Of course not."

The calm words brought Georgiana up short. One moment she was about to dissolve in tears, the next she had turned and her eyes met his. "I beg your pardon?" she asked weakly.

Smiling sympathetically, Dominic said, "My dear, if my offering for you will cause you distress, then of course I'll not do it. I would never knowingly distress you."

The look which accompanied his words warmed Georgiana through and through, despite the total depression which now hung like a cold black pall over her. He was convinced. He was going to make it easy for her. Tremulously, she smiled.

Seeing this evidence that she had pulled back from

the brink, Dominic smiled back and possessed himself of one small hand.

Georgiana was so relieved that she only just stopped herself from leaning against him, so close as he was. Her head was spinning. Was it possible to feel so cherished and yet know one was unloved? She wasn't sure. In fact she was no longer sure of any number of things. But thankfully he had taken charge. She was sure he wouldn't press her for further words.

Words, especially from his beloved, were very far from Dominic's mind. He had no intention of giving her the opportunity to refuse him again. It occurred to him that there were other routes to his desired goal. The time had come to consider alternatives—his patience was wearing wafer-thin. On impulse, he raised the hand he held and touched it to his lips, then, yielding to a need he was endeavouring to subdue, turned it and pressed a kiss to her palm. He heard the sharp intake of her breath, and glanced up to smile reassuringly at her.

"My dear, you're overset. I give you my word I'll press you to do nothing unless it is your wish, urge you to nothing beyond what is in your heart to do. Remember that."

Georgiana blushed. As a parting speech, it held a note of promise entirely out of place with its supposed intent.

Dominic watched her confusion grow, turning her eyes a deeper shade, like toffee. Repressing the all but overwhelming urge to kiss her, he reluctantly released her hand, adding in a conversational tone, "It's very likely I'll be out of town for the next few days, but I'll see you before you leave town." It would take a day or two to organise his trap, but he had no intention of letting her escape.

The hack turned into a square and pulled up before an imposing mansion. Within minutes Georgiana was ushered inside to find Bella anxiously waiting.

"DUCKETT? What the devil are you doing here?"

Slouched in the armchair before the fireplace, Dominic frowned as his head butler, whom he had supposed still at Candlewick, entered the room. Unperturbed by his greeting, Duckett held a long taper to the fire and proceeded to circumnavigate the room, lighting candles as he went.

"Timms is ill, m'lord. You'd given orders to shut up this house, so the lad very properly sent for me."

Dominic snorted. Lad? Timms was all of thirty-five if he was a day. But he was one of Duckett's protégés and, provided he obeyed Duckett's guidelines to the letter, would always be assured of the head butler's protection.

Turning the fragile glass balloon he held so that the candlelight caught and reflected from the golden liquid within, Dominic found himself staring at the glowing colour, the same colour as her eyes. With an effort, he withdrew his gaze and found his head butler engaged in the demeaning task of making up the fire.

"Duckett, I have a problem."

"My lord?"

"A problem with a lady, you understand."

"I understand perfectly, my lord."

"I sincerely doubt it," replied Dominic. He eyed his henchman appraisingly. It wasn't the first time he had unburdened himself to Duckett, and doubtless wouldn't

be the last. Duckett had started service as a stableboy
with his grandfather. He had rapidly progressed through
the ranks, reaching his present position shortly after
Dominic had attained his majority. They'd been firm
friends forever, it seemed, despite a good twenty years'
difference in age.

"I'd value your opinion, Duckett."

"Very good, m'lord." With the fire blazing, Duckett
rose and unobtrusively busied himself, straightening
books and stacking magazines.

"The situation," said Dominic, "can only be described as delicate. The lady in question is both young
and innocent. The crux of the problem is that she has
great difficulty in believing herself to be loved."

Dominic waited for some response, but none came.
He turned and saw Duckett flicking the dust from a
book before replacing it on the shelf.

"Are you listening, Duckett?"

"Naturally, m'lord."

Dominic let his head fall back against the chair.
"Very good." Taking a moment to gather his thoughts,
he went on, "This being so, the said lady invents the
most tortuous reasons to account for my wanting to
marry her, and for refusing my suit. The first was that
I was in love with a courtesan and intended marrying
her. Having convinced her this was untrue, I then found
she believed that I wished to marry her in order to gain
title to the Place, which she owns. Owned, I should say,
because today I bought it from her. The title-deed now
resides in my strong-box and has lost all relevance to
the proceedings. The last twist in the tale is that she
now perceives that I feel I must marry her because,
due to the public nature of my pursuit of her, not to

do so would leave her open to the usual opprobrium."
Dominic paused to take a swig of the fiery liquid in his
glass. "You now have the facts, Duckett. I am presently
searching for ways and means of removing her to a suitably isolated locale, sufficiently private to allow me to
convince her that I do in fact love her while at the same
time rendering her opinion on the subject irrelevant."

A slight frown marred Duckett's majestic countenance. "I take it the young lady returns your affections,
my lord?"

"The young lady is head over heels in love with me,
if you must know."

"Ah," said Duckett, nodding sagely. "Just so."

Dominic eyed his impeccable retainer through narrowed eyes. Duckett's gaze was fixed in the far distance.
Then, quite suddenly, a smile quirked at the corners of
his mouth.

"What are you thinking of, Duckett?"

The soft question brought Duckett to himself with
a start. Then he smiled at his master. "It just occurred
to me, m'lord, that now that you own the Place you'd
want Jennings and me to put our people through it—to
tidy it up, as it were."

Puzzled, Dominic nodded. "Yes, but—"

Duckett held up a restraining hand. "That being so,
m'lord, I dare say there'll be personal belongings—
things to do with the Hartleys—that we'd need to know
what to do with. And, I should warn you, old Ben says
the snows are no more than a few days away."

Dominic's eyes, vacant, remained trained on his butler's face as the grandfather clock in the corner ticked
on. Then, to Duckett's relief, the blue gaze focused.
Dominic smiled wickedly. "Duckett, prince of butlers,

you're a rascal. I'd be shocked, if I weren't so grate-
ful. No wonder I pay you so well." Struggling upright,
Dominic drained his glass and handed it to the waiting
Duckett. "We'll set out at first light."

"Very good, m'lord," replied Duckett.

CHAPTER TWELVE

BEING TRULY ALONE again was worse than Georgiana had expected. Bella's brother had come to fill a void in her heart she hadn't even known existed. Until he was gone.

Idly plying her needle over the slippers she intended leaving as a parting gift to Arthur, Georgiana stifled a despondent sigh. The day outside was dull and grey, but no more dismal than the state of her heart. Bella, reclining on the *chaise* in the middle of the room, flicking through the latest *Ladies' Journal,* seemed almost as subdued as she. But, in her friend's case, there was a peacefulness in her quiet which Georgiana, in her tortured state, could only envy.

The Season had come to an end two days before. During the last ball, at Lady Matcham's, there had been much talk of country visits and plans for the annual festivities. Georgiana had listened and tried to summon an enthusiasm she could not feel. To her, the future looked cold and bleak. She waited for Arthur's decision on when they would leave Green Street, Bella and he bound for Candlewick, she for the Continent. He had asked her if she would stay until his business in London was completed, to keep Bella company. Naturally, she could not possibly refuse such a request. Particularly now that Lord Alton had left London.

He had sent a short note to Bella, simply informing her he had business in the country and would welcome her to Candlewick whenever she chose to quit town.

There had been no word to Bella's protégée.

Casting another glance at Bella, Georgiana couldn't help feeling guilty that she had not been able to satisfy her friend's ambition, and, worse, would not be returning to London to continue their friendship. Arthur would have to find some other distraction for his wife next Season. Georgiana knew she would never return. She would never be able to face Lord Alton's bride. He would eventually marry—an inescapable fate for one such as he. Already she felt a potent jealousy for the beautiful woman who would be his wife. Feeling despair weigh heavily on her shoulders, she forced away her unhappy thoughts and bent over her embroidery.

The door opened.

"A note for you, miss."

Frowning, Georgiana reached for the white rectangle on Johnson's salver, images of Charles and Lord Ellsmere in her mind. But one glance at the strong script emblazoned across the white parchment dispelled those weaker images, replacing them with a handsome, dark-featured face with warm blue eyes.

With the unnerving sensation of having her heart in her throat, Georgiana nodded a dismissal to Johnson and broke open the seal.

"What is it?" asked Bella, struggling to sit up.

Slowly Georgiana scanned the single sheet. Then, absent-mindedly, she said, "Your brother wants me to go down to the Place. His people want to know what to do with the furniture and so on."

Bella, now sitting, nodded. "Yes, of course. You must tell them whether you want anything set aside."

"But I don't think there could possibly be anything I would want—" Georgiana began.

"You can't tell that," said Bella seriously. "Who knows? They might even stumble across those paintings of your father's."

Bella put her head on one side, the better to view her friend. To her mind, something was not entirely right between Georgiana and Dominic. Why on earth Georgie should fall into such a lethargy just because Dominic repaired to the country for a few days she could not imagine. As she saw it, it was only to be expected that her brother would want to see his affairs at Candlewick organised before he took his intended bride down for a prolonged stay. Despite the fact Dominic had apparently not as yet proposed, Bella was quite sure he would and that Georgiana's plans for removal to Italy would never be realised. She knew her brother well enough to be certain he would view any interference with his schemes in a dim light. But, in this case, her confidence in the eventual outcome was supreme. Consequently, she was waiting with perfect equanimity for the time to come for them to leave for Candlewick.

"When are you to go?" Bella asked.

"He says he'll come and fetch me tomorrow," answered Georgiana, still struggling with conflicting emotions. The note was little more than a polite summons, its wording leaving no room for manoeuvre and even less for escape. Lord Alton would give himself the pleasure of fetching Miss Hartley at ten the next morning. He would undertake to return her to town that evening.

"Perhaps I should come down with you," Bella suggested. "There's nothing to keep me here, and I would like to see Jonathon."

Georgiana readily agreed. In her present state, spending two hours and more in a closed carriage alone with Lord Alton was an undertaking too unnerving even to contemplate.

But when the subject was broached with Arthur that evening he surprised them both by vetoing his wife's part in it.

"I'm afraid, my dear, that I would prefer you to remain in London for the next day or two. As Dominic plans to bring Georgiana back the same day, I really don't think you should leave Green Street just yet."

Put like that, it was impossible to argue the point.

Georgiana retired for the night, trying in vain to quell the entirely inappropriate leaping of her heart whenever she thought of the morrow. All was at an end between Lord Alton and herself. Why, then, did anticipation run in tantalising shivers down every nerve?

PRECISELY AT TEN the next morning, Lord Alton's travelling chaise pulled up outside Winsmere House. Strolling unannounced into his sister's back parlour, Dominic could not repress a smile at the picture that met his eyes. On the window-seat, his beloved sat, perfectly ready, fingers nervously twisting in the ribbons of her bonnet. Her gaze was fixed on the garden, a dull prospect beyond the glass.

His sister lay on the *chaise,* staring at the ceiling, a slight frown puckering her brows. It was she who first saw him.

"Oh!"

With that exclamation Bella sat up, putting up a hand to straighten the wisp of lace she had started experimenting with atop her dark curls. Dominic held out a hand to assist her to right herself, bending to drop an affectionate kiss on her cheek. Then he stood back and eyed her headgear.

Bella held her breath.

After a moment, Dominic's brows rose. "Has Arthur seen that yet?"

"No," said Bella.

"In that case, I suggest you burn it before he does."

"Oh!" Spots of colour flew in Bella's cheeks, eliciting a chuckle from her unrepentant brother. "If you've a mind to be disagreeable, I'll leave you," she replied haughtily.

But Dominic only smiled. "Don't trouble yourself. It's I who am about to leave you. If Miss Hartley is ready?"

Finding herself the object of his calm blue gaze, Georgiana nodded and rose. Within a matter of minutes her cloak had been gently placed about her shoulders and she was settled in the luxury of his carriage, a warm brick at her feet, a soft rug wrapped protectively about her knees.

Taking his seat beside her, and giving the order to start, Dominic turned and smiled. "The journey should not be too tedious, I hope."

At his smile, all Georgiana's fears dissolved. She smiled back.

They preserved a comfortable silence as the coach wended its way through the crowded streets. Once the outskirts of town were reached, and the power of the four horses began to make itself felt, Dominic turned to Georgiana. "Have you heard of Prinny's latest start?"

She hadn't, of course. Without effort, he entertained her with stories of the *ton* and other suitable anecdotes, until she had relaxed enough to ask some questions of her own. These, not surprisingly, were focused on the Place. Perfectly content with the topic, Dominic described the actual land attached to the Place, and how it related to his own far-flung acres.

"So, you see, the Place all but cuts my holdings in two, at least in that area. It has meant that my people constantly have to route all their movements around the Place, often tripling distances. Aside from being purely a nuisance, it has in recent years become an eyesore—a blot on the landscape. It's been irritating to me, as much as to my farmers, to see good land go to ruin."

Georgiana nodded, the memory of the Place as she had last seen it vivid in her mind.

Dominic paused to glance once more out of the window. The one subject he was most assiduously avoiding was the weather. He had ensured that Georgiana was seated on the left on the carriage, so her gaze, should it wander, dwelt only on the relatively clear skies to the west. On his side the eastern horizon was obscured by slate-grey clouds of the peculiar quality which, to one country-bred, denoted but one outcome. Snow. By nightfall.

The temperature was starting to fall precipitate, even though it wanted half an hour to noon. He did not think Georgiana would notice, wrapped up as she was. Still, it wouldn't do to become too complacent on that score. With a wicked grin, he turned to her once more, his brain making a rapid inventory of the latest *on dits,* selecting those suitable for his purpose.

By his order, the coach took them direct to the Place. It was well after noon when he alighted and handed Georgiana down. His steward, Jennings, and Duckett were there to meet them.

"I'll leave you with Duckett, my dear," Dominic said. "I'll be with Jennings if you need me."

Recognising Duckett, Georgiana was relieved to have his comforting presence beside her as she walked the old rooms of the Place. There was no piece of furniture she remembered with any particular affection. When appealed to, Duckett suggested the vicar's wife, who managed the local charity, and promised to convey the furniture to her.

"There's just one more matter, miss," said Duckett, pausing at the top of the stairs.

Dominic, having finished his instructions to Jennings, approving the steward's suggestion that the Place be made over as a single unit into a farm, came to stand at the foot of the stairs. Spying Georgiana and Duckett in the shadows at their head, he ran lightly up to join them.

"I was just telling Miss Hartley, m'lord, that when our people went through the attics they found one of them sealed up. An old cupboard had been moved across the door. Took three men to shift it. Then it was a struggle to force the door—looked to have been left locked for years. The room inside seems to have been used for painting—bits of rag and dabs of paint all over. There were lots of old paintings stacked by the walls. We didn't know what to do with them, so we left it until you came. Would you care to take a look, miss?"

Her father's paintings? His studio at the Place? Georgiana simply stared at Duckett.

Correctly gauging his love's reaction, Dominic took her hand and drew it through his arm. "Lead the way, Duckett."

Escorted in Duckett's wake, Georgiana drew a deep breath. "Oh, Dominic! If only…"

He glanced down, smiling, inordinately pleased to hear his name on her lips. "Patience. A moment and we'll see."

He helped her up the narrow stairs to the low-ceilinged attics. A white patch on one wall of the first room showed where the old cupboard had been. Now the concealed door stood ajar.

Duckett pushed it open and stood aside to allow Georgiana to enter. Dominic released her and, when she hesitated, gave her an encouraging nudge.

Dazed, she stepped over the threshold, lifting her skirts free of the dusty floor. There was little doubt this had been her father's eyrie. Long windows all but filled the outer wall. Now half covered with creeper, clear, they would have allowed light to flood the large room. An easel stood in the middle of the floor, empty; a paint-stained rag hung on a nail at one corner. Georgiana gazed about. The odd smell of old paints was still detectable, wafting like a ghost about the room.

For one instant, reminded so vividly of the life that had been, she felt the past threaten to engulf her. She struggled to keep back the tears. Then she heard a soft movement behind her and Dominic was there, his hands closing gently on her upper arms, comforting by his touch, by his solid warmth so close behind her. Like an anchor, he held her in the present, defying the past to claim her.

Georgiana drew a deep breath. Calm once more, she put up a hand to touch one of his. Her gaze fell on the canvases, stacked against the side-wall. She moved to touch them and he released her immediately, following her across the floor.

Without words, they set about the task of examining her father's last legacy.

Most of the portraits were of adolescent youths. After a pensive moment, staring at one of a gentle-eyed young man with reddish tints in his hair, Dominic grinned. "Ah! Now I understand."

Patiently Georgiana waited to be educated.

Dominic's smile warned her. "Your father was clearly an astute man. He wanted to leave you something which was sure to retain its value, regardless of the vacillations of fashion. So he left you these." Still Georgiana waited. Displaying the canvas in his hand, Dominic said, "This one's William Grenville as a young man." When Georgiana still looked blank he explained, "Grenville was one of our recent Prime Ministers. His family will pay a small fortune for this. And," he continued, replacing the portrait and picking up another, "unless I miss my guess, this one is Spencer Perceval, another Prime Minister. That one," he said, pointing to another study of an earnest young man, "could be Castlereagh, though I'm not certain." He bent again to flick through the portraits.

There were sixteen in the series, and Dominic could put a name to nine and guess at the others. But the three portraits at the bottom of the pile, once they were uncovered, claimed his and Georgiana's complete attention.

The first was of a young woman, with a sweet face crowned by masses of brown hair. Her eyes, startlingly clear hazel, shone out of the canvas, bright and clear. It was the portrait of Georgiana's mother.

Leaving Georgiana to gaze on her mother's face, Dominic pulled the next from the pile. A young baby rolled playfully on the grass beside the same woman. A gentle smile, full of love, curved the woman's fine lips.

Wordlessly offering this picture to Georgiana, Dominic reached for the last. This showed a young girl, of six or so summers, long golden hair hanging in plaits down her back, honey-gold eyes alight with mischief. A dusting of freckles was scattered across the bridge of her pert nose. Dominic smiled. Turning to Georgiana, he put one finger under her chin and turned her face towards him. After a careful examination, which ignored her brimming eyes, he stated, "You've lost your freckles."

Georgiana smiled tremulously, recognising his attempt to lighten her mood and grateful for it.

Dominic smiled back and released her, gently flicking her cheek with his finger. He glanced about them. "Now that this room has been opened again, I rather think these pictures should be removed from here."

Georgiana looked blank.

"Shall I get Duckett to pack them up and take them to Candlewick? You can decide what to do with them later."

Still dazed by their discoveries, Georgiana nodded her agreement. Duckett began to move about her, carefully stacking the paintings into smaller piles to be carried downstairs by his minions.

"And now," Dominic said, coming once more to stand beside her, "you must be famished. I'll take you to Candlewick, and Mrs Landy can feed us."

Quite forgetting the long trip back to London, Georgiana, happiness filling her heart, and enjoying the novelty of having someone to share it with, allowed herself to be escorted downstairs and into the carriage.

Mrs Landy had a meal waiting. She scolded Dominic for keeping Georgiana so long in the cold, causing Georgiana's brow to rise. But Dominic only laughed.

When they had eaten, he left her in Mrs Landy's care while he went out to talk with his bailiff.

It wasn't until, over tea and scones in the housekeeper's rooms, she noticed the day drawing in that Georgiana started to become uneasy. As the hour dragged by and Dominic did not return, her sense of premonition grew.

The light had faded to a premature dusk when he finally appeared. He came into the drawing-room, where she had retreated, stamping his feet to restore the circulation. He crossed to the fire and bent to warm his hands. Straightening, he smiled at her reassuringly, but his words dispelled the effect. "I'm afraid, my dear, that we won't be able to return to town tonight. The weather's turned nasty and the roads are freezing. There's snow on the way, and I doubt we'd make the Great North Road before we were stuck in a drift."

At the sight of his satisfied smile, Georgiana's eyes grew round. He'd planned this, she was sure. But why, for heaven's sake?

But her host gave her no opportunity to ponder that vital question. He challenged her to a game of chess, to which she had admitted fair knowledge, and, by the time Georgiana had conceded her king, Mrs Landy was at the door, smiling and waiting to take her to her room to freshen up before dinner. The clouds of worried questions that flitted through Georgiana's mind seemed ridiculous when faced with the solid respectability of that worthy dame.

A sense of unreality hung over her during dinner, eaten in the large dining-room. The huge table, which Mrs Landy had informed her could seat fifty, had thankfully had all its leaves taken out, rendering it a suitable size for household dining. She was seated on Dominic's right, and so attentive was her host that she had no time to question the propriety of the proceedings. The food was delicious, and the wine Dominic allowed Duckett to supply her with was cool and sweet. A discussion of the portraits her father had left her occupied much of their time, until, with the removal of the last course, Dominic pushed back his chair and rose, waving Duckett aside and coming to assist her to her feet. "Come. We'll be more comfortable in the drawing-room."

The presence of Duckett behind her chair had soothed her troublesome conscience, pricking with half-understood suspicion. Now, as the drawing-room door closed and she realised he was no longer in the room with them, her jitters woke afresh. Her nervousness spiralling upwards, she crossed the room towards the *chaise* angled before the big fireplace, conscious that he followed close behind.

"Georgiana."

The single word, uttered in the most compelling of tones, stopped her before the marble hearth. Recognising the futility of attempting evasion, Georgiana turned slowly to meet him. He was closer than she had realised.

She found herself enfolded in his arms, like delicate porcelain. Looking up, she felt her eyelids automatically drop as his head lowered to hers and he kissed her, so gently that the caress captivated her senses. This time, the kiss did not end, but went on to steal her breath, and her wits. Her nervousness disappeared, chased away by the warm glow of desire which spread insidiously through her veins. In response to some inner prompting, she slipped her arms free of his hold and twined them about his neck. His lips firmed against hers, until she parted her lips in welcome and, by imperceptible degrees, the kiss deepened.

Suddenly her mind, all alive to every incoming sensation, registered the restraint in his body, the tightness in the muscles holding her so gently, the iron control which stopped him from crushing her to him. She moved closer, letting her body press, soft but firm, against his.

Dominic stiffened with the effort to hold his passions in check. He raised his head to look down into her face. In surprise, he viewed hazel eyes smoky with desire, lips parted slightly in flagrant temptation. The siren he had glimpsed in the Massinghams' library stood within the circle of his arms, her body pliant against his. And it was all he could do to draw breath and, his voice husky, demand, "Marry me, Georgiana."

His words slowly penetrated the fog of desire which swirled through Georgiana's mind. They made no sense. Nothing made any sense any more. He had the Place. This wasn't supposed to be happening. Georgiana ignored his talk and, instead, tightened her hold on him, forcing his lips back to hers.

With a groan, Dominic recognised her state. But he

was powerless to resist her blatant demands. His lips closed on hers and he tried very hard to think of other things—anything other than the slim form snuggling so invitingly against him. His plan of gentle wooing had not taken into account the possibility of such responses on her part. In the dim hope that her mind would return presently if he kept their lovemaking in a frustratingly light vein, he rained gentle kisses on her lips and face, ignoring her attempts to ensnare him in a deeper caress. Gradually her flaring passion abated somewhat—enough, at least, for him to try again.

"Georgiana?"

"Mmm." She moved seductively against him, and he caught his breath.

"Marry me, love. Say yes. Now."

"Y... What?" Abruptly Georgiana's eyes focused. Slowly her mind followed. Then, still dazed, she shook her head.

To her amazement, she found herself looking up into eyes darkened with desire but lit by underlying sparks of anger.

"I do hope, my love, that you are not going to tell me you won't marry me."

The clipped accents sobered her. The warmth of his arms still surrounded her, making it difficult to think. Her hands on his shoulders, Georgiana tried to ease from his embrace, only to find the arms holding her so gently were, in fact, made of steel. "I can't think," she murmured protestingly.

"Don't think," came his voice, so close that his breath caressed her cheek. "Just say yes."

Again she shook her head, not daring to meet his eyes. Unequal to this battle, she leant her forehead against his shoulder. She felt his arms come up to draw her closer against him, his solid warmth comforting rather than threatening. Ridiculous, she thought, to feel so wholly at peace in the arms of a man who did not love her.

"Why?"

The question drifted softly, a murmur in her mind.

"Because you don't love me." She answered aloud without realising it.

"What?"

Abruptly he held her from him, staring at her in stunned disbelief. His eyes searched her face, then his lips twitched. Closing his eyes in exasperation, Dominic drew her head back until it was once again pillowed on his shoulder.

Georgiana snuggled against him, still dazed from his kisses, still wanting more, but not, at this juncture, daring to tempt him further. His insistence on marriage baffled her. Her own responses confused her even more. How wanton she became, with him.

Dominic waited until he had regained some measure of control over his reeling senses before asking, in a perfectly amiable tone, "Do you think, my love, you could explain to me why you think I don't love you?"

The effort required to return their interaction to an acceptable footing was entirely beyond Georgiana. She contemplated attempting to retreat without explaining herself, but doubted she had the strength to win free of his arms, let alone his presence. So when his lips found her ear and nuzzled gently, inviting her confidence, she sighed and said, "You don't really love me, you only say you do. I saw you kiss Lady Changley once. You never kiss me like that."

Put into words, it did not sound particularly rational, but it was the best she could do, with him so close.

Silence greeted her revelation. After a moment she glanced up to find him regarding her, an odd expression in his eyes.

"Do you mean to say that *that* is why you've held me off for so long? Because I *didn't* kiss you the way I did Lady Changley?"

His voice sounded strangled. Georgiana looked up at him in concern. When she neglected to answer, he shook her slightly. She nodded.

A groan rewarded her honesty. "Georgiana!"

Then she was swept into his arms and ruthlessly kissed, passionately kissed, until her legs collapsed under her and she had to cling to him for support. And still the kiss went on, demanding, commanding and utterly devastating. When at long last she was allowed to emerge, she was shaken to the very depths of her being.

"Oh!"

It was all she could say. She looked up at him, love, joy and wonder dancing in the golden flames of her eyes.

With a wordless groan, Dominic crushed her to him once more, burying his face in her silken curls.

"But why?" asked a dazzled Georgiana. "Dominic, why didn't you kiss me like that before?"

To her amazement, she felt his shoulders shake.

Dominic could contain his laughter no longer. And, although his love struggled in his embrace, he held her tightly until he felt rather less crazed and more capable of answering her sanely. Only then did he ease his hold enough to allow her to look up into his face.

Reassured at seeing her own love reflected in his blue eyes—eyes which held warmth and gentle affection as well as the passion she had not recognised before—Georgiana smiled and waited patiently.

Drawing a deep breath, Dominic sought for words to explain how her innocence had tripped him up yet again. "I was most careful, I'll have you know, not to expose you to my desire, because my sweetest love, it is generally held that innocent young ladies are not—er—sufficiently robust to withstand such raw passions."

The incredulous widening of his love's innocent stare nearly had him in stitches again.

"Aren't I supposed to like...? No, that can't be true."

Dominic was nuzzling her ear again. "I assure you it is," he murmured. "If I'd kissed any of the gentle debs as I've just kissed you, seven out of ten would faint dead away and the other three would have had the vapours."

Georgiana giggled.

Then she felt the arms around her shift slightly and one strong hand found her chin, tilting it up so that he could gaze into her eyes, his own burning again with the dark lights she now understood. A sensuous shiver ran through her.

A slow and infinitely wicked smile curved Dominic's lips. When he spoke, his voice was husky and deep. "Enough of the rest of this crazy world. Come, let me see if I can convince you of just how irrevocably I love you."

His lips closed over hers, and Georgiana, swept away on a tide of passion, gave herself up wholeheartedly to that enterprise.

"Ahem!"

The discreet cough from the doorway brought Dominic's head up. "What the devil?" Frowning direfully, he turned his head and located the intruder. "Duckett?"

At the door, Duckett stood correctly to attention, his gaze fixed on the far wall. "I'm sorry to interrupt, m'lord, but I thought you'd want to know that Lady Winsmere has just arrived."

"Bella?" Dominic's incredulous question hung quivering in the air, but Duckett had already gone, leaving the door ajar.

Brows flying in disbelief, Dominic looked down at the woman still held securely in his arms. "I suppose we'd better go and see what your chaperon has to say."

Georgiana smiled. "I wonder why she's come."

"Precisely my question. We'd better ask her." Keeping Georgiana within the circle of his arm, Dominic strolled to the door.

In the doorway, they paused to take in the scene. Only one of the large double doors was open, with one of the footmen standing in its protection with a branch of candles, trying to cast some light on to the steps outside. Blasts of cold air hurled into the hall, bringing swirls of snowflakes to flutter and melt on the tiles. On the porch a carpet of snow, already some inches thick, bore witness to the intensity of the storm outside. As Georgiana and Dominic watched, two footmen emerged from the darkness, bearing Bella between them. Duckett followed immediately behind, the shoulders of his dark coat already dusted with snow.

As soon as everyone was inside, the footmen slammed

the door shut against the elemental fury ravaging the night.

Immediately her feet hit the floor, Bella glanced about. Her eyes found Georgiana and Dominic, side by side in the drawing-room doorway. "There you are! Really, Georgie, you're going to have to be more careful!" She bustled up and embraced Georgiana before turning a censorious look on her brother. "And you, of all people, should have known better!"

Intrigued, Dominic allowed one brow to quirk upward. Holding the door wide, he bowed slightly, ushering both Bella and Georgiana into the drawing-room. He closed the door firmly.

"Now, Bella, cut line. What on earth made you leave Green Street in this hoydenish fashion?"

In response to her brother's crisp question, Bella simply stared.

"*Hoydenish?* Dominic Ridgeley! To call me hoydenish when you've all but compromised Georgiana by unthinkingly bringing her here when you might have guessed the snows were coming on. Why, if I hadn't set out as soon as the first snowflake fell, she'd have had to spend the night here with you unchaperoned. I would have thought with all your experience you would have seen the danger as well as I."

"Precisely."

The exasperated tone brought Bella's eyes to his face. Her confidence faltered. "You knew…" Bewildered, she glanced from Dominic's face to Georgiana's, then back again. "I don't understand."

Dominic sighed. "Before your arrival interrupted us, Georgiana and I were examining a number of the reasons for our impending marriage. As my affianced wife, she most definitely does not need the services of a chaperon when with me."

"Oh." Bella looked at Georgiana, but her protégée was watching Dominic, a strange little smile on her lips.

Dominic, meanwhile, had crossed to the bell-pull. "Yes. *Oh!* And, what's more, you'll have brought your husband out in these foul conditions—"

"But Arthur doesn't know," Bella interrupted to assure him.

"Most assuredly Arthur didn't know when you left Green Street. However, he will certainly have found out long since and be close behind you. Talking about people who should know better, dear sister, in your condition you have no business to go gallivanting around the country in snowstorms."

Bella gasped. "My condition? Whatever do you—?"

"My lord?"

Dominic turned to the door. "Ah, Mrs Landy."

But before he could give any orders, there came again the sound of the great front doors opening. Voices, all masculine, were heard in the hall.

Bella put a hand to her lips.

Dominic glanced at her but said nothing, his attention returning to the door.

Arthur walked in. One glance was sufficient for everyone to see he was displeased. He nodded a wordless greeting to his brother-in-law, then fixed his wife with a stern eye. "Bella, what's the meaning of this?"

Small hands fluttering, Bella went quickly to his side. "Arthur, you're frozen." When her husband's gaze did not waver, she hurriedly explained, "But really, you must see. If I hadn't come, Georgiana would have been alone here with Dominic."

"My dear, your brother is perfectly capable of managing his own affairs. You're my affair, and I cannot condone your careering across the countryside in this fashion. Not in your condition."

For the second time that evening, Bella was struck dumb.

· Before she could recover her wits, Dominic smoothly intervened. "I suggest you let Mrs Landy take you upstairs, Bella. You should get to bed immediately."

"Quite so," agreed Arthur, turning to nod to Mrs Landy, still standing by the door. "My lady is expecting and needs to rest."

Abruptly Bella found her voice. "Whatever do you mean? I'm not—"

"Yes, you are!" said two male voices in emphatic unison.

Bella blinked. Then, as the truth dawned, she smiled beatifically. "Oh," she said.

"Arthur," pleaded Dominic, in a tone of desperation, "take her away. Please?"

Arthur smiled.

Mrs Landy took her cue and bustled forward. "Now if you'll just come along, Miss Bella, we'll get you nicely settled…"

Within a minute, an unresisting Bella had been borne away.

"I'm sure Duckett can organise some dinner for you," said Dominic to Arthur.

Arthur nodded. "If you don't mind, I'll take a tray upstairs with Bella. But first I think I'll go and find some of that excellent brandy you keep in your library."

The shrewd grey gaze came to rest on Georgiana's face. "I'm glad to see you've come to your senses, Georgiana. You belong here, my dear." With a smile and a nod to each of them, he left.

"Now where were we?" asked Dominic, as he came to stand once more in front of Georgiana and drew her back into his arms.

Georgiana stared up into his face, her eyes alight with love and laughter. "Did you really plan to compromise me?"

From under heavy lids, Dominic's blue eyes watched her. He smiled, slowly, knowing what it did to her. "Mm-hm," he assented, nodding solemnly. "After all, you did beg me not to offer for you. If I couldn't get you to agree any other way, then I was quite prepared to compromise you shamelessly."

Returning the smile, his golden angel turned into a golden siren and wound her arms about his neck. "Shamelessly?"

It was the last word Georgiana uttered for quite some time. A log crashing into the stillness of the room finally broke the spell that held them. Dominic raised his head and glanced around to make sure the log had not rolled from the hearth. Turning back, he surprised an impish smile on his love's face. One dark brow rose in question.

Georgiana saw it. She hesitated, then, her smile broadening, she explained, "I was remembering the first time I saw the Fragonard." She inclined her head in the direction of the masterpiece above the fireplace. "I wondered then what sort of man would hang such a painting in such a place."

A rakish smile lit his face. "The same sort of man who has two other Fragonards."

Her golden eyes begged the invitation.

"Would you like to see the other two?"

"Mm-hm," Georgiana murmured, one tiny fingertip tracing the line of his jaw. "Where are they?"

"Upstairs," Dominic said, in between dropping tantalising little kisses along her lips. "In the master bedroom."

"Ah," said Georgiana, far more interested in his kisses than in any painting. After a moment she moved closer and asked, "Does that matter?"

With mock-seriousness, Dominic considered the point. One brow rose sternly. "It occurs to me, my love, that, as you have yet to formally accept my offer, such an excursion would be highly improper."

Georgiana smiled, letting her fingertip wander to trace the line of his lips. She glanced up at him through her lashes. "And if I were to accept your offer?"

The blue eyes gleamed. "That, of course, would cast an entirely different light on the matter."

Their gazes locked. For one moment, all was still. Then a slow smile twisted Dominic's lips.

"Georgiana, my love, will you marry me?"

Her face alight, Georgiana squealed as his arms tightened about her. "Yes!" she said, laughing. Then, as his head bent to hers, "Oh, yes."

Much later, curled on his lap, warm and secure and pleasantly intoxicated, Georgiana recalled the paintings. She looked into his face. His eyes were closed, but as she watched they opened. One brow rose in query.

Suddenly shy, she dropped her gaze to where her

fingers played in the folds of his cravat. "Will you take me to see the Fragonards?"

As a deep chuckle rumbled through his chest, she blushed vividly. But when she glanced again into his face, his expression was perfectly serious.

"Maybe you should see them. Just so you know what kind of man you're marrying."

His lips twisted into a smile that held a gentle promise. The glow in his eyes thrilled her to the core. Feeling suddenly light-headed, her heart thundering, Georgiana managed to nod her agreement.

A few minutes later they left the drawing-room with some semblance of normality and started up the stairs, Georgiana going ahead. On the landing they met Duckett, on his way down. As he drew abreast of his butler, Dominic paused to murmur, *sotto voce,* "Just remember, Duckett, this is all your fault."

Duckett's rigidly correct demeanour did not alter. He inclined his head. "Very good, m'lord."

Duckett continued down the stairs, pausing at their foot to listen to the soft murmur of lovers' voices, cut off by the closing of a door overhead.

Then he smiled. "Very good, m'lord."

* * * * *

REQUEST YOUR FREE BOOKS!

2 FREE NOVELS
FROM THE ROMANCE COLLECTION
PLUS 2 FREE GIFTS!

YES! Please send me 2 FREE novels from the Romance Collection and my 2 FREE gifts (gifts are worth about $10). After receiving them, if I don't wish to receive any more books, I can return the shipping statement marked "cancel." If I don't cancel, I will receive 4 brand-new novels every month and be billed just $5.74 per book in the U.S. or $6.24 per book in Canada. That's a saving of at least 28% off the cover price. It's quite a bargain! Shipping and handling is just 50¢ per book.* I understand that accepting the 2 free books and gifts places me under no obligation to buy anything. I can always return a shipment and cancel at any time. Even if I never buy another book, the two free books and gifts are mine to keep forever.

194/394 MDN E7NZ

Name	(PLEASE PRINT)

Address		Apt. #

City	State/Prov.	Zip/Postal Code

Signature (if under 18, a parent or guardian must sign)

Mail to **The Reader Service:**
IN U.S.A.: P.O. Box 1867, Buffalo, NY 14240-1867
IN CANADA: P.O. Box 609, Fort Erie, Ontario L2A 5X3

Not valid for current subscribers to the Romance Collection
or the Romance/Suspense Collection.

Want to try two free books from another line?
Call 1-800-873-8635 or visit www.morefreebooks.com.

* Terms and prices subject to change without notice. Prices do not include applicable taxes. N.Y. residents add applicable sales tax. Canadian residents will be charged applicable provincial taxes and GST. Offer not valid in Quebec. This offer is limited to one order per household. All orders subject to approval. Credit or debit balances in a customer's account(s) may be offset by any other outstanding balance owed by or to the customer. Please allow 4 to 6 weeks for delivery. Offer available while quantities last.

Your Privacy: Harlequin Books is committed to protecting your privacy. Our Privacy Policy is available online at www.eHarlequin.com or upon request from the Reader Service. From time to time we make our lists of customers available to reputable third parties who may have a product or service of interest to you. If you would prefer we not share your name and address, please check here. ☐

Help us get it right—We strive for accurate, respectful and relevant communications. To clarify or modify your communication preferences, visit us at www.ReaderService.com/consumerschoice.

MROM10R

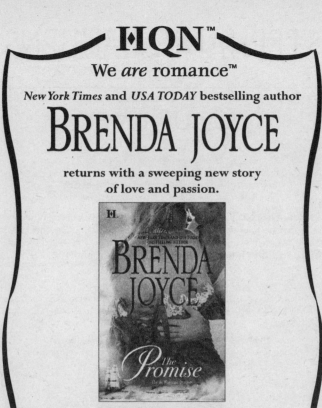

STEPHANIE LAURENS

77309 FOUR IN HAND   ___ $7.99 U.S.   ___ $7.99 CAN.

(limited quantities available)

TOTAL AMOUNT $ _____
POSTAGE & HANDLING $ _____
($1.00 FOR 1 BOOK, 50¢ for each additional)
APPLICABLE TAXES* $ _____
TOTAL PAYABLE $ _____

(check or money order—please do not send cash)

To order, complete this form and send it, along with a check or money order for the total above, payable to HQN Books, to: **In the U.S.:** 3010 Walden Avenue, P.O. Box 9077, Buffalo, NY 14269-9077; **In Canada:** P.O. Box 636, Fort Erie, Ontario, L2A 5X3.

Name: _____
Address: _____ City: _____
State/Prov.: _____ Zip/Postal Code: _____
Account Number (if applicable): _____

075 CSAS

*New York residents remit applicable sales taxes.
*Canadian residents remit applicable GST and provincial taxes.

HQN™

We *are* romance™

www.HQNBooks.com

PHSL1110BL